A Wish for Christmas

The Happy Holidays Series, Volume 3

Michele Brouder

To God be the Glory

For Jen & Bec,

Not only my sisters but my best friends

CHAPTER ONE

Monday, November 27th

"I can do this," India Ramone whispered to herself. She stood outside the door of the luxury lakefront apartment, nervously glancing up and down the corridor with its tropical plants, expensive wallpaper, and plush carpeting. There was not one Christmas decoration in sight. There was also no one around.

She had three options: ring the doorbell, press the intercom buzzer, or use the brass knocker rendered in the image of a roaring lion. India raised an eyebrow. Not too hospitable. The doorbell seemed the most straightforward choice and the most refined. Closing her eyes, she drew in a deep breath, wondering if it was possible to channel Audrey Hepburn or Grace Kelly for a little bit of confidence and that certain je ne sais quoi. She pressed the bell and heard it ringing distantly in the depths of the apartment. How large was this place?

The door was opened abruptly by a man who looked as though he'd been born in a boardroom. His short, precisely trimmed black hair was damp from a recent shower and he wore a crisp white button-front shirt with black trousers with a sharp crease and a conservative silk tie. He held his suit jacket in one hand. With his cell phone pressed to his ear, he made the briefest of eye contact with her, his blue eyes blazing. Her new employer as of this morning: John Laurencelli.

He placed his hand over the phone "You're late." Without another word, he turned on his heel and headed back into his apartment.

Whatever little bit of confidence India had possessed quickly evaporated. She remained on the doorstep, unsure as to whether she should follow him inside.

He turned around and said, "You'll get nothing done out there. Come in and close the door behind you."

India's eyes widened and her mouth formed a silent 'oh.'

She took a good look around the place as she followed him through the marbled front entrance with its expensive-looking console table, and down a long, wide hallway that was bigger than some of the rooms in her own home.

India couldn't help but overhear the conversation he'd resumed on his cell.

"I am very clear on my intent to buy that company," he said to whomever was on the other end of the line. "I can't make it any clearer."

Her mouth fell open when they stepped into the expansive open-plan space that included the kitchen, dining room, and living area. There was a bank of floor-to-ceiling windows overlooking Lake Erie, and to the left was another hallway which she presumed led to the bedrooms. She was stunned at the spaciousness of it; the home she lived in with her family would easily have fit into this space twice over.

"Tell him to stop being coy and ask him what he wants. Is it more money?" Mr. Laurencelli asked. His voice was tinged with frustration. "All right. I'll see you at the office."

He ended the call and turned his full attention to India. She tried to still her nerves and gave him a smile. There was a small, barely discernible lifting of his mouth in response. Not for the first time she wondered if this job was a good idea. Then she reminded herself that she had no choice.

"I expected you fifteen minutes ago," he said. Despite his quiet manner, she sensed impatience in his voice.

"Um, Mr. Laurencelli, I was told to be here at six," she said. She was covering for Marta, his personal assistant, who had broken her wrist and would be out of work for six weeks. Although a temporary position, it was perfect because it fit around her classes and it would provide a much-needed injection of cash for Christmas. This job had been the answer to a lot of prayers.

He looked at her as if she had challenged him. "Yes, it's a six o'clock start, but I'll expect you here by five forty-five. I'd hoped Marta would have explained all that." He paused. "Think you can handle it?"

"Yes," she said firmly, aware that she was shaking. The thought of having to get up fifteen minutes earlier on a cold, dark winter morning made her feel even more tired than she was. She chided herself. She could deal with it. It was only temporary.

"I'm sorry, what was your name again?" he asked, frowning. The photos she'd seen of him in the newspaper didn't do him justice. In person, he was even more handsome, which hardly seemed possible. He had a beautiful face: all planes and angles, a firm jaw, and sharp cheekbones. But it was his piercing blue eyes framed by dark lashes and brows that gave India pause. They made his handsomeness weapons-grade dangerous.

"India. India Ramone," she replied, casting a glance around in an attempt to look at anything but those eyes.

"I'm sure Marta's told you that I can be difficult," he said quietly.

She didn't know whether she should confirm or deny this. She decided to go with more or less what her friend had told her.

"No, not those words exactly," she replied. "Just that you like things a certain way."

He gave her a faint smile. "That sounds like something she would say. I do like things done a certain way," he said.

There wasn't anything to say to that so she remained silent.

"I also like to keep things professional, so I'd like you to address me as Mr. Laurencelli. Understood?"

She nodded, concluding that looks weren't everything. She didn't even think she was going to like him much. "And I would like to be addressed as Ms. Ramone."

He studied her for a moment. He gave her a slight nod and said, "As you wish."

She smiled. "Thank you."

"Also, one more thing. I'm the employer, you are the employee," he continued. "So please don't get any ideas about a personal relationship or friendship of any kind."

India felt her cheeks go scarlet. Wow, this guy was on some kind of power trip. She wanted to tell him his attitude was nothing to be proud of, but she needed this job more than he needed her working for him. However, it was enough of an insult to stop the shaking and fire her up. "I can assure you, Mr. Laurencelli, that any notions of any kind of personal interaction have already been dismissed."

He regarded her sharply but didn't say anything. Instead, he turned and walked away. She hesitated only briefly before following him, in case he issued any more directives, but she pulled up short when he opened the door to what was clearly his bedroom.

"I'd like a four-minute egg on lightly buttered toast and a small glass of freshly squeezed grapefruit juice in exactly eight minutes." He paused in the doorway and added, "And coffee. One cream, one sugar." The door closed shut.

India let go of a breath she felt like she'd been holding since he'd first let her into his apartment.

What had she gotten herself into?

INDIA DIDN'T HAVE MUCH time to get his breakfast on the table. She pulled her favorite vintage apron out of her backpack—she'd brought it along for good luck—and tied it around her waist. Looking quickly around the kitchen, she searched through the cupboards for a small pot. She found one, filled it with water and set it on the stove, turning on the burner. Marta, who had been Mr. Laurencelli's personal assistant for more than five years, had provided India with cheat sheets and photos of what his breakfast setting should look like. India knew from all the stories from Marta's sister Patti, that Mr. Laurencelli was exacting. Marta had said from the beginning that although the job would pay exceptionally well, it certainly wasn't for the faint of heart. India sighed. She was still shaking inside but she had managed to quell her nerves. She needed this job. It was only for a month. Surely, she could manage that without any screwups. She had to; she was going to give Stella, Petey, and Gramps the Christmas they deserved.

She heard Mr. Laurencelli come out of his bedroom just as she poured the fresh-squeezed grapefruit juice into his glass. She took one last glimpse of the photo on her phone and compared it to the table setting. It looked identical. She stood back and admired her handiwork.

John Laurencelli took a quick look at his watch, sat down, and unfurled The Wall Street Journal with such a loud snap that it startled India. He studied the breakfast she had laid out before him. Standing beside him, India held her breath.

He looked up and ran his eyes over her, from head to toe and then back up again, his face expressionless. India's cheeks colored under his scrutiny. "Can I ask what you are wearing?" he asked.

Uncertain, she looked down at herself and wondered if her turtleneck sweater and jeans had offended him. Marta hadn't mentioned a uniform.

He didn't hide his exasperation. "No, that thing around your waist."

She fingered the frilly holiday waist apron she'd picked up from Vintage Rose, the shop at the end of her street, owned by Patti, Marta's sister. She had loved this apron when she saw it. It was so 1960s. "Oh, this was a find at the thrift shop."

"It seems . . . superfluous."

India bit her lip and steadied her voice. "Marta did not mention a dress code to me. Is there one?" She held his gaze and hoped everything wasn't going to turn into a fight.

He shook his head.

"Then if it's all the same to you, I'll continue to wear it," she said. She tried to control the angry tremor in her voice but she wasn't sure how successful she was. "Unless you find my apron politically or religiously offensive in some way?"

"Of course not," he said, either missing or ignoring her sarcasm. "I'm just not accustomed to frivolity. There's no place for it in my world."

"Then why don't we agree that I'll wear the apron and you don't have to," she put forward bravely. Who did this guy think he was, anyway?

He set the paper down on the table with an exaggerated sigh and made no further comment. He surveyed the breakfast laid out before him. She wondered if he was looking for fault. Finally, he picked up his juice glass and sipped from it. He set it back down in exactly the same place it had been.

He tapped the egg in the egg cup and cracked the top half of the shell loose, then carefully scooped out the soft-boiled egg and spread it across his buttered toast. India began to walk away, thinking she wasn't about to stand there and watch him eating, especially when her own stomach was growling. She had skipped breakfast due to nerves.

"Ms. Ramone?" he started.

She backtracked.

"May I make a few suggestions?"

"Of course."

He picked up his butter knife and ran it along the edge of his toast. "This is a bit too dark for my liking." The area was browned but definitely not burnt.

"All right, Mr. Laurencelli. Will I fix you another piece of toast?"

"It's not necessary," he said.

India took a step back.

"Also," he said, moving his knife to the egg. India took a step forward. Again. "Part of the white is too runny. Tomorrow give it thirty seconds more and we'll see how that turns out."

"All right," she said quietly. She hesitated, then asked, "Is that all?"

"Is the coffee ready?"

As if on cue, the coffeemaker on the counter beeped, prompting India to respond, "Yes, as a matter of fact, it is."

India headed toward the kitchen to clean up, trying to reconcile three things about her new boss: his exacting ways, his quiet manner, and most especially, those amazing blue eyes.

MR. LAURENCELLI STOOD up from the breakfast table and went into the other room without saying a word. India was left standing there, her mouth hanging open. She had never met anyone like him. He soon returned, carrying a briefcase. He opened it up on the console table behind the sofa.

"Ms. Ramone, would you come here for a moment, please?" he asked.

Wiping her hands on her apron, she hurried over and stood next to him. His briefcase was filled with papers and folders. He pulled out two sheets of paper and scanned one of them before handing it to her.

"This is the confidentiality agreement I ask all my employees to sign," he said. He handed her a pen.

India studied the pen. It was an expensive fountain pen, unlike the ten-for-a-dollar pack she favored from the discount store. She bent and placed the document on the console to sign it.

"Are you not going to read it?" he asked, raising his eyebrows.

"I assume it says I'm not to discuss anything I see in here with anyone," she said.

"Yes, but—"

"I don't need to read it," she assured him.

"I insist that you do."

She shrugged. He was the boss. She straightened up and leafed through the paper, but it was all in legalese. By the second paragraph, her eyes began to glaze over.

She went to sign it but he stopped her. "If you don't mind, I would prefer if you'd put something underneath the paper before you sign it," he said.

Bewildered, she asked, "Mr. Laurencelli?"

He pulled a folder from his briefcase and set it under the form. "It saves the wood from being marked."

"Oh," she said. She thought of the old coffee table at home, all marked up with water rings.

"There are two copies. We'll both sign them and we each keep one," he said. He gave her the briefest of smiles.

Once she'd signed them, he handed her one and folded the other, tucking it into the pocket of his briefcase. He pulled out a housekey and handed it to her. "Here is a key to the apartment so you can let yourself in."

She nodded. "Thank you."

"Also, there is an envelope in the kitchen drawer with grocery money in it. I'll leave items on the list that I need when you do the grocery shopping. You'll also find a weekly menu there so you'll know what to make for my dinner." He snapped the briefcase shut and headed toward the door.

"I'll see you tonight, Ms. Ramone," he said.

"All right. Have a good day, Mr. Laurencelli," she said. She cringed. What on earth made her say that? As if he were a child going off to school. India stood there for ten minutes just staring after him. Finally, she recovered and started on the rest of the tasks she'd need to complete before leaving for her clinical at the hospital.

Her senses were on such high alert she was too nervous to even look around the bedroom. She wanted to but was too anxious; he probably had cameras installed everywhere. She did not miss, however, the king-size four-poster bed with its high-thread-count sheets. Why did one person need such a big bed? The sheets were smooth and lovely to the touch, unlike the sheets at her house which tended to pill after a few washings. After stripping the bed, she headed toward the marble bathroom. Steam still misted the shower doors. There was a lingering scent of expensive aftershave and the room had a decidedly masculine feel to it with its walls and accents done up in sand and walnut. Gathering wet towels from the towel rack, India couldn't help but feel that she had walked right into the lion's den and that the lion would pounce any minute. She carried the laundry to the other side of the luxury apartment where a utility room was located discreetly off the kitchen. She opened the closet, which housed the ironing board. On the inside of the door were taped explicit laundry instructions. She looked at her load of towels and located the directions for them. She sighed. This wasn't going to be easy. Once the load was in, she hurried back to the dining room and cleared off the table. Glancing at the clock in the kitchen, she realized she had to hurry. After loading up everything in the dishwasher, she took a quick look around to make sure she hadn't missed anything.

She took her bag and headed to the bathroom off the hallway. Quickly, she changed into her white nursing scrubs and slipped on her white sneakers. After she folded her clothes and tucked them into her bag, she took one last look in the mirror to make sure she looked presentable. Removing her hairband, she pulled her brush through her hair and put it back into a ponytail. She threw on her coat and grabbed her purse. Locking the door behind her, she was momentarily relieved that she had gotten through the first morning with Mr. Laurencelli. She'd be back this afternoon, after her clinical, to cook his dinner.

As she walked down the hallway with its plush carpeting, she pulled out her cell phone and called home.

Petey answered the phone.

"Are you all ready for school?" she asked. After the Thanksgiving holiday weekend, she knew Petey would be dragging his feet to go back. And even though Gramps would give the kids breakfast and see them off to the bus stop, she just wanted to touch base with them.

"Yeah," he replied. Petey was her twelve-year-old brother. Their mother had been dead for less than two years. Their father had died when Petey was a baby.

"What did you have for breakfast?" she asked, trying to make sure he hadn't pulled a fast one and convinced Gramps that orange soda and orange juice were the same thing.

"The usual suspects: cereal, toast, and juice."

"Is Stella awake?"

"Yeah."

"I've put her gym bag by the door. Make sure she doesn't forget it," India said into the phone.

"I won't. Gramps said he'd drive us to school," Petey said.

"Why?" India asked. She pictured the three of them crammed into the front seat of Gramps's old but reliable 1978 El Camino, an auto with serious identity issues. It didn't know whether it wanted to be a car or a pickup.

"He offered," Petey explained. "Who am I to refuse an old man?"

India rolled her eyes. "Okay but tomorrow please take the bus." Gramps was eighty years old. It was bad enough they had to impose on him when he should be enjoying his golden years but these were the circumstances they found themselves in. Hopefully, only temporarily.

"Don't forget your clarinet," she added. "You've got band practice after school."

"As if I would," he said. "I live for music."

That was evident in the band posters all over his walls and the music blaring out of his room when Gramps wasn't in the house.

"Anything else, boss?" Petey asked.

"Please feed Jumbo before you leave," India remembered.

"Oh, he already ate," Petey said.

India closed her eyes. "Whose breakfast did he get?"

Petey laughed. "Gramps's. He had two fried eggs, some Polish sausage, and some toasted Italian bread."

India groaned. "Was Gramps mad?"

"He was swearing under his breath and stuff, but he didn't tie him to a stake or anything like that," Petey said.

India glanced at her watch. If she didn't hurry, she would definitely be late.

"Petey, put Stella on the phone."

There was some grappling for the phone and then Stella was at the other end of the line.

"Hi, Mommy," Stella said cheerfully.

India's heart bloomed at the sound of her daughter's voice. "Hello, buttercup," India said. "Are you all ready for school? Did you eat your breakfast?"

"Yes, and yes. When will you be home?"

"I'll see you tonight when I get home from work," India said.

"Oh, Mommy, that late?" Stella whined.

"Yes, just for a few weeks, until after Christmas," India reminded her, the way she'd likely be reminding herself every day.

"Okay, Mommy, see you later," Stella said and hung up the phone.

THE BLACK MERCEDES, with John Laurencelli behind the wheel, rolled out of the parking garage beneath his building. He hadn't even arrived at his office and he was already unnerved. He had come to rely heavily on Marta for the smooth running of his personal life. He realized things happened—people got sick, they needed time off—and he had no problem with that. He wanted his staff to be at their optimum so it was better that they stay home when they were sick so they could give one hundred percent plus while working.

India Ramone had caught him off guard—a feeling that was not familiar. Marta had told him that her friend could cover for her while she was out. John had assumed that her replacement would be someone like Marta: fiftyish and matronly but efficient. But when he opened the door earlier to India Ramone, he had been startled to see that her replacement was nothing like her. With her dark hair and eyes and dimples, India Ramone was pretty to the point of distraction. Luckily, John prided himself on not mixing business with pleasure. That would only be disastrous. Initially, when he saw the frilly apron, he suspected that she may not be up to the task but decided to give her a chance and see what happened. He was lots of things, but most of all, he was a fair man. And if she wasn't up for the task, he'd give her sufficient notice and find a replacement. It was all he could do.

He felt better about the attractive Ms. Ramone now that he had a plan.

As he neared his office building, his thoughts turned to work—namely, the two businesses he was in the process of buying out: a relatively new and one-of-a-kind magazine devoted to sea glass and a mom-and-pop whiskey operation in Scotland. These thoughts—the pursuit of something that interested him, weighing up the pros and cons and formulating a plan to acquire his object of interest—these were the types of thoughts that relaxed him.

CHAPTER TWO

India would have to run if she didn't want to be late for her morning clinical. On Mondays and Wednesdays, she had to report to the hospital for her clinical rotation for the seven-to-three shift and then it was back to the college on the rest of the days for lectures in her various classes: Nursing 401, pathophysiology, microbiology, and statistics. It was a heavy load, which was why she had chosen yoga for an elective. But as it turned out, yoga wasn't as easy as it looked. There was one more week of classes and clinicals followed by a week of final exams for the semester. The pressure was on. She had visions of herself collapsing on her sofa the week before Christmas. And then it was on to the spring semester, graduation, and then sitting for the NCLEX, the nursing boards for New York state.

After parking in the hospital ramp, India hoofed it to the fifth floor to the lounge her instructor had designated as their morning meetup area prior to the start of clinicals.

Breathless, she sat down with a thump in the only remaining chair, nodding to the rest of her classmates. Her friends, Becky and Amber, waved to her from across the table. The clinical group was comprised of nine of her classmates.

India was still wound up from the events earlier that morning. She'd skipped her morning coffee thinking she was already plenty hyper. Taking some deep breaths in an effort to settle down, she wondered if she could do this job—personal assistant to John Laurencelli. When the opportunity first came up, she'd thought it was the answer to her prayers. She'd been so stressed over finances and paying bills and then all the extras that were Christmas that she was no longer sleeping at night. Once she'd secured the job, she had had her first good night's sleep in a month. But after the first morning with him, she could understand why he had already gone through two replacements and had basically chewed them up and spat them out. That's what Patti had said.

India had heard a lot about John Laurencelli. Mostly from Patti. The only thing Marta would ever say was, "He just wants things the way he wants them."

And then Patti would butt in. "Don't be evasive, Marta. He's difficult and you know it." In response, Marta would shrug, give a smile, and make no further comment. India figured he couldn't be that bad; after all, Marta had been with him for years.

When she had accepted the job, Patti had warned her, "He's definitely eye candy, but sour in the middle." More like a fireball, India thought.

It didn't matter how much she did or didn't like him. Or how nervous he made her. He was going to pay her in cash every week and already in her mind she was buying Christmas presents for Stella, Petey, and Gramps. There'd even be enough to get one of those pet stockings for the dog, Jumbo, and the cat, Mr. Pickles.

Her thoughts were soon interrupted by the door to the lounge being flung open and the entrance of their nursing instructor, Mrs. Stratham.

"Good morning!" she boomed. She was a big, tall woman with blonde hair. India had liked her as an instructor. She removed her winter coat and laid her armload on the table in front of them. "How are we this morning? It's a beautiful winter day, isn't it?" She could be over the top with the cheeriness, which didn't bother India but grated on the nerves of some. India thought it could always be worse; it could be someone who was mean.

"We're wrapping things up and today is going to be a good day on the floor," Mrs. Stratham enthused. She put her cheaters on and scanned a sheet of paper in front of her. "Let me tell you what we have for today. All good, I assure you!"

They waited. India held her breath. Clinicals made her anxious.

"I've spoken to the nurses and of course, they're happy you're here to lighten the load. Today, we've got a thirty-five-year-old female, status one day post-op for a tummy tuck—mmm—with a surgical drain! Oh, how exciting! There's also a seventy-one-year-old male, three days post-op of a below-the-knee amputation—" Here she paused to grimace. "And we have an eighty-four-year-old female who has an order for a Foley catheter to be inserted." Mrs. Stratham could barely contain her glee.

She looked around at all of them gathered before her, probably to see if their facial expressions matched hers. Unless she was full of anxiety, India doubted it.

"Also, don't forget, I want you each to write a note on your patients. This isn't going into the chart or anything like that. It's just to get you into the habit of writing a nurse's note. I just ask you to remember two things when writing your notes." She paused. "First, use correct medical terminology. If your patient has a nosebleed, for example, I want to see the term 'epistaxis.' And secondly, remember when writing your note that it is a legal document, therefore be concise. And if you mention a problem, don't forget to record your intervention and its outcome. No cliffhangers, please!"

She rifled through her papers and picked one up and read it.

"Now, I have two opportunities for students to go off the floor. There's an opportunity to observe an autopsy today. Mmm. Sounds great. Anyone like to go to that?"

Amber's hand shot up.

"Good, Amber, off you go to the basement to the morgue!" Mrs. Stratham sang. "When you're finished down there, please return up here."

Amber nodded, grabbed her things, and exited the room.

"Also, is there one of you interested in going down to the operating theatre for the day? I should add that there is a lot of standing involved." She looked around the table. Malcolm slowly raised his hand.

"Off you go," she said.

Once he was gone, she looked at the rest of the group, sighed, and with a dreamy look on her face, said, "It's a good day to be a nursing student."

INDIA STOOD AT THE bedside of the elderly woman with Mrs. Stratham at her side. India introduced herself and explained the order for the Foley catheter.

"I've had these before, so go ahead," the woman said. "Is this your first time doing it?"

India hesitated, afraid to confess that it was, in case it made the woman nervous. Finally, she admitted, "Yes, it is."

The woman nodded. "It's okay. Everyone has to learn somewhere."

India relaxed a little bit.

"The most important thing to remember when inserting the Foley catheter is to maintain your sterile field," Mrs. Stratham said. "Gather your supplies and set them up."

Mrs. Stratham walked her through it.

India opened the kit and carefully took out the sterile drape, opened it up, and emptied everything from the kit onto the drape. She paused and looked at everything laid out before her and took a breath, thinking about what she was going to do. Carefully, she opened the packet with the sterile gloves and pulled them on. Conscious not to lean over her sterile field—until the day she died she would always hear or see the words, 'sterile field'—she paused, reviewing the steps in her head as she had been taught. Hands trembling but determined to get through it, she prepped the area and proceeded to insert the catheter. When she was finished and there had been a return of urine, she hooked up the catheter to the drainage bag, letting go of the breath she'd been holding.

She cleaned up and glanced at Mrs. Statham, who was smiling. "Very good, India. Excellent sterile technique."

INDIA MANAGED TO GET through the rest of the day. But by the time three o'clock rolled around, she was tired. At the end of clinical, she gathered her belongings, said goodbye to everyone, and headed toward the hospital parking lot. She had to get back to the apartment on Lakeshore Drive. First, she had to pick up Mr. Laurencelli's dry cleaning. Marta had instructed her on that. Every Monday, the bag of shirts and suits were to be dropped off and the dry cleaning picked up. There was a lot. She had to put all of it in the backseat.

She slid in behind the steering wheel of her ten-year-old car. She buckled up and turned the key in the ignition. The engine shuddered, then stalled.

"Oh, come on, Betsey," she whispered. "You can do this."

She turned the key again and the engine shuddered as it had before, but then it turned over weakly.

"Thank you, God," she said.

The doorman opened the front door of John's complex for her. It was odd to see a doorman in this city. New York City, yes, but in Buffalo?

He wore a scarlet uniform with gold braiding. India pegged him to be in his thirties. He had brown hair and his eyes were slightly too close together.

"Here, let me give you a hand with that," he said, relieving her of one stack of the dry cleaning before she could reply.

"Thank you," she said.

He seemed pretty adept at this. He strolled to the bank of elevators, whistling a Christmas tune. He held the elevator door open and accompanied her inside, pressing the button for Mr. Laurencelli's floor.

"So, you're taking over from Marta," he said. The doors slid closed and the elevator began its ascent.

"I am." She smiled.

"How long will she be gone?"

"A few more weeks," she answered, beginning to feel uncomfortable with all the questions.

"Mr. Laurencelli is one odd duck. But I'm pretty sure Marta has already clued you in."

"Oh really?" Clued in? After one morning with John Laurencelli, India felt more clueless than anything.

He nodded knowingly. "He can be quite abrupt and moody at times. Big man on campus and all that."

Well, he is the big man on campus, she thought.

"Then I guess I'm lucky that I'm not here to make friends with him," India said.

Mercifully, the elevator came to a stop and the doors opened.

"Here we are," she said. She removed the house key from her pocket and walked toward the door. The doorman followed her.

She unlocked Mr. Laurencelli's apartment and stepped inside. "Thank you so much for helping me," she said, relieving the doorman of the remainder of the dry cleaning.

He tipped his hat. "No problem. By the way, my name is Martin if you ever need anything." He extended his hand.

With some awkwardness, she shifted the dry cleaning and reached out to shake his hand. "India. India Ramone."

"Pleasure to meet you, India. Like I said, if you need anything, just let me know."

She thanked him again, closing the door behind her.

She laid the dry cleaning on the arm of the sofa. She put her coat on a chair in the dining room. After she had changed out of her nursing scrubs and washed her hands, she rifled through her purse for the stapled paperwork Marta had given her. From there, she flipped furiously through the pages until she saw "Dry Cleaning" in italics. She glanced at the big clock on the wall. It was just after four. Mr. Laurencelli wasn't due until seven. She had some small chores to do and then she could sit down at the dining room table and get started on her assigned reading for her nursing lecture. That was another perk of this job. There was going to be some down time so she could study in peace. Graduation in May couldn't come soon enough. She continued to visualize herself walking across the stage in her black cap and gown and receiving her diploma. Sometimes, when she was thinking grandly, she added a bouquet of roses. If only her mother and father had lived to see it.

She owed it to her mother, her decision to pursue nursing as a career. Her first attempt at college had been a half-hearted effort to study fashion, even though she knew enough about herself to know she didn't have the competitive drive she'd need to succeed in that field, and she'd never want to leave the Buffalo area. When she became pregnant in her second year, she'd dropped out and hadn't gone back. Stella was just learning to walk when India's mother was first diagnosed with cancer. India became her primary caregiver, and despite the sorrow of knowing her mother's death was looming, it had been a pleasure for India to look after her. Her mother made her promise that one day she would return to college.

After her mother's death, she distracted herself from her own grief with the care of Stella, Petey, and Gramps. Gramps's sorrow had broken her heart. Her mom had been his only child and after her death, he had been lost for a long time. When Stella turned four, India began to look around at nursing schools to attend as a 'mature' student. She had loved that phrase. She'd only been twenty-five at the time and whenever she'd heard the word 'mature' she always thought of a retiree with white hair.

India carried the dry cleaning into the bedroom. The room was spacious and was decorated in the same sand and walnut tones as the bathroom. She thought it odd that there were no framed photos anywhere. In fact, there was only one piece of abstract art on the wall that made India dizzy if she looked at it too long. On the nightstand was a fancy, hi-tech clock that had no numbers on it.

She opened the door to the walk-in closet and gasped. There were two tiers of clothing. Clothes ran along three sides of the interior of the closet. On the top row were the shirts. Along the bottom were the suits. The majority of the clothing was suits and dress shirts but there was some casual wear there as well. The suits were grouped by color: blue, black, and various shades of charcoal and gray. There was a handful of brown suits but India frowned at them. Somehow, she couldn't picture Mr. Laurencelli in a brown suit. She fingered the sleeve of one of the jackets. Expensive.

India swallowed hard. She had never seen so many expensive clothes in one place before. There had to be thousands and thousands of dollars' worth. Who had that kind of money? No one from her working-class background, certainly, but obviously Mr. Laurencelli did.

Following Marta's detailed written instructions for the automated wardrobe lift, she went about the task of hanging up the shirts and suits she had picked up from the dry cleaners in the order of Mr. Laurencelli's preference. Pressing one of the buttons on the panel, she waited as an upper rod descended. She hung the shirts on it neatly and pressed another button to put it back in place. It took her twenty minutes.

Once that was done, she ironed the sheets before replacing them on the bed. It seemed redundant to her. However, Mr. Laurencelli was particular about his bed linens; he liked them changed daily, and he liked them crisp. To each his own, she thought.

Finished in the bedroom, she retreated to the kitchen. Expensive gadgets lined the counter and were set against a herringbone-effect backsplash. A five-burner gas stove anchored the island in the center of the room. It was a kitchen to die for. She thought about all the cooking shows she liked to watch, a guilty pleasure of hers. Somehow, she doubted Mr. Laurencelli cooked. Or entertained, for that matter. But if he was fussy about his laundry, he was even fussier about his food. Marta had made that very clear. India looked at the menu selection Marta had left for her. On Mondays, he liked poached salmon, grilled asparagus, and wild rice. Very basic, she thought. She had never poached anything other than an egg and she realized that in all the cooking shows she had watched, she hadn't once seen anything about poaching. She googled it and found an instructional video that wasn't too long, so she watched it. It was nearing five. She didn't have to have his dinner ready to serve until seven. She had a little bit of time to prepare for tomorrow's nursing lecture and go over her notes. This way she could have everything done by the time she got home so she could spend some time with Stella and Petey.

It took her five minutes to realize there was no kettle but there was a boiling water tap next to the sink. She made herself a cup of tea and settled in at the dining room table with its magnificent view of the lake. She pulled out her notebook from her backpack and began to review the previous week's notes. Glancing at her watch, she figured she had about an hour to study before she had to start preparing dinner. She soon found herself distracted by the falling snow. Resting her chin on the palm of her hand, she watched it listlessly. Suddenly, she felt overwhelmed and exhausted. She'd been so nervous about this job because Patti had practically scared her off of it with all sorts of tales of the very difficult John Laurencelli. And initially, India had been dismissive but now after the first day with him, she knew there had to be a kernel of truth there. She realized she had been wound tighter than a drum all day and now that she had time to sit down, she felt herself uncoil without warning. The snow against the darkening sky was hypnotizing and her eyelids began to get heavy. Her shoulders sagged and she laid her head down on her open textbook. She thought, I'll just close my eyes for a minute . . .

AT THE END OF ANOTHER productive day, John was tired. He was looking forward to some dinner and a quiet evening. He came up through the parking garage and was greeted by the doorman. Martin was a schmoozer and if there was one thing that annoyed John it was schmoozers and hangers-on.

"Good evening, Mr. Laurencelli," Martin said.

John gave him a curt nod.

Martin pressed the 'up' button for the elevator. "I see you've found a replacement for Marta."

"Temporary fill-in," John corrected. He was counting the days until Marta returned.

"Her replacement isn't too shabby to look at," Martin remarked with a wink.

"I didn't hire her to look at her," John replied smartly.

"Of course not," Martin backpedaled.

The elevator bell dinged and the doors opened. Martin went to step in.

"No need to accompany me. I've been managing elevators by myself now for some time," John said, sidestepping him and getting into the elevator. Before Martin could respond, John pressed both his floor number and the 'close doors' button. The elevator ascended with a quiet whoosh.

John had noticed that India was pretty—how could he not? He'd have to be half-blind not to. She was downright striking. But he was not one of those men who derived enjoyment from objectifying women. He was fortunate enough to have been brought up in the company of two exceptional females: his mother and his sister, Bridget. Women were to be loved and cherished. If you were inclined to go out and find one, that is. They also needed time and attention and at this point in his life, he did not have that kind of time to give to any woman. Nor the inclination. And besides, India Ramone was his employee and he was strict about keeping his business life separate from his personal life. It was best business practice to keep those boundaries up.

He turned the key in the lock and as the door swung open, he was surprised to find his apartment in complete darkness. At the opposite end of the hall, he could see that the floor-to-ceiling drapes on the panoramic window remained open, with the inky black night and the lake spread out beyond. The vastness of it tended to give him a lost feeling. Marta had known to draw the drapes as soon as the darkness came.

"Ms. Ramone?" he called out.

No answer. She hadn't even lasted a day. He had to admit to being disappointed. Marta had given him several assurances that she was up for the job and only as temporary fill-in. After five years with Marta, he had grown to trust her. She hadn't even bothered to give him a phone call or a text to say she wouldn't be back.

He flipped on a light switch, illuminating the foyer. He removed his scarf and overcoat and hung them in the closet. His thoughts turned to dinner and he began to make other plans. He was hungry. He'd eat first and then he'd call Marta.

Entering the spacious living room, he switched on a table lamp behind the sofa and set his briefcase down on the floor. Looking up, he was startled to see India, sound asleep at his dining room table.

For a disturbing moment, he was afraid she might be dead, but when he heard the light snore, he was momentarily relieved to discover she was just asleep. First, he was relieved. And then he was angry. He was paying her good money to take care of him and here she was snoozing. He glanced around the kitchen. There was no dinner in sight.

Angrily, he strode toward her with the intention of waking her and then firing her. Her head was planted in profile on the heavy textbook, the notebook open next to her. He remembered something Marta had told him about the girl being in her final year of college. Something medical. He glanced at the notebook. Each line was filled with neat, feminine handwriting.

He studied her for a moment. Her dark hair spilled over her shoulders and her thick black lashes lay in contrast against her creamy porcelain skin.

He cleared his throat loudly.

She was out cold. He wondered if she was a drinker or a drug user. That would really be terrific. Marta had assured him she was nothing of the kind. But then Marta hadn't assured him that she wouldn't be sleeping on the job.

"Ms. Ramone," he said loudly.

India's head snapped up and at first, she looked at him with heavy-lidded eyes, unsure of her surroundings. With the dawning realization of where she was, a look of horror soon replaced her uncertainty.

IN HER DREAM, INDIA had been helping her mother decorate a Christmas tree. Her mother was handing her an ornament to place on the tree and she was smiling at her. She always looked so much younger in India's dreams. And so healthy.

A decidedly male voice broke through the dream. "Ms. Ramone."

At the sound, India lifted her head abruptly. The happy image of her mother disappeared, replaced by the vision of a handsome man, scowling at her. He looked vaguely familiar. India stared at him in confusion.

John Laurencelli.

She bounced out of her chair and gathered her books, shoving them into her backpack. All the time apologizing. She shook so hard, she couldn't look at him.

"Oh, my . . . Mr. Laurencelli, I am so sorry. I must have dozed off. What time is it?"

"It's just after seven."

She closed her eyes, put her hand to her forehead and exhaled. "Your dinner. I am so sorry."

"Ms. Ramone," he said a little louder over her near-hysterical voice.

She stopped. Her heartbeat thrummed so hard it threatened to slam against her chest. India burned with shame. She was so hot with embarrassment she could have single-handedly melted the polar ice cap.

"Ms. Ramone," he said again.

She was unable to read him. His face showed no emotion but she definitely picked up the edge in his voice.

"Yes?" she asked, her voice just above a whisper.

"You can certainly understand my position," he started. "I need someone I can depend on." He hesitated and then added, "I'm not paying you to nap."

India felt her face redden all over again. She had no defense. What she had done was inexcusable. She cringed. She prided herself on being a responsible person.

"I'm afraid I'm going to have to let you go," he finally said.

"Oh no," she whispered, instinctively reaching out her hand to touch him but then pulling back when she saw the expression on his face. She tried to control the tremor in her voice. "Mr. Laurencelli, what I did was awful. Everything you said is true. I want to apologize without justification."

He picked up her coat and her backpack and walked to the front door. India had no choice but to follow him. Panic set in as she realized her newfound employment and all the hopes and dreams attached to it were going up in smoke. All thoughts of a happy Christmas for Stella, Petey, and Gramps flew out the window.

Without another word, he opened the door for her and handed her her coat and bag. Before she could protest, she was outside in the hall, humiliated, with the door closed behind her.

"No," she said to no one in particular. Tears stung her eyes. She had just wanted to give her family a happy Christmas. And she had messed it up on the first day with no one to blame but herself. She thought for a moment. If she went home, jobless, that pretty much ensured they were going to have a miserable Christmas. Petey and Stella deserved better than that. Gramps needed some new cardigans and a new pair of house slippers and she had planned to make a nice Christmas dinner. Turkey. Or ham. Or both. She needed this job, more than she needed anything else.

She swallowed hard and rapped on the door.

CHAPTER THREE

John had just reached the end of the foyer, thinking how he was starving. But even if he could cook, he'd be too tired to do it. His plan was to go down to that little corner restaurant in the old house on the west side that was nothing to look at on the outside but served a mean ribeye.

As he opened the hall closet to get his coat, there was a sharp knock on his door. He rolled his eyes. He strode to the door with the intention of firing India a second time if he had to.

Ms. Ramone stood there with her dark hair still smashed to one side of her face from sleeping on it. Her eyes were wet with tears and she was trembling. He steeled himself. He was not going to give in to her. He had made a stand and he would stick to it. Like he always did.

"Mr. Laurencelli, I wanted to apologize again," she started. Her brown eyes were huge in her face.

He sighed, exasperated. "To apologize a second time dilutes the original apology."

She protested. "But I really am sorry."

He crossed his arms over his chest. "Now it's getting redundant."

"Please," she said softly.

"Look, Ms. Ramone, apology accepted. But you can't have your job back. I need someone I can depend on and I don't think you're it," he explained. "It seems with school, you already have enough on your plate."

"I promise you it won't happen again," she said.

"I'm sorry," he said. "Goodnight." He began to close the door but she stuck out her foot, blocking it. He looked down, surprised that such a small foot could contain so much force.

"Look, I really need this job," India said firmly. "My family depends on me to provide for them."

He could feel his resolve waver, hating himself for that. And he was annoyed with her for making him feel that way.

"How many people are depending on you?" he asked.

"Three," she replied.

He raised his eyebrows in surprise. "You have three children?" She looked to be in her twenties, but closer to thirty than to twenty. She had been busy.

She shook her head. "No, no. There's Gramps, he's eighty. My brother, Petey, who's twelve and my daughter Stella, who'll be six on Christmas day."

"Your brother and your grandfather? Where are your parents in all this?"

There was a look of surprise on her face as if he had caught her off guard. Without looking away, she said, "My parents are dead."

They stared at each other for a moment. Her eyes were a beautiful shade of brown—dark like espresso in her heart-shaped face. To cave in to her attractiveness would be a sign of weakness.

He closed his eyes. "I should say no. We've already gotten off on the wrong foot."

"Yes, but don't you believe in second chances?" she asked, eagerly.

He opened his eyes and said evenly, "No, I don't." Her face crumpled. "Against my better judgement, I will give you another chance." He was surprised when she threw her arms around his neck.

"Thank you so much!" she said, a smile lighting up her face.

He stiffened and removed her arms from around his neck. "But if I ever catch you sleeping on the job again, I will fire you immediately and I won't care if you're the sole support of a third-world country. Understood?"

She nodded eagerly. Her face was full of excitement, like a little girl on Christmas morning.

"Will I throw a dinner together for you?" she asked.

He shook his head, appalled at the thought that she would 'throw' his dinner together. "No, thank you, I've made other plans." He paused, beginning to close the door. "I'll see you in the morning at five forty-five."

"I'll be here with bells on. And whistles," she said, beaming.

"I seriously hope not," he said.

She laughed. "Good night, Mr. Laurencelli." She dashed down the hall and when she reached the elevator, she turned back, waved and smiled. "You won't regret it!"

He closed the door behind him, thinking he already did.

INDIA TURNED ONTO NARAGANSETT Street where she lived. It was Gramps's street, really, with its two-story brick or clapboard houses and its row of towering old oak and elm trees running parallel to the curb. They'd moved into Gramps's small brick home after India's mother had died. She pulled into the driveway behind the El Camino and circumvented the brick archway leading to the front porch, instead going in through the side door. As she did, she turned off the outside light, flipped the deadbolt and headed up the three steps to the interior kitchen door.

As soon as she opened it, they all came at her at once, including the dog, Jumbo, who barked.

"Mommy, I need help with my hair," Stella whined, holding out a brush.

"Do I have to take peanut butter and jelly again tomorrow? I'm sick of it. Why can't I have turkey or ham?" Petey complained.

"You're late, India," Gramps said, pointedly looking at the clock.

"Hello everyone," India breathed out, removing her scarf. "And how was everyone's day?" she asked, smiling.

"The usual horse—," Petey said.

"Petey! What did I say about swearing?" India admonished.

"Mommy, I missed you," Stella said, wrapping her arms around India's waist.

"I missed you too, sweetie pie." She gave her daughter an extra hug before disengaging. "Has anyone fed Mr. Pickles?"

Gramps nodded. "Everyone, human and animal, has had dinner."

"Thanks, Gramps," she said.

"Will you have a cup of tea?" Gramps asked. "Tell us all about the urbane John Laurencelli."

"Don't worry, Gramps, I'll get it," she said, heading toward the kettle on the stove.

Gramps waved her away. "Sit down. I can certainly make a cup of tea."

"That sounds lovely," she said, sinking into a kitchen chair. Despite the nap at Mr. Laurencelli's, fatigue overwhelmed her and threatened to pull her under. Again.

Gramps set down a cup in front of her with a teabag in it. When the kettle whistled, he poured boiling water into her cup.

"What did you have for dinner?" she asked.

"I made them meatloaf," Gramps answered.

"Oh, how nice," India answered.

Behind Gramps, Petey ran his finger along his neck and stuck his tongue out. India scowled at him. Gramps was many wonderful things, but cooking wasn't his forte.

"I'm sure it was delicious," India said, relieved that they had all had a hot meal. As she spooned sugar into her tea, Stella climbed into her lap.

"Guess what, Mommy? I ate all my peas!" Stella said.

"Good girl. You know Santa's watching," India told her. She poured milk into her tea.

Stella reached for it but India held it out of reach. "Wait a minute, it's hot."

Stella nodded. India undid the ponytail in her daughter's hair and began to brush it.

"Well, India, is he stinking rich?" Petey asked.

"Yes, as a matter of fact, he is," India answered. She thought of the spacious floor plan layout. Of the hundreds of suits and shirts. Of the electronic clothes rail in the closet. Of the fine, soft cotton sheets and towels. Of kitchen drawers that glided instead of coming off the track and getting stuck.

"Money isn't everything," Gramps said.

"It is when you don't have it," Petey said.

India laughed. "Gramps, how was your day?"

"Good. Went to breakfast with Cal and Harry. Then went to the VFW for the afternoon to play cards."

"Anything new with them?"

Gramps shook his head.

From behind her, Jumbo, their hundred-and-twenty-pound Old English Sheepdog/Great Dane mix, appeared carrying their five-pound ginger cat, Mr. Pickles, by the scruff of his neck.

India reached around Stella and scratched Jumbo behind his ear and then did the same for Mr. Pickles.

"Hello, dog. Hello, cat."

"Hey, India, you know what I saw? Maybe we can get one of those laser lights for outside," Petey suggested. Petey had grand ideas for exterior illumination at Christmas. However, his ideas and India's budget were on opposite ends of the spectrum.

"Maybe," she said in a non-committal tone. "Any notes from school for me?"

Petey handed her his note about the parent-student luncheon the Friday before Christmas, and Stella's note was about her Christmas pageant which was also Friday, the twenty-second of December. She sighed. Of course, they would be on the same day. No point in anything being easy. She sipped her tea as she read both notes.

"I'm going to be a star," Stella beamed.

India leaned forward, kissed the top of her head, and whispered, "You are a star, darling."

They were interrupted by a knock at the side door. The doorbell had broken ages ago and it was on the list with lots of other things that needed fixing.

India peered at the clock. It was almost eight at night. Who'd be here so late on a school night?

Petey ran down the steps to answer the door. He returned with a big grin on his face. He made smooching noises and whispered, "It's Warren." He batted his eyelashes.

"Behave," she said. She tried to sound stern but she knew she had failed. Petey just made her laugh too much.

Warren appeared in the doorway, lanky and lean, his hair combed straight back from his head and wearing black glasses that were too big for his face. He removed his overcoat and set that and his briefcase down on one of the kitchen chairs. India often wondered what he kept in that briefcase as he never went anywhere without it. Petey joked that it could only contain one of two things: nothing or the nuclear codes.

She stood up, setting Stella back down on the chair and letting her finish her mug of tea. She'd forgotten about Warren and their arrangement to meet up tonight to practice for the charity dance, also scheduled for Friday, December twenty-second. Marta and Patti were running it, with all the proceeds to go to the neonatal unit at the hospital. India had let them rope her into it despite already having a full plate. She felt she could hardly turn them down after they went through all the trouble to get her the job with Mr. Laurencelli. The only problem was that India wasn't a great dancer, and her partner by default—Warren—wasn't much better.

Warren had been her best friend since the fourth grade when she was the new student and he'd sat behind her. He used to pull on her braids but one good wedgie from India had cured him of that. They had been inseparable ever since, except when Warren had gone away to college to major in math while India remained at home, choosing to go to a local college. When they didn't have dates for the high school prom, they went together. Warren had stood by India's side when her college boyfriend had gotten her pregnant and subsequently dumped her. And when she had mentioned her desire to go back to nursing school, it was Warren who had gone on the tours with her and helped her fill out applications for admission and financial aid.

She was always happy to see him but tonight she was tired. No, she was exhausted. Almost on a criminal level. All she wanted was to get Stella to bed, watch a one-hour program with Petey and then take a nice long soak in the tub. She saw the bath thing flying out the window. But the reality was their dancing needed work. And if last week's practice was anything to go by, they needed lots of it.

"Hey, Warren, how are you?" she asked.

"Good. Hey, Gramps," he greeted.

"Warren, how's the job?" Gramps asked.

India inwardly cringed. The one topic you couldn't get Warren off of was his job as an actuary for a local insurance company. He didn't just love it. He lived and breathed it.

"It's great, Gramps, just great. How lucky am I that I get to spend my whole day, all day with numbers? I was just checking my stats today at the office and at the end of the month I'll have been there three years! I'll get my one-percent raise and I've only two more years until I'm fully vested in the company's 401k plan."

And we're off, India thought. She could tell by the glazed-over look on Gramps's face that he was off, as well.

"Come on Warren, we'd better get practicing," India said, leading him to the living room in the front of the house. She looked over her shoulder and said, "Stella, go get ready for bed."

"Oh, Mommy, do I have to?"

"Yes, Stella." She turned to Gramps and Petey. "Gramps, we won't be long. Petey, have you finished all your homework?"

"Most of it," he said.

"Why don't you work on finishing all of it?" she suggested. "And let Jumbo out one more time for the night."

Petey rolled his eyes.

Gramps spoke up. "I'll let the dog out. Petey, you finish your homework."

With one eyebrow lifted, India looked pointedly at Petey, who finally said, "Thanks, Gramps."

Warren pushed the sofa and the coffee table back to clear the area. India pulled out Gramps's record player from the corner and selected an album she'd picked up from the charity shop. She removed it from its jacket, laid it on the turntable, and set the needle down. She loved this record player.

Warren frowned. "Why don't you let me bring over my wireless speaker? That sounds so scratchy."

"I know, that's what I love about it," she said, smiling.

He scratched the back of his head. "You're a rare bird, India."

"Why, thank you, Warren. Shall we get started?"

"I've been giving this a lot of thought . . ." He sat down on the sofa, popped his briefcase open, and removed a few sheets of paper. He laid them out on the coffee table. India leaned down to take a better a look at them. Warren had drawn diagrams—images of footprints with numbers assigned to each one in a one-two-three-four pattern.

"I think if we count out our steps together, we might be more co-ordinated. In better sync."

"Sounds like a plan," she agreed. She'd do anything to avoid making a fool of herself or Warren in front of a crowd. Even if the crowd was going to be family, friends, and neighbors.

"All right, let's begin," he said.

India stood in front of him. Warren held out one arm and placed the other on her waist. He craned his neck to view the diagram behind him on the table.

"Okay, it's a simple step like this," he said. He went off in one direction, counting 'one, two, three, four,' as he showed her the basic dance step. "It's fairly easy as you can see."

Easy for him to say. She had to do everything he did, but backwards. They attempted it a few times but India realized sadly they still had a long way to go. Their movements were mechanical. Warren wouldn't or couldn't stop counting. She counted, too, but she managed to do it silently. After an hour and with no real improvement, she pulled away.

"I'm done for the night I think, Warren," she announced. "I have to be up early."

He nodded and smiled, pushing his glasses up on his nose. "I think we're making progress." He picked up the diagrams from the table and handed her one. "I'll leave you with a copy so you can review it during the week."

She wanted to burst out laughing but refrained. When would she have time to review his little penciled-in footsteps? She had a test on Friday and she had to get a better grasp on the subject of acid-base balance. It was confusing and she had a tendency to overthink things. But still, she had to buckle down.

"Hey, how is the new job?" he asked.

She thought briefly about how she'd almost lost it but decided to shove that out of her mind. "Good, so far. It's only the first day."

Warren smiled brightly. "At least you didn't get fired—that's encouraging."

She cringed inwardly. "Oh, it's encouraging all right."

She walked him to the door and he put on his coat, hat, and gloves.

"Don't be discouraged, India, we can do this," he said. "I know you're busy but a few minutes each day will do the trick. We'll be Fred and Ginger in no time."

Somehow, she doubted that but she smiled regardless, not wanting to rain on his parade.

JOHN LAURENCELLI FINALLY undid his tie and hung it up on one of the many tie racks in his closet. He turned out the lights in the bedroom and headed toward the small bar tucked away in the living room. He pulled open the cabinet doors to reveal a recessed wall with deep mirrored shelves and many bottles of top-notch liquor. He took down one of the crystal tumblers and poured from a bottle of Macallan 25. Gulping it, he appreciated the slow burn it gave him. He carried it over to the sofa and sat down, staring into the distance and thinking of nothing in particular. He simply enjoyed the moment and the whiskey.

Annoyance filled him when his phone rang, disrupting the quiet moment. He glanced at it. It was his sister, Bridget. He swiped the 'decline' icon and leaned back against the sofa cushions, but no sooner had he settled than his phone rang again. Sighing, he picked it up as the name 'Angela' flashed across his screen. He frowned at that. Angela was his work colleague, and she had started making the odd call to him in the evening over the last two months. They had been classmates in college and after graduation had started up their business together. She had used her trust-fund money and John had the money from the proceeds of his late father's house. Much like his own mindset, she was all about her career: ambitious, driven, and smart. She had no more time than he did for romance or marriage, which worked out well when they had to attend business or charity functions, as they accompanied each other. He closed his eyes before declining that call as well. He wasn't in the mood to chat. Besides, he'd see her in the morning. Angela was picking him up and they were driving out to meet the woman who owned the start-up magazine they were looking to purchase.

He got up and poured more whiskey into his glass. All he had to do was just get through this next month. That's it. The time of year he hated most of all. He couldn't wait for the whole Christmas season to be over with. Every year, he managed to get through it one day at a time until his favorite day, December twenty-sixth, heralded the end of the holiday for another year. For the rest of the month, he'd dodge invitations to Christmas parties, ignore anyone's mention of the holiday and their plans and definitely not contribute to any water-cooler conversations. He'd avoid all the Christmas treats that were brought into the office. And he'd refuse any staff member's suggestion of including him in the Christmas party or gift exchange. His employees knew not to expect any bonuses at the end of the year. In July, he threw a huge Independence Day office party and bonuses were handed out then.

He finished the remainder of his drink in one gulp. He frowned, closed his eyes, and put his finger to the area between his eyebrows, working hard to push any thoughts or memories of Christmas past from his mind to the outer recesses.

CHAPTER FOUR

India knocked on John Laurencelli's door at five forty-five sharp the following morning. She had already consumed two cups of coffee prior to her arrival.

"You're on time," he noted. "That's a good start."

She nodded, smiling.

"You can let yourself in with your key in the mornings," he said.

"All right."

He did up one of his cuff links as he turned and headed back into the apartment. "I hate to put you under pressure, but I've got an early meeting." Cuff link done, he looked up at her. "I'll need my breakfast right away."

Up close and personal, India got a good look at him. His blue eyes were framed by almost-black lashes and eyebrows. The contrast was striking. His eyes were striated with flecks of gold. They were beautiful, like looking at the earth from space.

She pulled herself together and replied, "No problem. I'll get it now."

"Good, I'll be out in five minutes."

She nodded and headed toward the kitchen while he returned to the bedroom, a faint, heady cloud of aftershave trailing behind him.

She was just setting his breakfast down on the table when he entered the dining room. He draped his suitcoat over the back of the sofa and proceeded to sit down. He took in the front page of The

Wall Street Journal before turning his attention to the breakfast she had laid out. India held her breath.

He picked up his fork and knife and tucked into his breakfast without comment. If India was looking for praise, she'd wait a long time, she realized. She turned it around in her mind—at least he hadn't criticized it. She returned to the kitchen and began cleaning up, putting away the toaster, the carton of eggs, the butter, and the bread.

Ten minutes later she heard a knock on the front door. She looked over to him, eating at the dining room table. "Will I answer that?"

"Please."

She opened the door to a tall, beautiful woman a few years older than she. Her copper-colored shoulder-length hair had both highlights and lowlights. Her green eyes were sharp, intelligent. Everything about the woman, from her clothes to her hair to her makeup, screamed money. Lots of it.

"You must be Marta's temporary replacement," the woman said.

India nodded and stuck out her hand. "India Ramone."

The woman took her hand in a firm grip and shook it. "Angela Preston."

"Nice to meet you," India murmured.

Angela followed her in and strode to the dining room.

John stood up from the table and laid down his linen napkin.

"Good morning, Angela," he said. "I'm ready."

Angela glanced at her watch. "She's expecting us at seven."

"Plenty of time. I'm hoping she's come to a decision on her price . . ."

India tried not listen to their conversation but it proved difficult in the open-plan setting.

"Ms. Ramone, we're leaving now," John announced. He took Angela by the elbow and guided her toward the foyer, where he carefully put on his cashmere overcoat.

They were a power couple, that was for sure, India thought as they left the apartment. His girlfriend was definitely his equal in the looks and status department.

AS THEY HEADED TOWARD the elevator, John asked, "Will I drive?"

"No, that's all right. I'll drive out to the lake," Angela replied.

"Very good," he said and he held open the elevator doors for her. She stepped in and he followed her.

"How's it working out with Marta's replacement?" Angela asked.

John sighed. "It got off to a bumpy start but I'm hoping today will be better than yesterday."

She smiled. "That well? I'm surprised you didn't fire her."

They stepped off the elevator into the lobby. John acknowledged Martin with a nod as the doorman ushered them outside, then turned his attention back to his colleague. "I did. But she talked me into giving her a second chance."

Angela raised an eyebrow. "You're becoming soft in your old age. You're going to need a lot more backbone when dealing with Mannion Industries."

John groaned. "He's holding out for more money. But by the time I'm through with him, he'll sell the company to us for a song."

She laughed. "Take no prisoners."

He shrugged, opening the passenger-side door of her car. "I'm here to make money, not friends. A deal's a deal. We already had an agreement in place. I want Mannion Industries but I won't be manipulated into giving him better terms. The terms are generous enough as it is."

They buckled themselves into their seats.

"He must be reading all that press about you and believing it," she said, referring to the recent newspaper articles that described him as being a billionaire. "And he's trying to squeeze us a little bit more."

"Easy come, easy go. There's always another company waiting to be bought."

Angela pulled out of the parking lot and headed out toward Route 5 which would take them out to Evangola, almost an hour away on the shores of Lake Erie.

"There's the folder on this company," she said, indicating a manila folder tucked between the front seats.

John pulled it out and opened it. "I want to take a look at her numbers again."

Angela pulled down the visor. "It's impressive. She's taught herself everything from the ground up regarding magazine publication."

"Who knew there was such a large community around beach glass in the US," he said, absentmindedly. "Remind me again, why we have to meet her at the crack of dawn?"

Angela chuckled. "Apparently, she keeps odd hours. Works at night. She heads to bed by nine a.m."

"Hopefully, she can stay awake for our meeting."

"Hopefully." They fell into companionable silence for part of the way.

Angela spoke shortly after they passed Hamburg. "Before I forget, that opening of the VIP club is this Friday night. Will you go with me? I know how you feel about these things but since we have a majority share in this new venture, it would look good."

"It's not a problem, Angela. I'll be your plus one."

"Can you pick me up at ten?" she asked.

He looked over at her. "Will you be ready?" Angela, outside of work, was notoriously late for just about everything.

She laughed. "All I can do is give it a college girl try."

"I'll settle for that."

"SWANNIE, IS THAT YOU?" asked the high-pitched voice.

India laughed at the photographer's nickname for her. "Yes, it is, Rupert, what can I do for you?" India buttoned up her coat. With her phone tucked between her ear and her shoulder, she pulled on her gloves. She was getting ready to head to class.

Rupert huffed. Rupert was always huffing about something. "Mr. Bachmann has decided he wants to run a full-page ad in the News. Now. I told him last month if he wanted to do anything for Christmas to do it then. But did he listen? No, no one ever listens," Rupert moaned. "He's missed the Black Friday weekend and now he wants a rush job. He claims he knows someone at the News to be able to get a back-page advertisement."

"What can I do to make your life easier?" she asked with a smile. Rupert could be a drama queen at times.

"It's obvious. I'll need to use your neck, darling, for the brand-new diamond choker he wants to showcase," Rupert explained.

"You need me to stop by your studio," she said.

"And a mind reader to boot. What did I do to deserve you?"

India couldn't tell if he was being sarcastic or not. "When did you need me to stop by?"

"Now, if possible!" he said.

She smiled. "I can't. I'm on my way to class."

"Can you skip it?" he asked.

She laughed and then she realized he was serious. "You do know I'm in my last year of nursing, right? Where every multiple-choice question has two right answers and I have to choose the best one."

"Why are you putting yourself through all that?" Rupert said. India could practically hear the contempt coming across the line.

"Because I want to."

"It makes me squeamish just thinking of all the things you're going to have to do," he said and then added, "Yuck!"

"Anyway, getting back to my neck," she said.

"Yes, right," he said. "I'm so easily distracted."

This was true, India thought, and could definitely be maddening at times.

"Do you have any free time today?"

"I have some time between three and four. But I have to be at work at four."

"Where are you working?" he asked.

"I'll tell you when I see you," she said, getting him back on track. "Will that work? I could come after seven if that's better." She didn't want to go after seven, she'd want to go home by then and have her pajamas on, but this job would mean some easy money. This would be the fourth time Rupert had used her neck in an ad in the last two-and-a-half years. The nice thing about it was that no one knew it was her, as her face was never shown.

"All right then, come at three even though I usually power nap from two to four," he pouted.

"I'll see you at three, Rupert."

"Signing off now, Swannie," Rupert sang and hung up.

India shook her head and threw her phone into her bag. She exited the apartment, locking the door behind her and let out a sigh of relief as she realized she had managed to get through the morning without any major catastrophes. Humming a Christmas tune, she left the building, waving to Martin as she did so, and headed toward her car.

She had plenty of time to get to class but it would be nice to get there early for a change. She might even have time to grab a cup of coffee.

INDIA PANICKED WHEN her car didn't start on the first go or the second. She laid her head against the steering wheel and whispered a prayer. So much for being on time or early. She sat back and turned the key in the ignition one more time, but the response was the same: nothing.

She pulled her phone out of her purse and looked at the time. Even if she were to call someone, there'd be no way she could get to class on time. She had prided herself on not missing one class this semester. And now with finals drawing closer, she definitely couldn't afford to miss any school. She could call Gramps but he was twenty minutes away and his car would need fifteen minutes just to think about warming up. She could ring one of the girls in her clinical group but they were probably already en route and surely wouldn't treasure having to loop back, pick her up, and be late for school themselves. She looked up from her phone to see Martin approaching her.

She rolled down the window.

"Trouble?" he asked, peering in.

She nodded. "It won't start and I've got to get to class."

"Do you have jumper cables?" he asked.

She shook her head.

"Hold on, I'll get my car," he said and turned away from her, disappearing inside the building.

Soon the bay from the underground parking garage for the tenants opened and she could see Martin behind the wheel of a newer but sensible car. What she herself wouldn't give for a newer, more reliable model than the one she was driving. Hopefully, in the next two years, once she was working, she'd be in a better position to afford one. It was always someday with her. Never now. It was hard not to be discouraged.

Martin parked his car in front of hers so that the two vehicles were nose to nose. His hood popped open and he stepped out of his car. She leaned forward, felt underneath the steering column for the latch, and released the hood of her own car. She stepped out and joined him. It didn't seem right to sit in the car while he did her a favor.

It was frigid outside. A blast of arctic air had descended from some northern place and everything seemed colder and crisper.

He placed jumper leads on his battery and hers.

"Okay, let's see what we can do," he said. He gave her a smile. He wasn't bad looking, she thought. "Try starting your car."

India slid behind the wheel and turned the key in the ignition. When the familiar thrum of an engine starting came to life, she breathed a sigh of relief.

Martin removed the jumper cables attached to both cars and slammed the hoods shut. He walked over to her.

"You're all set," he said.

"Thank you so much." She smiled. "I can't be late for class."

"Of course not," he said. "Happy I could help. Listen, do yourself a favor and pick up a pair of jumper cables."

She nodded. She could add that to her ever-growing list along with a million other things that were needed. She waved and smiled at him as she pulled out of her parking spot. The clock on the dashboard told her she could still make it in time. She could forget about the coffee, though. She smiled, thinking how thoughtful the doorman was to help her out.

"THE ADDRESS IS 5823," Angela said, peering through the windshield.

"I think it's that one over there," John said, pointing at a two-story, white farmhouse.

"I haven't been out this way since our college days when we used to go drinking out at the lake in the summer," Angela said. She pulled into the narrow asphalt driveway and parked her car behind an SUV.

John gave a small chuckle. "Long ago and far away."

They exited the car and John looked around. The houses had originally been built as simple summer cottages but had long ago been converted to year-round living. There were no cars on the street and no one around. It was quiet.

"Let's hear what she has to say," Angela said as they stepped up onto the porch.

Whenever acquiring a business, if it was at all possible, John liked to visit the premises and talk to the employees—if there were any—to get a better feel for the company. It was on a trip to Scotland that he had come across a homegrown whiskey and decided he had to have it. He'd rescheduled his flight to meet with the company's founder and tour their distillery. He had been impressed and before his flight took off, he had negotiated an offer and signed papers.

There'd be no employees to talk to here; it was a one-woman show. There were no premises to view as she worked out of her home. John was skeptical. Magazine publications were tough and competitive. But his intuition was telling him to at least check it out, make sure he wasn't missing anything. To make sure it wasn't a hidden gem.

Angela pressed the doorbell and they waited.

Brenda Boker was a middle-aged woman with short, graying hair. As John and Angela crossed her threshold, three dogs jumped and barked with excitement at their arrival.

"Get down," Brenda told them. "Kitchen." And the dogs scurried out of the front room, their nails scrabbling along the hardwood floor.

After general introductions were made, she frowned at Angela's feet or more specifically her black stiletto boots. "I was hoping to take you down to the beach but I see you're not wearing the right kind of boots."

John and Angela exchanged a look.

"You go down to the beach in the winter?" Angela questioned.

Brenda nodded. "I go down to the beach, every morning, three hundred and sixty-five days a year."

"Maybe another time," John suggested.

Brenda nodded. "Maybe." She indicated they should follow her. "Come on back to my shop."

They followed her through the kitchen where the three dogs sat patiently waiting for further instruction and some wonderful aroma wafted from the oven. Out back, was a converted garage with lots of light and space. The entire room was dedicated to beach glass and glassing projects, including the magazine.

"Let me show you what I do here," she said and she closed the door behind them to keep out the cold.

AFTER THE FIRST NURSING class, India practically bolted from her seat to get to her next one. Her two friends, Becky and Amber, caught up with her in the hallway.

"Where's the fire?" Becky laughed.

"Just trying to get to patho," India said.

"We all are," Amber pointed out. "But you always act like your hair's on fire or something."

"Sometimes, it feels like it is," India replied.

"Look, we're going out Friday night and we want you to come with us," Amber said. "That new VIP lounge has opened and my brother's been hired as a bouncer. He promised to get us in."

India looked at her friends and envied their lifestyle. They were both twenty-one and although they, like India, had the pressure of nursing school, they really had no outside pressures. They worked part-time jobs and were able to go out on the weekends. And although she was only five years older, she sometimes felt like she could be their mother. They both lived with their parents so they didn't understand the demands of raising a young daughter or a younger brother, or the more imminent demand of paying the past-due on the cable-internet bundle before the whole thing was shut off.

"I can't," she said. "As much as I'd like to." And she would like to. Just to let her hair down for one night and go drinking and dancing. Just for a few hours.

"Yeah, that's all right," Becky said. "We expected that answer from you."

India looked at her, curious.

"And we're not taking 'no' for an answer," Amber said.

"See you in patho," Becky said as they dashed down the hall, the two of them giggling.

"But I have nothing to wear!" she protested, calling out after them. Everyone passing in the hall glanced at her. She looked at one kid and said, "Well, I don't."

CHAPTER FIVE

"What did you think?" Angela asked as they emerged from the house in Evangola over two hours later.

John buckled up and stared through the windshield at the unimposing house, its front door an unassuming white bearing a burlap wreath bedecked in ribbons and beach glass. "It's hard to believe all that's going on inside."

Angela agreed. "We never know what's going on behind closed doors."

John thought about everything they had observed over the last couple of hours. Brenda Boker epitomized the American dream: she'd built a business from the ground up and made it profitable. She was single, with no kids but the three dogs. After they toured the shop out back, she invited them to sit down for something to eat. She'd had a nice spread laid out for them: coffee and tea with homemade blueberry muffins and lemon drizzle cake. But she'd also prepared a polished and professional information packet for each of them.

"She has a lot of passion for what she does," he noted. The woman drank, ate, and breathed the beach and everything on it. They had commiserated over the weather and she'd said it was a shame they had come in the winter when the local beach was covered in snow. She would have liked to walk them down to the shoreline to show them the various pieces of tempered glass the tide washed in every day.

There had been a lot of information to process. She had explained to them the history of beach glass, where some of the best beaches in the country were to find these items and the enthusiasm of the beach glass community. Unfortunately, Lake Erie had been a dumping ground for more than one hundred years. The conditions of the lake were favorable for the tempering of the glass. The most common color of beach glass was white with the reds and oranges being more elusive. She'd even found a cannonball dating back to the War of 1812, which she had donated to the historical society. She'd gone into detail about how she had self-taught herself everything from copy writing to layout to printing, to pare down the expenses.

"But is it viable long-term?" Angela asked as they pulled back out onto Route 5.

"That is the question, isn't it?" John asked.

RUPERT LIVED IN A NARROW, three-story red brick townhouse with his wife, Barbara, on Delaware Avenue. Originally destined for the wrecking ball, it had been abandoned for decades when the Bachmanns had rescued and lovingly restored it. Their living quarters were on the first two floors, while Rupert ran his photography business—shooting mostly weddings, communion photos, portfolios, and hi-gloss ads—out of his third-floor studio. India never tired of looking at the before-and-after photos of the restoration that were displayed on the exposed-brick interior wall.

She dashed up the stairs to the third floor, slightly breathless when she finally reached the top.

Rupert looked up from the middle of the room where he was setting up his cameras and lights.

"You're not sweating, are you?" he asked, panic beginning to take hold. "Because nobody wants to see a diamond choker on a sweaty neck." Rupert had a two-packs-and-a-bottle-of-whiskey-a-day voice, still, even though Barbara had made him give up those vices many years ago.

India laughed. "No, I'm not sweating." Just to be sure, she wiped her neck with her scarf.

"Don't do that, you'll make your neck red," he said, looking through his camera lens.

India removed her coat and scarf. Rupert was all decked out in his signature colors: black and gray. Gray hair and goatee, black T-shirt, black leather vest, black jeans, and black hi-tops.

"Barbara, put the kettle on, Swannie's here," he shouted down the stairs. He looked up at her, gave her a once-over, and frowned. "Are you losing weight?" He walked back over to the banister, leaned over and yelled, "Bring up some of that cake you made this morning. She's looking a little thin. Actually, bring two slices."

He studied her for a moment. "You look exhausted, Swannie. Too much on your plate."

"It's only temporary," she said with a shrug.

"Come here, I want to show you something," he said, with a wave of his arm. She joined him at a side table and he lifted a navy-blue velvet box from the table. On the outside of the box, the words Bachmann Jewelers were embossed in gold lettering. He opened the heavy lid and India gasped at the diamond choker. It was pure brilliance.

He lifted it out and handed it to her. "Twenty grand." She was surprised at the weight of it. "Let's take a couple of preliminary shots while we're waiting for Barbara."

India fastened the clasp of the diamond choker behind her neck and realized that as magnificent as it was, she didn't like the way it felt. It was as if she had a collar on.

"I told Lenny, the next time he pulls this, I won't do it for him, not last minute like this," Rupert complained. "And at Christmas, too!" He looked up from his camera and said to India, "He takes advantage of me because I'm his little brother." Rupert complained incessantly about him and yet when the jeweler had had emergency open-heart surgery three years ago, Rupert had never left his side and had ended in up in such a state he'd almost needed hospitalization himself.

"Come on, Swannie, get up on your perch," Rupert said, nodding toward the stool in the middle of the room, surrounded by all sorts of lights.

India climbed up onto the stool.

Rupert bent to look through his lens again, then straightened up. "Do you have a hairbrush? You look like the wreck of the Hesperus."

India stepped down from the stool and made her way to her purse, pulling out her brush and tugging it through her hair.

When she returned to her stool, Rupert stood there with his hands on his hips. "You'll need to take more care than that if we're ever going to get you a man."

India laughed. "I don't want a man."

Rupert looked thoughtful for a moment. "A woman, then?"

India shook her head. "I don't have time for anyone in my life."

Rupert's wife entered the studio.

"Hello, India," Barbara said. "How are you? You're looking well."

"No complaints."

Barbara made her way over to the dumbwaiter in the wall, opened it, and removed a tray bearing a teapot, cups, and plates of cake. India hadn't had time for lunch so she was looking forward to the cake.

If ever there was a case of opposites attracting, it was Rupert and Barbara. India found it baffling. Barbara was three years older than her husband and they had been married for thirty years. There were no children but India thought that living with Rupert was probably a full-time job for Barbara. Where Rupert was always dressed in blacks and grays, Barbara favored airy pastel colors of mint, pink, and lavender. She wore her blonde hair long, always pinned at the top of her head. For whatever reason, their marriage worked. More often than not, it left India scratching her head.

"Thanks, my love," Rupert said, taking the tray and setting it down on the side table.

"Rupert mentioned that you were working," Barbara said, pouring tea into the cups. She looked to India. "Sugar and milk?"

India nodded. "Heavy with both."

"Come on, tell us about the new job," Rupert chimed in.

From her perch, India sipped the tea that had been handed to her. She hadn't realized how thirsty she'd been.

"It's only temporary. I'm covering for my friend, Marta, who broke her wrist."

Rupert dug into his cake. "Doing what, pray tell?"

India hesitated. "I'm John Laurencelli's personal assistant for a few weeks until Marta gets back."

Both Rupert and Barbara ceased their activity and exchanged a look. This reaction was the reason India was hesitant to tell anyone about her temporary position.

"What?" India asked, glancing back and forth between them.

Rupert raised his eyebrows. "We've heard about him. They say 'difficult' is an understatement when it comes to John Laurencelli."

"Is it true?" Barbara asked.

India felt uncomfortable giving her opinion on her new employer, especially when he was paying her a great wage.

"You don't get to be a billionaire without stepping on a few toes," Rupert noted, sipping his tea.

"Lots of toes," Barbara concurred.

India thought of how Mr. Laurencelli had given her a second chance when she had messed up big time and said, "All I can say is he seems like a fair, decent man."

Rupert and Barbara raised their eyebrows and looked at each other.

"Would you two please stop with the conspiratorial looks?" India took a bite of Barbara's cake and closed her eyes. "This is divine, Barbara."

"You need to be at work by four and I need to get back to my sofa for my nap. Now finish up and let's get to work, Swannie," Rupert said. "Time to take pictures of that beautiful neck of yours."

AS SHE MADE HER WAY to the stairs, Rupert took her by the arm and pressed an envelope into her hands. India frowned.

"It's payment for today," he said quietly.

"For today? But I wasn't expecting anything until January," she said, confused. That had always been their arrangement. When the vendor paid him, he paid India.

"I know you weren't, but it's Christmas time and I thought you might be able to use it now," he explained.

She felt the tension draining from her body. She'd be able to pay the past due on the cable bill and the electric bill. She flung her arms around his neck. "Thank you, Rupert!"

"Never mind that now," he said. "Besides, I know you've got a cast of thousands at home depending on you. Cecil B. DeMille would have had a field day with your crew." He raised his eyes to heaven.

"Oh, Rupert!" She laughed. For all his gruff, hysteric exterior, he was just a big old softie inside.

WHEN INDIA ARRIVED home, she found Petey at the kitchen table doing his homework. After a hug from Stella, she sent the little girl upstairs to get her pajamas on. Jumbo followed India around, demanding attention, and once she'd petted him, hugged him, and given him a dog cookie, he settled down.

Having a little bit of time, she decided to do some decorating for the holiday. She pulled a Nat King Cole Christmas album out of its sleeve and placed it on the record player. She dug out a roll of red foil wrapping paper and covered the entire front door with it. Then she created the effect of a white ribbon, crosswise, with a bow in the center. She stood back and admired her handiwork. She hung stockings from the mantle for each one of them: herself, Stella, Petey, Gramps, and smaller ones for Jumbo and Mr. Pickles. There were some lovely ceramic Christmas decorations that had been her mother's that she placed strategically around the living and dining room, remembering to keep them out of harm's way—namely Jumbo's tail and lumbering body. She smiled at the results. It wasn't much but it definitely provided some extra cheer.

When finished, she checked on Petey in the kitchen to see if he needed any help with his homework. Stella reappeared, looking very Christmassy in her red-and-white striped pajamas and red robe.

"Mommy, what can I do?"

"You know what you can do?" India said. "You can make your wish list for Santa Claus."

Stella jumped up and down, clapping. "Oh, goodie! I'm going to draw Santa a picture."

"That's nice. He'll like that," India said. "Get the crayons and Petey will give you some paper from his notebook."

"I need a list from you, too, Petey," she said. "I'm going to mail them in the morning."

Petey looked up from his homework. "If I don't believe in Santa, will I get less gifts?"

"If you don't believe, you don't receive," India sang.

Petey rolled his eyes. "I just don't want to get all clothes."

Stella came running around the corner and India put her finger to her lips and looked meaningfully at Petey. "Shh."

He nodded.

Stella climbed up onto the chair next to India. She laid out the paper and crayons in front of her.

She tapped the red crayon to her chin, deep in thought. India chuckled at the sight of her.

"Mommy, I don't know what to put on my wish list," she finally said.

"What would you like Santa to bring you?" India prompted.

"A doll!" Stella said, her eyes lighting up. "And a stroller for the doll."

"Wait a minute, Stella," Petey said. He stood up from the table and left the room. He reappeared shortly with a catalogue in his hand. "Take it from your Uncle Pete, you'll want to refer to this when you're making up your list."

Stella's eyes grew wide when she opened the book. India made a face and mouthed, 'thanks a lot' to Petey.

"No problem, sis, what are younger brothers for?"

Gramps entered the kitchen and went about making himself a cup of coffee. "What's going on here? You all look very industrious."

"I'm making my wish list for Santa," Stella informed him.

"Good girl," he said. "I ran into an elf the other day at the store and he told me he'd heard you'd been very good this year."

Stella looked at him with wide eyes. "How did he know that?"

Gramps chuckled. "Oh, Santa knows everything."

"Gramps, are you going to make a wish list for Santa?" she asked.

"I'm still deciding what to ask for," he answered.

"You better hurry up—Santa will be here soon!" she warned him.

"Will do, young lady."

Stella took one sheet of her lined paper and handed it to India. "Here, Mommy, you need to do your own wish list," she said.

India took it from her and smiled.

"You can use my crayons if you want," Stella said.

"Thank you," India chose a crayon from the box. Magenta.

"Remember, only put down what you truly want for Christmas."

"Okay." India laughed. She looked at the blank page and wondered what it was she truly wanted for Christmas. She looked around the table at her family. Gramps, sitting across from her drinking his cup of instant coffee. Petey on one side of her doing his homework and darling Stella on her left, leafing through the catalog.

India began doodling on the paper. She drew candy canes and Christmas tree. She tried to peek over Stella's shoulder to see what she was writing down.

Stella caught her spying and clutched her note to her chest. "Hey, Mommy, no peeking. Only Santa can see this." She peered at India's paper. "You don't have anything written down."

"I'm working on it, honey," India said. Prompted by her daughter, she scribbled down some ideas, starting with the obvious:

1. *To give Stella, Petey, and Gramps a great Christmas.*

2. *To do well on my nursing finals.*

She thought about number three and decided to shoot for the moon. What was the saying? If you shot for the moon and missed, you still landed among the stars. She was having fun with this and decided to go for the unattainable. To dream big, as her father used to say.

3. *To meet the love of my life.*

She looked around the table again and made an addition to her list:

3. *To meet the love of my life and have him accept all of us as a package deal.*

India stared at her third wish and drew some stars around it. She folded up her note and slid it in an envelope.

"All done, Mommy?" Stella asked.

India nodded. She licked the envelope and sealed it shut.

"I'm done, too," Stella said. She folded her list unevenly and struggled to get it into the envelope.

"Here, let Mommy do that for you," India said. "I promise I won't read it."

Stella peered at her and said, "All right, but remember Santa's watching."

India laughed and slid her daughter's list into an envelope. "You need to put Santa's address on these envelopes."

"Okay, what is it?" Stella asked, picking up a red crayon.

"Santa Claus on the first line. S-A-N-T-A, that's right," India said. "then C-L-A-U-S." India checked her daughter's work. The 'S' and the 'N' were backwards but she was confident Santa would still get them. "Then below that, on the second line, write 'The North Pole,' N-O-R-T-H, that's right, and then P-O-L-E."

Stella addressed both their letters and handed them to India, who said, "Good job."

"Wait a minute, Mommy," Stella said. She took the envelopes from India and handed India her own. "You forgot to seal it with a kiss. That's the magic." And she kissed her letter. India laughed and planted a pink-lipsticked kiss on the seal of her envelope. She tucked them into her purse.

"Now, twinkle toes, it's time for bed."

"Will you read me a story?" Stella asked.

"I will. Go on up and I'll be there in five minutes."

"Okay. I've got to find Mr. Pickles."

"Okay, you do that."

India stood up. "Come on Jumbo, let's go out one last time before bed."

The giant fur ball got up and ran to the door, almost knocking India down.

"You know, he's like a small farm animal," Gramps said, shaking his head. "He doesn't realize his size or his strength."

"He's still awesome, though," Petey said.

"I suppose in some ways he is," Gramps said and then muttered, "I just haven't seen any evidence of it yet."

Once Jumbo was in for the night, India went upstairs. She found Stella in bed, with the light still on. Mr. Pickles was all tucked in the doll cradle on the floor next to her. Stella had put a doll blanket over him like she did every night. For some reason India couldn't fathom, the cat always went along with Stella's ideas. One was never seen without the other.

Stella smiled at India and handed her a book, 'Twas the Night Before Christmas, which had been India's when she was a child. It was a large hardcover copy with colorful illustrations. Christmas was still almost four weeks away but Stella's eyes glistened with excitement.

CHAPTER SIX

"Gramps, are you sure you don't mind?" India asked again, clipping on a rhinestone teardrop earring. She felt guilty about going out on a Friday night and leaving him to watch Stella and Petey, especially since he looked after them all week while she worked and went to class.

He shook his head. "I'm positive. Go out. Have a good time. And don't worry about a thing."

"I know, but—" she started, hopping around on one foot, trying to locate her other heel in the pile of shoes in the hall closet.

"No buts about it," he said sternly. "You deserve a night out. You work hard, and then you've got college. Please go out with my blessing."

"All right," she said, sounding unconvinced. "I won't be late."

"India, be as late as you like," he said.

Stella came into the room and stopped. "Mommy, you look beautiful!"

India was pleased with her outfit, a sleeveless, curve-hugging red velvet dress with a V-neckline she'd found on the rack at Patti's shop. Despite it being from the 1960s it felt as if it had been made just for her. She'd worn her hair down around her shoulders instead of in its customary hairband.

"Thank you, honey," she said, swooping down, picking up her daughter, and hugging her. "Be good for Gramps tonight. And go to bed when he tells you." She added firmly, "No stalling."

Stella laughed. "Okay, Mommy." India put her down and she ran off to the other room. India got the broom from the closet and banged it on the dining room ceiling.

"What?" responded Petey's muffled voice from his upstairs bedroom.

"I'm going!"

"Yeah, bye!"

"I guess he's not going to come down," she said, sighing. Petey had been quiet since he arrived home from school. He had days like that sometimes. It worried India to no end.

"He'll be all right," Gramps said. "What time are you meeting your friends?"

"I'm meeting them at nine."

"Then you better get a move on," he said.

She pulled on her coat and slipped her hands into her gloves. It had been a long time since she'd dressed up and gone out. Family weddings didn't count. She tried to think when she was last out for an evening. It was probably Warren's birthday party last winter. The thought brought a frown to her face; she really needed to get out more.

She opened the outside door and stepped out, careful of her heels in the snow.

SHE SAW BECKY'S CAR pull into a lot across from the VIP lounge and followed her into it, paying the attendant and parking her car next to her friend's car. She was appalled at the price but she could hardly complain as it meant she wouldn't have to walk far in her high-heeled shoes. She got out of the car and locked it, then walked briskly to catch up with Amber and Becky. She noticed a line of people snaking out the door of the lounge. Her heart sank. She did not want to stand out in the freezing cold in just a dress and a light coat. She wondered how long she would have to hang out before it was suitable for her to make her exit. She had visions of her family at home on the couch with a big bowl of popcorn and a good Christmas movie.

"I would have picked you up," Becky said when she reached them.

India smiled at her. "I know but I might not stay out as late as you and I wouldn't want to spoil your fun by making you leave before you're ready," she explained.

"You're not going to pull a fast one?" Becky asked.

"What do you mean?" India asked, all innocence.

"You know, leave without saying goodbye?" Amber said. "Remember that?"

"Or how about the time when she said she was going to the restroom and she slipped out the back door?" Becky chimed in.

"Suspicious, are we?" India asked, laughing.

"Suspicious with good reason!" Amber huffed.

"I promise I won't leave without a proper goodbye."

"Come on," Amber urged, crossing the street. "I see my brother."

India followed her friends as they bypassed the line cordoned off by a red velvet rope and headed straight to the two bouncers standing at the door. India did not miss the outraged stares from those waiting in line. She wished she could disappear.

Jason stood at the door, dressed all in black, looking somber. The other man was also dressed in head-to-toe black. They looked like twins with their similar outfits, their short-cropped hair, their over-pronounced muscles, their thick necks, and their non-stop gum chewing.

Jason barely acknowledged his sister or her friends. He simply unchained the velvet rope from the steel pylon to allow the three of them in. He didn't even say hello to them as they walked past.

JOHN REALLY WASN'T in the mood for the club scene. He felt he'd outgrown that but it was business, after all, and one had to put in the effort. Besides, he'd promised Angela, and even though he knew it would fuel the rumor mill—people often speculated, wrongly, on the true nature of their relationship—he wasn't about to let his colleague down.

"Good evening, Mr. Laurencelli," said Frank, his long-time driver. A personal chauffeur had been one of John's first indulgences when the company had started pulling in serious profits, and even though the novelty had soon worn off and John had realized he preferred the freedom of driving himself, he'd kept Frank on, calling on his services only occasionally. Since he was going to be drinking tonight, he definitely didn't want to drive.

John climbed into the backseat of the car. There was a bar there but he decided he'd wait until he arrived at the club before he had a drink. "How are you, Frank?"

"Can't complain," he answered.

"How's Estelle?" John enquired. He'd only met Frank's wife once or twice, back when Frank first started driving for him, just before she'd been diagnosed with multiple sclerosis.

"She's had a good few days. The new treatment seems to be working," Frank said.

"I'm glad to hear that," John said.

"She wanted me to thank you for the basket of chocolate that came after her last hospitalization," he said.

John waved away his gratitude. "That was no problem. I know how much she likes her chocolate."

"That she does," Frank agreed, laughing.

Frank picked up Angela at her apartment and dropped them off a short time later in front of the glittering lights of the VIP.

Before exiting the car, John leaned forward to address his driver. "Frank, I'll call you when we're ready to go if that's all right."

"It certainly is," Frank agreed.

"We won't be late," John promised.

"Whenever you're ready, no matter what the time," Frank assured him.

JOHN ESCORTED ANGELA into the lounge—purportedly the newest, hottest nightspot in town. It had better be, for the money they'd invested in it. He glanced around, taking in the place, seeing what their investment had bought them. They were greeted by the manager, Jimmy, who was all smiles. There was a lot of hand shaking, but it was the backslapping that annoyed John. The manager took their coats and gave them to the coat-check girl. Jimmy spoke to Angela as he led them toward their reserved table. John couldn't hear what he was saying and he was okay with that. To him, nightclubs were all the same: pulsing lights and too-loud music that made conversation impossible. He was getting too old for this. Their table had an excellent view of the dance floor, which would be a good point for observation. Angela waved and nodded to people. She had talked him into this project and although it wasn't an acquisition he would have championed, business partnership was about give and take.

Jimmy wished them well. They slid into their booth and a server soon appeared to take their order.

"Shall we order champagne? Celebrate our newest venture?" Angela asked John, glancing around the club with keen eyes.

"Fine," he said. Then he said to the server, "A magnum of your best champagne."

Angela settled next to him and took in her surroundings with a smile on her face. "It looks good," she announced with an approving nod. "I like that idea—the balcony looking down on the dance floor so you can watch all the goings-on below," she said, indicating the balcony above them that wrapped all the way around the ceiling.

Every available seat was taken. He would have expected a good crowd on a Friday night, but the real test would be a Tuesday in the middle of winter. Could you still fill the place? It remained to be seen. As unobtrusively as possible, he scanned the crowd, recognizing some players from the city's professional football and hockey teams and their entourages.

The music continued to blare and John could feel the bass thumping along the floor beneath his feat. He leaned back and tried to relax but found it difficult.

"Oh look, there's Billy Johansen from the city council," Angela said with a wave of her hand. "I'll go over and say hello." She cast a glance at her business partner and friend. "It's a good thing one of us likes to socialize and network."

"Yes, it is," John agreed. She slid out of the booth and made her way toward the councilman. John found small talk painful. It was one of Angela's strong suits and he was perfectly happy to let her do the networking for the business. He brought his own strengths to the partnership, such as his penchant for travel, which meant that Angela didn't need to face her unnatural fear of flying. When there was traveling for business—and there was a fair amount of it—John went. He didn't mind. He liked going to new places and seeing different things.

He turned his attention to the dance floor, the crowd of bodies pressed together in an overpowering mixture of cologne, body odor, and sweat. He didn't know how they all stood it. He'd done it, too, when he was younger but . . . no thanks. Lately, he was starting to gain a new appreciation for the ballroom dancing his mother had insisted he learn as he was growing up. He'd resisted at the time but his mother had been right; there was something classy and refined about those waltzes and foxtrots that you didn't see in a crowd like this. Mom. He pushed away the thought of her as soon as it arrived. This was hardly the place. It was funny how memories came at you out of nowhere because of a seemingly innocuous thought. The unpredictability of it unnerved him.

To distract himself, he scanned the crowd. A group of three women caught his attention, whooping it up at the far-left corner of the dance floor. One of them, the dark-haired one in the dynamite red dress, slid away from the group as if she did not want to be noticed. She picked up her drink from a nearby table and stood at the edge of the dance floor, sipping her cocktail through a straw and watching her friends with a smile. He thought she looked a little lost. When she turned in his direction, he was surprised to see it was India Ramone.

His eyes remained on her, studying her, and it was clear to him by the look on her face that she'd rather be anywhere else but here. He knew how she felt. Her friends beckoned her to come back to the dance floor but she shook her head and sipped her drink.

INDIA WONDERED IF IT was too early to say her goodbyes. She'd only been there an hour and she felt as if she'd already had enough. It was a new club and it was easy to see it was going to be trendy. Her friends shouted at her to come back to the dance floor but she declined, wondering if they'd notice if she just got her coat and left. Her feet were killing her in these shoes. She didn't wear heels often and when she did, she always paid for it. And she would pay for it dearly tomorrow, she knew.

She had the distinct feeling she was being watched. As casually as she could, she glanced around at the dance floor, at the people seated at the bar, and at the booths and tables that circled the dance floor's perimeter. Her eyes soon locked with those of John Laurencelli. A little gasp escaped from her lips. Now that they had made eye contact and each knew the other was there, India felt she could hardly ignore him. That certainly wouldn't be polite. She decided to go over and just say hello. As she approached his booth, he slid out of it and stood up, and she wondered if he was going to bolt, but then she realized he had stood up for her.

"Ms. Ramone, how are you this evening?" he yelled over the music.

"I'm fine, thank you," she answered. Although he was dressed casually in a sport coat with his dress shirt open at the neck, she thought he still looked elegant. Expensive. She herself felt confident in her vintage-shop find. With its designer label, she was pretty sure it had been expensive also, fifty years ago.

"Will you join me?" he asked, indicating the booth.

She hesitated, not wanting to impose. Finally, she said, "Sure, why not." She'd only stay a few minutes.

"Would you like a glass of champagne or would you care for something else?"

India had never tasted champagne before and decided she'd try it.

"I'll have a glass of champagne."

He indicated to the server that he needed another glass and when one appeared promptly, he poured the champagne for India and handed to her.

"Thank you," she said.

"I'm surprised to see you here," he said.

She raised her eyebrows. "I'm surprised to be here, too."

He appraised her. India squirmed under his gaze, suspecting she didn't meet his standards. But what did she care? It was what it was. He was a billionaire and she . . . well, she was not.

"This usually isn't my kind of thing," she explained.

"I feel the same way," he answered.

"Then why are you here?" she asked.

"We're investors in the enterprise, so it's has more to do with public relations and goodwill and all of that," he explained.

She nodded. It seemed to have gotten hotter since she'd sat down in the booth. She felt perspiration threatening to bead along her hairline.

"Why are you here?" he asked.

"My friends," she said, inclining her head in the direction of the dance floor. She sipped the champagne. The bubbles tickled the back of her throat.

"This is the first time I've tried champagne," she admitted.

"What do you think?" he asked.

"It's all right. But I can't see what all the hype is about."

"That's disappointing—that bottle cost nearly a thousand dollars."

She was mortified, pretty sure she had committed a faux pas at best and at worst, insulted her boss. "I'm so sorry. I didn't mean to offend you." She was definitely leaving now. If she said any more, she'd certainly lose her job and she hadn't even finished her Christmas shopping yet.

"Don't give it another thought," he said. "I'm grateful for your honesty. There should be more of that in the world, don't you think?"

"As long as it doesn't hurt someone's feelings," she added.

Leaning toward her, he said conspiratorially, "To be honest, I'm not crazy about the stuff either."

In response, she giggled and took another sip, but decided her opinion hadn't changed.

"Can I get you something else?" he asked.

She shook her head, thinking this was her cue to exit. She slid to the end of the booth to stand up.

"I better get going. My friends will wonder where I've gone off to," she said.

But she was interrupted by his girlfriend, Angela, who had arrived back at the table with a man India had seen in the papers. She couldn't recall his name. They both stared at India and she was acutely aware that she was being sized up.

"Oh, hello," Angela said. "I'm sorry—I can't remember your name."

Initially, India thought she was being mean, but her conciliatory expression appeared to be genuine.

"My name is India Ramone."

"Oh, that's right," Angela said. She turned to her male friend and said, "She's John's assistant."

The man extended his hand. "Billy Johansen."

Ah! That was it, India thought. He was a member of the city council.

"It's a pleasure to meet you, India Ramone." The councilman held India's hand and her gaze a little longer than necessary.

India colored, withdrew her hand, and managed to get out of the booth. "I really should go."

"What district do you live in?" the councilman persisted.

John frowned, and even Angela's good humor was visibly waning.

"Um, South Buffalo."

"Not my district, which is a pity," he said, his eyes traveling the length of her. India felt uncomfortably warm under his gaze.

"Goodnight, Mr. Laurencelli. Ms. Preston," she said. She avoided making eye contact with the councilman. He looked at her as if he knew what she looked like with her clothes off.

Before they could respond, she hurried away. She was leaving. Now. That Billy Johansen was old enough to be her father. She shuddered. Searching the dance floor for her friends to tell them she was leaving, India was startled when her arm was grabbed.

"Ms. Ramone," said a deep voice.

She turned to find her arm in the stiff grasp of the councilman.

"Why are you rushing off? I'd like to buy you a cocktail and get to know you better," he said smoothly.

"No, thank you," she said, forcing a smile. "I really must be going." India tried to pull her arm from his grip but his hold tightened on her.

He leaned in closer. "Not yet. Come on." His warm breath smelled of onions, making her slightly nauseous.

India looked him square in the eye and said firmly, "I said no." She kicked him in the ankle bone with her stiletto. He grimaced, let go of her arm, and looked at her angrily before hobbling away.

India became aware that John Laurencelli had been standing right behind him. He wore an amused smile. "I came over to see if you needed any help. But I see you took care of the problem."

She shrugged. "He didn't seem to be getting the message."

"Are you leaving, Ms. Ramone?"

"Absolutely. I've had enough for one night."

"Let me escort you to your car," he offered.

Shaking her head, she said, "Not necessary, Mr. Laurencelli. It's right across the street." Before he could protest, she added, "I'll see you Monday morning."

She slipped away into the crowd to find her friends and say goodbye, then picked up her coat from the coat check and made a hasty exit, not even stopping to button up. A blast of bitter air hit her right in the face and she teetered carefully in her high heels to her car.

Luckily, there hadn't been many confrontations with men like the councilman, but the few she'd experienced had always made India feel small and insignificant. But now she was just too busy to put up with that kind of nonsense. Besides, she had to set a positive example for Stella.

Pushing the unpleasantness out of her mind, her thoughts wandered to what she was going to purchase with her pay packet. Mr. Laurencelli had left a long white envelope discreetly tucked behind one of the counter appliances earlier that morning before he'd left for work. Inside were crisp bank notes. She was going to catch up on the cable bill and buy just a few extra goodies when she went grocery shopping, like lunch meat for Petey instead of his usual peanut butter and jelly. She planned on doing some Christmas shopping tomorrow, excited that she actually had some cash to do it.

Her mind drifted to Mr. Laurencelli. She usually found his presence intimidating but tonight, sitting next to him in the booth and chatting over a glass of champagne, he had seemed normal. She reminded herself that she didn't have to be cowed by his wealth or his personality—he put his socks on one at a time, just like she did.

When she pulled into the driveway, she noticed all the lights were out. It was almost twelve-thirty. She couldn't wait to wash her face, throw her hair back in a ponytail, don her pajamas, and climb into bed.

"UGH, THAT BILLY JOHANSON is a real turd," Angela mused in the car on the way home from the club. "I hope he didn't upset your assistant too much."

John grinned, thinking about it. "It turns out, Ms. Ramone is no shrinking violet. She was able to manage him all by herself."

"Good for her." Angela turned and looked out the window at the city skyline. "Do you feel like going out for something to eat?"

It was almost one in the morning. John didn't want to keep Frank out any later than he had to; his wife required a lot of care. He shook his head.

"I'm going to pass," he said.

She nodded, unoffended. Their friendship was easy, which was probably why they had remained friends for so long. She made no demands on him and he didn't make any on her.

Angela's apartment loomed on the horizon and he knew he'd be home ten minutes after dropping her off. He was tired; he was looking forward to going to bed.

When the car pulled up in front of her building, she appealed to him again. "Will you come up for a drink?"

He declined but climbed out of the back of the limo and came around to her side to help her out.

Her hand in his, she seemed to hesitate. She looked up at her building then back at him. She opened her mouth and then closed it.

"Angela?"

She scratched her forehead, frowning. "John, I want to talk to you about something. Run something by you."

"That sounds serious."

"It is." She gave a brittle laugh. "Kind of."

"Then let's talk properly tomorrow instead of in the middle of the night when we've been drinking and we're half asleep," he suggested, smiling kindly.

She smiled back at him. "Always so practical. Aren't we working tomorrow?"

He shrugged. "We work every Saturday. We can talk over lunch."

"True, all right then, lunch it is," she said. She bid him goodnight and headed toward the front door of her apartment building. She looked back at him. "Thanks, John."

He gave her a wave. He got back into the limo and sighed. What on earth did she want to talk to him about?

CHAPTER SEVEN

B y Saturday afternoon, John felt he'd done enough, workwise. He sent off a quick text to Angela asking if she was ready to go to lunch. She responded immediately and it wasn't long before they were heading up to a pub on Elmwood Avenue. John dropped her off at the door and went and parked the car.

What was it she wanted to talk to him about—was she going to try to sail that web-design business by him again? She had been all excited about it last year but after meeting the owner and reviewing their numbers, John had not been impressed. Angela had really pushed for it, trying to talk him into it. But their long-standing agreement was that before any endeavor could be presented to the board, it had to be agreed on by both of them. It was a system that had worked well for them.

By the time he arrived at the table in the corner, she had already ordered him coffee. They talked about what they had worked on that morning until the server took their orders and left. Angela looked nervously around the restaurant.

John sipped his coffee and leaned back in his chair. "You've got my curiosity piqued."

She laughed anxiously. He had never seen Angela like this. She was usually so confident and sure. About everything.

"There's something I want to talk to you about," she started. She fiddled with her napkin. Finally, he reached over and placed his hand over hers.

"Are you all right? Are you ill?" he asked.

She said brusquely, "Of course not. Don't always think the worst."

He shrugged. "Can't help it."

She leveled her gaze at him. "You could if you tried."

"Too late. I'm an old dog and all that," he said. "Anyway, what did you want to talk to me about?"

She drew in a deep breath and sipped her wine. "We've been friends a long time," she said.

He nodded. "More than a decade."

"And why do you think our friendship works?" she asked.

"Because we're alike. Our ambitions are similar," he said. "We have the same goals."

She looked away, staring at something on the wall. "I've been thinking a lot about my life. I've been very successful in business." She looked quickly at him and added, "We both have. I have sacrificed my personal life because of it. There was never any time for relationships. And I didn't mind—I still don't mind."

John squirmed in his seat. He, like Angela, didn't have much of a love life. But he didn't like to think about that too much; it might be better for Angela to do the same.

"The thing is this: I don't want the business to be all there is in my life. I feel as far as business is concerned, I've reached the summit."

For a brief, uncomfortable moment, he wondered if she was thinking of quitting. "We've still got a lot more mountains to climb," he said.

Angela started to speak but they were interrupted by the waitress, who laid their lunches in front of them. Once she was assured they had everything they needed, she departed.

Angela looked meaningfully at her business partner and spoke. "I want more than just a career."

John blanched. Was she looking for a boyfriend and tagging him for the part? What a way to ruin a perfectly good friendship. He cleared his throat. "Angela, if you want a life outside of the business that's perfectly understandable, but I'm not sure a relationship between us is a good idea. I mean—"

She burst out laughing. "A relationship? With you? Of course not! Come on, you know me better than that."

John breathed a sigh of relief.

Angela continued to chuckle. "You should see the look on your face. Like a man who's just been given a stay of execution."

Even John had to laugh. "Well, you did have me concerned. You know I don't like to mix business with pleasure."

She stopped smiling. "Me neither. No, John, I'm not looking for romance. What I want is a baby and I want you to father it."

THE TEMPERATURES CLIMBED slightly Saturday afternoon, and there was a drip, drip sound of melting snow falling from the rooftops to the sidewalk as India walked to her part-time weekend job at Vintage Rose.

"Come on, tell me how the first week went with Buffalo's most eligible billionaire," Patti prompted when India arrived at the shop.

Buffalo's only billionaire, India thought.

Patti stood in front of her, eager, her eyes wide with anticipation. Patti had been the owner of the vintage clothing shop on Abbott Road for as long as India could remember. India's mother used to bring her here as a child, indulging their shared love of all things vintage. India had never grown out of it, and now she helped out at the shop once a week, on Saturdays.

India removed her coat and hung it on a hook in the back room. She saw three cardboard boxes stacked against the wall by the back door.

"A new drop off?" she asked, anxious to look through it herself to see if there were any treasures.

"Mrs. Patterson had another cleanout. You know, just when you think that old woman has no more to give, more boxes show up. She's a sandbagger, that one," Patti said.

"Remember those two Emilio Gucci outfits from the sixties she brought in last time?" India enthused. "I wonder what she has for us this time?"

Patti waved her hand. "Never mind that right now. I'm dying to hear all about your week with John Laurencelli." Patti was a large-sized woman who favored colorful caftans and turbans. She wore a red-and-gold one today and India thought it looked very Christmassy. She'd been a showgirl in Las Vegas many, many years ago. India had seen the photos and Patti had been a knockout. Twice divorced and widowed once, she had even dated a bodyguard of Elvis Presley's—or was it Frank Sinatra's? India could never remember. Although almost seventy, Patti still had it going on. If the right song came on the radio, Patti could be known to do a couple of high kicks just to get into the spirit of things.

India shrugged. "It went fine."

Patti threw her hands in the air. "Fine! Is that all you can say? You're as bad as Marta!"

"I guess. But it did go fine," India said, laughing.

"I don't want to hear 'fine.' I want details, girl, and the more explicit the better," Patti said, her eyes gleaming.

"What kind of details are you looking for?" India asked, knowing with Patti that was a dangerous question.

A look of glee spread over Patti's face. "Have you seen him naked yet?"

"No!" India said, laughing.

"That's too bad. Has he made a pass at you?" the older woman asked, practically rubbing her hands together.

"No, he isn't like that," India replied.

Patti's face fell, her excitement deflated. "He isn't?"

India shook her head. "No, he isn't. He's a consummate professional. Besides, I'm not that kind of assistant."

Patti's shoulders sagged. "What fun is that? I mean, he's a good-looking man and rich to boot, and you're a pretty girl, and all the two of you are doing together is being professional?"

India wanted to laugh at the level of disappointment on Patti's face but refrained. "I'm afraid so."

"But don't you feel just the slightest bit attracted to him?" Patti asked.

India shook her head. "He's my boss, Patti. That makes him not my type."

"Well, honey, he's not my type, either, but his money makes him my type." She laughed. Then she sobered up and eyed India. "I can see you're not going to be cooperative, so I guess we'll have to do some work."

"I guess so," India agreed happily. She looked toward the boxes Mrs. Patterson had dropped off, anxious to open them up. "Will I start with those?"

"Yeah, kid, go ahead."

AFTER WORK, INDIA DROVE over to the mall to get a few presents for Gramps, Petey, and Stella. She did well and felt a sense of relief she had never felt before. Usually, she was scrambling around at the last minute trying to get together some nice gifts. Gramps did what he could but he was on a limited income. In the past, Patti had helped out by letting her have first pick of the second-hand toys that invariably came in. India would bring them home and give them a good scrub with disinfectant and then distract the receiver of the gift with pretty wrapping paper and a nice big bow. Petey knew the deal and now Stella was getting to be an age where she was going to know, too.

Once home, she snuck by everyone and ran up two flights of stairs to the attic to stored her purchases, locking the door behind her to keep her nosy brother out.

JOHN LOOKED DISINTERESTEDLY at his plate; he had lost his appetite. "You want me to do what?"

"Oh, don't look at me like that. It would strictly be a business transaction," Angela explained. She picked up her fork and tucked into her lunch.

He didn't know what he had a harder time believing: discussing the prospect of having a baby as a business transaction or trying to picture Angela with a diaper bag or doing the school run. Neither image could he reconcile in his mind.

"I've given this a lot of thought," she said.

"I'm sure you have," he said.

Angela was nothing if not thorough. He was sure she had mountains of research somewhere. This wasn't something she would have thought up on a whim. No, this was the result of a lot of thinking, studying, and planning. And that's what worried him. Somehow, he had ended up in the crosshairs of her scope.

She leaned forward and lowered her voice. "I want something more than just my title and my job and my money. I want an extension of myself."

"Why me?" he asked.

"Because you're the perfect candidate," she said. "Besides, you're a good friend of mine. Why shouldn't you help me out?"

"It's a little more than helping you out," John pointed out. "Giving you a ride into work when your car breaks down is helping you out. This is a lifetime commitment."

She shook her head. "No, John. You wouldn't be beholden in any way. We would sign papers to protect your anonymity. And you know I don't need any child support. I don't want the hassle of the father wanting to have a say in how my child is raised. All I need from you is a donation. Once I'm pregnant, you walk away."

She made it sound so clinical, so straightforward. He could think of a hundred different ways this could go wrong.

"Why don't you try a sperm bank?" he suggested.

Angela scowled. "Oh no, you don't know what you're getting, do you? I don't want my issue's father to be a petty thief or something like that. No, I look at you, and you tick all the boxes."

"I tick all the boxes," he repeated. "What about work?"

"I'd only be off for six weeks after the birth of the baby. I've already started looking for a nanny."

Wow, she didn't play.

"Look, Angela—" he started.

"Wait," she said. "Don't say anything. Just tell me you'll think about it."

"I've already thought about it—"

"No, John, don't say another word," she said. "Please. I wouldn't ask for your help if I didn't need it."

ON SUNDAY, THEY AWOKE to two feet of fresh snow on the ground, and India promised Stella and Petey that after she finished studying, she would walk them to the park to go sledding. But first, they had to promise to occupy themselves for the better part of the morning because she had to get her reading assignments done. Monday was the start of her last week of clinicals and classes. She had to buckle down. They were both pretty good about it. Gramps read the Sunday paper in the recliner with his feet up and a cup of instant coffee. Petey was tasked with cleaning his room. He was supposed to do it Saturday but had never gotten around to it. India warned him that there would be no sledding unless his bed was made and the room cleaned up. He grumbled and muttered things under his breath but he dragged himself up the staircase to his room.

She parked Stella at the coffee table with the big plastic tub of crayons and markers, and some coloring sheets she had printed up from the internet of Christmas trees, Santa Claus, and candy canes.

"We need some decorations for the walls, Stella, so will you color these for me?" India asked.

Stella's eyes lit up, happy with her task. "Sure, Mommy."

AFTER LUNCH, INDIA helped Stella into her pink snowsuit and wrapped a scarf around her neck. The tricky part was trying to get her fingers into the right holes of her gloves. Petey came downstairs, dressed and ready to go.

The sled was stored up on a ceiling rafter in the garage. India dragged out the stepladder and asked her brother to hold it while she clambered up. Carefully, she pulled down the sled, trying not to let the weight slide toward her and topple her.

The three of them trudged through the calf-deep snow on the sidewalks with Petey leading the way. Some walks had been shoveled but most had not. It wasn't long before Stella's legs got tired and India ended up having to pull her on the sled.

India stopped at the corner of Naragansett like she did every time she walked down this street. Like she had been doing since she was a young girl and her mother had stopped in the same spot each time they passed. She placed her hands on the rotted picket fence, the paint long gone, and looked at the old Van Doren house. It was a two-story house with dormer windows in the attic. On the left side was a round tower room. The porch railing was hanging off and the steps to the porch were long gone. It had been abandoned and left to ruin for as long as India could remember. But there was something wonderful about this old house. Something magical. She could close her eyes and almost see it at its best: long summer evenings sitting on the front porch, drinking iced tea and listening to the sounds of children playing in the neighborhood. In the winter, there'd be a roaring fire in the front parlor and more than once she imagined two great wreaths on the double doors at Christmastime. If it were her house, she'd repaint the outside in a pale yellow and replace the old picket fence. She sighed, with a smile on her face. This was one of her dreams. It was important to have dreams; they were what kept you going during the tough times. And there were plenty of those.

Petey circled back and stood next to her. "What are you doing looking at that old dump?"

"It's my dream home," she answered, knowing that no explanation could ever make clear to him her love of the old place.

"Are you kidding?" Petey said. "Look at it. There's not a window left in the place. Everything about it is broken or dirty."

"I know," she conceded. "But at one point in its life, it was very majestic, I'm sure."

"Was that in this century?"

She shook her head. "It was a long time ago."

"I'd tear it down. It's a dump."

"It's like a lot of people: broken, abandoned, and just in need of a little tender loving care."

Petey rolled his eyes. "India, you are too much. Are we going to the park today or are we going to stand here, watching you drool over this junkpile all afternoon?"

"Mommy, I'm cold," Stella said from the sled.

"Okay, let's go," India said, pulling the sled behind her. She crossed the street and took one last look over her shoulder at the abandoned house on the corner.

WITH ONE WEEK UNDER her belt and going into her second, India felt as if she had started to get the hang of things as Mr. Laurencelli's assistant. The only thing she didn't like was the silence. The place was like a tomb when he wasn't there. There was no noise. At all. No footsteps above or slamming doors below or any muted sounds of traffic coming from outside. She never heard any voices or music coming from behind closed doors in the outside hallway. They were either a very sedate bunch of tenants or they were unconscious. India was used to noise. Lots of it. She liked it. Actually, she thrived on it. Standing at the solid wall of windows, she cast a glance out on the lake. Turbulent, dark waves crashed against the breakwater but she couldn't hear a thing. As beautiful as it all was, it left India feeling cast adrift, as if she were the only one left on the planet.

She remedied the sound barrier with two things: her own voice and the vacuum cleaner. She found vacuuming therapeutic; there was something very orderly and soothing about vacuuming one's self out of a room and seeing all those straight lines the vacuum had created. It was like a newly cut lawn with its mower stripes. But more than that, she relished the sound it made in the cavernous space. And when the vacuum was off, she either sang or hummed Christmas tunes.

At least when he was there, there was a little bit of conversation. India had concluded that the lack of chitchat wasn't because he was rude or condescending. It was because he was a quiet, thoughtful man, not prone to chattiness or small talk. He answered her questions politely when asked, but he didn't expound on anything. Sometimes, when India looked at him, he appeared to be lost in thought or a thousand miles away.

Anxious to hear another voice, she attempted conversation with Mr. Laurencelli.

"It looks like we're in for more snow," India remarked as he sat down to his breakfast.

"It is December, I guess it's to be expected," he answered, picking up his newspaper.

"Do you like snow, Mr. Laurencelli?" she asked.

"I don't have a strong opinion on that one way or the other," he replied.

He snapped his paper open but India continued. "I love winter. I love Christmas, always have, but more so now since it's Stella's birthday," she said brightly.

"So you said," he responded blandly.

"But I like summer, too," she continued, thinking out loud. "Actually, I like all the seasons. For different reasons, obviously."

"Obviously," he said drily.

"I guess I like the variety," she mused.

John put his paper down. "As fascinating as I find this subject, I really do like to read my paper before I leave for the office. In peace. And quiet."

"Okay, Mr. Laurencelli, I'm sorry, I didn't mean to ramble on," she apologized.

"That's all right."

She headed toward the kitchen, humming a Christmas tune. As she wiped down the counters, she sang the words to the chorus.

"Ms. Ramone!"

India turned toward him, seated at the dining room table.

"Yes?"

"The noise . . ." he prompted.

She looked around. "What noise?"

"The noise you were making. You're singing," he explained.

"Oh that," she answered. "I just find it so quiet around here. I'm not used to that at home." She added a nervous laugh.

"I prefer it like that."

"Really?" she asked, trying to hide her disbelief.

"Yes, really," he said. "Now can I enjoy my breakfast and my paper in a noise-free environment?"

"As you wish, my lord," India joked.

John scowled at her.

India mumbled, "Oops." She turned around and finished wiping down the counters, feeling his eyes on her. She was glad her back was to him because her face felt like it was on fire.

CHAPTER EIGHT

John looked at the call display on his landline. "I'll get that, Ms. Ramone," he called, taking the cordless phone into his bedroom and closing the door behind him before answering the call.

"Is that you, John? John Laurencelli?"

John sat down on the side of the bed and sighed. "Yes, Bridget."

"Is your cell phone not working?" she asked. He didn't miss the frustration in her voice.

"It's working," he replied, without adding an explanation as to why he wasn't answering her calls. They both knew the reason.

"I've been calling you and leaving messages," she started.

"And?" he asked.

"You're avoiding me," she said.

"I am not," he lied.

"Yes, you are, don't lie. We were raised better than that," Bridget said. No one knew him better than she. Four years older by birth, she had been able to cut through his crap since he was six years old.

"I've been busy," he said.

"Nobody is that busy, dear brother."

"I am. As a matter of fact, I have to go now as I have a very important meeting to attend," he lied again. He knew she probably didn't believe him but he didn't care.

She sighed on the other end of the line. Her disappointment upset him.

"You can't ignore me forever, John," she said softly.

"I'm not ignoring you—" John started to say, but she had already disconnected. He stared at the phone before putting down the handset. He and Bridget went around and around every December about his unwillingness to celebrate Christmas. It was a battle she'd lost every time. He had to give her credit; she kept coming back for more.

He sat on the edge of his bed, staring out the window at the lake. It was time to get to work and face Angela. He'd thought of nothing else over the weekend but her proposal.

Despite looking at her idea from every angle, he had not changed his mind. He did not want to become a father that way. Not as a donor. He couldn't just father her child, or any child, and walk away. What would that say about him? And he knew Angela would not want any interference; she'd want to do it all her own way. They'd end up butting heads over child rearing. Plus, he wasn't interested in becoming a weekend-and-holiday-only father. He'd never given it much thought before but he did over the weekend, and he concluded that someday he'd like to have kids. If he had put as much effort into finding a wife and having children as he had in setting up and growing his business, he'd have a nice family life and home right now. But it hadn't been the path he had chosen.

At least not yet.

INDIA HURRIED OUT OF Mr. Laurencelli's apartment. She had waited for him to leave, hoping she might be able to leave five minutes early to get to her clinical. But he had left a few minutes later than usual. And now she had to run if she wanted to be in time for her clinical over at the hospital. To save time, she changed into her nursing uniform before racing out of there.

Martin approached her when she stepped off the elevator. Oh, not now, she thought, because she didn't have time for chitchat. Despite this, she pasted a bright smile on her face.

"Hey what's the rush? Is something on fire?" he asked with a grin.

Why was someone always asking her that? She began to seriously wonder how she looked, dashing from one place to another.

Martin always seemed nice yet India was a little wary of him. For a doorman, he held a lot of power. He knew the comings and goings of everyone in this place.

"I don't want to be late for clinical," she said.

"Clinical?" he repeated.

She nodded. "I'm in my last year of nursing."

"How noble," he said.

She shifted on her foot, the exit in her sights. She could see her car out in the parking lot. If only she could get to it. She made a move but he held up his hand.

"Hold on a minute," he said.

A little flash of irritation coursed through her. She had just explained to him that she didn't want to be late and yet here he was, holding her up.

"Yes?" she asked, smile still firmly in place.

"I was wondering if you'd like to go out sometime?" he asked. When he saw her hesitation, he added, "Maybe dinner or a drink? Get to know each other better."

She had to let him down gently. She always felt it took a lot of courage to ask someone out because there was always a chance of rejection. "Wow, Martin, I am really flattered but I have to say no."

He stood there waiting and she realized it was his way of demanding a reason. She stifled a sigh, then trotted out her standard fabricated excuse: "I'm already in a relationship."

"Boy, that didn't take long," was his reply.

At first, India didn't understand what he was alluding to, but then it dawned on her. He was insinuating that she was involved with John Laurencelli.

She was aghast. "With Mr. Laurencelli? He's my boss! No, not him."

"My apologies," he said.

She didn't think his 'apologies' sounded too genuine. "But again, thanks, Martin," she said breezily as she sidestepped him and headed toward the exit.

She started her car and gave it the requisite ten minutes to warm up. It could be ornery like that. It tended to need a lot of coaxing.

Martin wasn't the first fella to ask her out since Stella's birth. And he wouldn't be the last. The last boyfriend she'd had had been Stella's father and he had made it very clear that he had no interest in becoming a father or a husband. He was gone before Stella had even been born. So, there was that. And when her mother had died, she just hadn't been in the mood to socialize, much less date. Now, with some time under her belt, she very much liked the idea of having a boyfriend, but it wasn't the right time yet. She had too much on her plate. It wouldn't be fair to ask someone to get in line behind everyone and everything else. But maybe someday. In the meantime, she was in a serious relationship with her family and most especially, her Nursing 401 textbook.

— ◦◦◦ —

INDIA WAS ALREADY TIRED of Mr. Laurencelli's pre-planned menu. How on earth did he eat the same thing every single Monday night? Ugh. She was determined to test out her culinary skills in his fabulous kitchen. Those cable cooking shows made it seem so easy and what they prepared always looked so yummy. They were on a budget at her house, so she couldn't afford to splurge on luxury ingredients or expensive cuts of meat, although she'd decided to take a little bit from her pay packet each week and tuck it away in her underwear drawer for the Christmas dinner. She was going to go all out. She had planned to have two starters, a turkey and a ham with all the trimmings, and some lovely, decadent desserts. Mr. Laurencelli had a kitchen to die for as well as a generous grocery budget he left her every Monday morning. It was a shame for it not to be used to its full potential.

She wondered if she could sneak something new into his menu without him noticing. Maybe a small side dish? Or perhaps a sauce for the fish? Maybe a mustard wine sauce or a creamy dill? It left her wondering. She didn't know about the rest of John Laurencelli's life, but his daily menu indicated he was in a rut. She hoped his life didn't resemble his dinner plan. If so, she was going to have to do a lot more than whip up a sauce for the salmon.

When she had a little bit of downtime, she began to search for recipes online, visiting her favorite haunts. She had hundreds of recipes stored on her phone. She had been saving them for the day when she could use them. After a while, she looked at the time and realized it was time to get the meal together.

"DID YOU EVER THINK of shaking things up a bit?" India asked John as she served his dinner.

John wondered what constituted 'shaking things up' in India Ramone's world.

"With regard to what?" he asked. "My choice of aftershave, my routine at the gym, or do you mean my love life?"

Her cheeks reddened slightly. "No, I meant your menu for dinner."

He bristled. "What do you mean?"

"What I mean is, today is Monday, so it must be salmon for dinner," she said, her arms flying about the place expressively. John wondered if she was able to talk without them.

"I like eating salmon on Mondays," he said.

"Yes, but what if you had the salmon on Wednesday and something else on Monday?" she asked.

"But I like eating salmon on Monday," he repeated.

"What would happen if you ate salmon on Wednesday?" she asked.

He shrugged. "Nothing, I suppose. But I prefer to eat it on Monday."

She rolled her eyes. "Could you humor me?" she asked, her arms flailing.

"I feel like I've been doing that since you started working for me," he said. "Do you need to be medicated for that?"

"For what?" she asked.

"Your arms swinging around like that? You're beginning to look like a windmill and I'm starting to feel dizzy," he said drily.

"Oh, I'm sorry," she said. "I tend to gesture when I talk."

"I noticed."

She pointedly put her arms at her side.

"Anyway, what would I have in place of the salmon?" he asked.

She looked excited and he hoped she hadn't taken his question for any kind of assent.

"For instance, sometime we have 'Sunday surprise' at our house," she started, warming to the subject.

He raised his eyebrows. "That sounds more questionable than mysterious." It also sounded suspiciously like a casserole. "Is it edible?"

"Don't be silly, of course, it's edible."

He had been called many things in his life, but 'silly' hadn't been one of them.

"Or sometimes it could be a casserole on Tuesday," she said.

He knew it. John Laurencelli was not a man who ate casseroles. He frowned. "Casserole? Isn't that the lazy cook's idea of a meal?"

She put her hands on her hips. "What do you mean by that?"

He put his hands up in mock surrender. "No offense intended, Ms. Ramone." He paused, choosing his words carefully. "It's like you put all the food together in one big dish and call it a casserole. No, I'm not a fan of that." Besides, his mother, God bless her, had been the casserole queen while he was growing up. He felt as if he had consumed his quota of casseroles in his lifetime.

"There's a lot of work with creating a casserole."

He was skeptical. "Anyway, as enlightening as this conversation has been, I think we'll stick to the pre-arranged menu."

THE FOLLOWING MORNING, John hunted around in the black lacquer trinket box for his Patek Philippe watch, his favorite. He frowned when he didn't see it immediately. A watch was hard to miss. It wasn't like a cuff link or a tiepin. He picked up the box and examined it more closely but didn't see it. He dumped the contents out on the top of the bureau but the watch wasn't there. He pulled out the heavy bureau to see if it had fallen behind, but there was nothing. He examined the carpet and looked under the bed, all clear. He went into the walk-in closet and pulled out drawers and rifled through suit pockets, but no sign of it. He tried to think when he had last seen it but concluded that it had been sometime last week.

John wrestled with the thoughts that came to him. He could easily replace the expensive watch; it was the idea of being stolen from that bothered him. He wondered about India. It was a vulgar supposition, but she was the only one here when he wasn't home. He knew she was financially strapped. But she seemed trustworthy so far, and he had a hard time believing Marta would recommend someone who had light fingers. It would explain things neatly as to the missing watch, though. And a Patek Philippe watch was a luxury item. If she had the right kind of friends, she could easily make a nice chunk of change for herself.

Once dressed, he exited the bedroom and found India laying his breakfast on the table. She looked up and smiled at him.

INDIA'S SMILE DISAPPEARED when she saw the stormy look on Mr. Laurencelli's face. She did a quick visual check of his breakfast; everything was there and she had laid it out exactly as he preferred.

"Ms. Ramone, you haven't seen my watch around the place, have you?" he asked. He remained standing and did not sit down.

She shook her head and immediately felt uneasy. "No, I haven't. Where did you see it last?" she asked.

He laughed but it didn't sound funny. "On my wrist. I haven't seen it since last week."

"I'll keep an eye out for it. Look behind the furniture and stuff," she volunteered. She tried to sound bright but something ominous skated along the edge of her mind.

He scratched his head and asked again, "Are you sure you haven't come across it?"

She was about to say no again, but there was something troublesome about his expression and the way he continued to stare at her. He said nothing, waiting.

Her mouth formed a small 'o' as it dawned on her. She couldn't believe it. She was horrified. "You think I took it?" she asked quietly.

"I didn't say that—"

"You didn't have to!" she said. Fury began building up within her.

"Look," he started. "I understand your situation. You're a single mother with a lot of people depending on you and in a not-so-great moment, you may have thought it would be handy to have a little more cash for Christmas. If I'm not paying you enough, just let me know. If you haven't sold it already, just give me back the watch and we'll say no more about this. I won't get the police involved."

India exploded. "You think I stole your watch? You think I took from you because I'm in desperate need of money?"

He began to stammer a response but she cut him off. "Look, Mr. Laurencelli, I am many things but I am not a thief! And shame on you for even thinking that! I'll save you the trouble of firing me because I quit!"

And with that, she grabbed her things and ran out the door, slamming it so hard behind her that the whole apartment shook.

Balling her hands up into fists, she gave a kick out with one of her legs and said, "Ugh!" Quickly, she opened his apartment door again and yelled, "You'll need to pick up your dry cleaning today. I didn't get to it yesterday. I was too busy cooking your pre-planned dinner!"

After slamming the door a second time, she turned on her heel and marched down the corridor toward the bank of elevators.

CHAPTER NINE

It took India a whole ten minutes to stop sobbing so she could put the car into drive and leave that place. Her body shook. To be accused of something you didn't do and know that your accuser didn't believe you—it was gut-wrenching. She hoped she'd never have to relive it. She wanted to smack herself for being so naïve. When he'd initially approached her about his missing watch she had just assumed he was asking her to keep an eye out for it, not implying that she stole it. And then when the truth of his implication dawned on her . . . it was akin to being kicked in the stomach. Foolishly, she had thought things were going well with Mr. Laurencelli. She had managed to stay awake and he hadn't fired her again. She had done what was required of her and there had been no complaints or criticism, at least none of a serious nature. He still wasn't much of a talker but he had seemed to be gradually coming around. Overall, she had thought she'd proved herself capable and efficient at taking care of him. After all, it was what India loved doing best: taking care of people. Before this morning, she even would have ventured to say he liked her. Ha! Not only didn't he like her but he thought she was a thief. She cringed at the thought of it. How horribly seedy!

Of course, now there was the other problem: she was out of a job. She had done the right thing in quitting because it was the principle of the matter. Besides that, how could she expect to go on working there when she knew he didn't trust her? She'd have to figure out a way to pay for Christmas. At least she had gotten a few things. Sickened, she decided to skip class. Her heart just wasn't in it.

By the time she arrived home, she had pulled herself together. She told herself to look on the bright side. There was always a bright side. Now she'd be home more often with Stella and Petey and she could do fun things with them in the evenings like put up more decorations or bake their favorite Christmas goodies.

She found Gramps at the table eating his breakfast, listening to a news talk show on the radio. He looked up at her, his mouth dropping open. "What are you doing here?"

"I forgot something for class," she lied.

He peered at her. "Why aren't you at work?"

She shrugged. "I had to quit that job."

"Quit? Why? What happened?" He studied her face. "He didn't try any funny business with you, did he? Cause if he did, I'll go down there and pop him one!"

She had to laugh in spite of herself at the image of Gramps driving down there in his El Camino and 'popping' him one. Or worse, bringing his BB gun along for the ride. She couldn't tell him the truth because she was too embarrassed. So instead, she said, "No, not at all. It just wasn't working out. Too much of a personality conflict."

"I'm sorry to hear that," he said. "But no job is worth making yourself miserable over. Life is too short."

"That is true," she agreed, except she hadn't been miserable. She had enjoyed taking care of Mr. Laurencelli. But Gramps was right; life was too short. They had all learned that the painful way.

Gramps finished his meal and stood up. "Sit down there. You've got time and I'll make you my breakfast special."

She laughed and plopped down on the kitchen chair. "That sounds good." Gramps's breakfast special was two eggs, sunny-side up; two pieces of Italian bread, toasted; and several medallions of Polish sausage. It was comfort food at its best.

Once she ate she felt better. The thought of skipping school no longer appealed to her as she hadn't missed one class or clinical all semester. The breakfast had reinvigorated her. She stood up, pulled her coat off the chair, and took the last piece of toast to go.

"Thanks, Gramps," she said, flying out the door with the toast in her hand.

THE UNPLEASANTNESS of India quitting on him was still stuck in John's craw by the time he arrived at work.

Janice, his secretary for the past ten years, read his mood instantly as he stomped into the office. She raised her eyebrows. "What's happened, Mr. Laurencelli?"

It bothered him that he was that transparent to her; it made him feel like a barometer.

He stood in front of her desk and lowered his voice. "I'm in need of a new personal assistant."

"I thought it was working out with Ms. Ramone," she said evenly, studying him. She wore big glasses and her hair, an unnatural shade of auburn, was piled into a twist at the back of her head.

"No, it isn't. She quit this morning," he confessed.

She frowned at him. "What did you do?"

"Nothing," he said.

"Try again," she commanded.

Janice had been eligible for retirement years ago. But she stayed with him and he was grateful for that, as she was super-efficient and could do the job with her eyes closed.

"It was a simple misunderstanding," he explained.

"Don't say any more," she said, holding up her hand. He didn't miss the disappointment in her voice.

"Do you know anyone looking for a temp job?" he asked.

"No," she said, then pursed her lips. "Besides, I wouldn't do that to my friends or family."

"Forget it," he grunted. At his office door, pausing with his hand on the knob, he turned to her and said, "Any chance you'd be willing to pick up my dry cleaning later this afternoon?"

She turned slowly toward him and leveled him with such a steely gaze, he wondered for a moment if she might need an exorcist.

"Okay, forget that too."

BEFORE LUNCHTIME, HE put out a call to Marta. She reiterated that she wouldn't be able to return to work until after New Year's. Then he ventured that he was looking to replace India and when she asked why he told her that India had quit, hoping she wouldn't pursue the reason. But of course, Marta did ask why India would quit a perfectly good job and he was forced to tell her.

"You did what?" she asked, her voice rising, clearly not happy. She was almost shouting, which was completely unlike her. John was forced to hold the phone away from his ear.

"India Ramone is not a thief," Marta said.

"Yes, so she told me," he said, wondering if it would infuriate her more if he just hung up. He decided to stay the course and bear the consequences.

"Mr. Laurencelli, do you really think I would recommend a criminal to step in for me?" she asked. "Frankly, I'm insulted."

Oh great, he thought. I've managed to ruffle the feathers of another female.

"I am sorry about that, Marta, but it still stands that I don't have a personal assistant."

"You had a perfectly good one until you accused her of stealing," Marta pointed out.

"Yes, could we get beyond that?" he asked, exasperated.

"I'm sorry, Mr. Laurencelli, but you're on your own with this one," she said. She bade him goodbye and hung up.

He closed his eyes. He was already lost without Ms. Ramone. After she had stormed out, he'd lost time cleaning up the kitchen and stripping his bed himself. He'd had to read the instructions on the inside of the ironing-board closet to figure out how to do his own laundry. He'd have to leave work early to pick up his dry cleaning. Worst of all, he was not looking forward to going home. There'd be no dinner on hand, ready to be served. But most of all, there'd be no one there, waiting for him.

INDIA HAD CALLED WARREN to bump up their dance practice.

He showed up while they were still eating dinner. India had just served herself another helping of shepherd's pie. Warren set down his briefcase, then removed his coat and laid it over the back of a chair. He said hello to everyone. Jumbo stood next him waiting to be petted. Once Warren obliged him, the dog resumed his position next to Stella in the lucky event she'd drop some food.

"Warren, will you have some dinner?" India asked.

He shook his head. "No thanks, I ate at home. I'm ready to practice."

"How was your day?" she asked.

"Surrounded by numbers, so I can't complain," he said.

"Would you two listen to yourselves?" Petey teased. "Just get married, for God's sake and put us all out of our misery."

Even Gramps raised his eyebrows.

"They can't get married because they don't kiss each other," Stella said knowingly.

It was India's turn to raise her eyebrows at Stella. Warren laughed nervously.

"We've been friends for so long we don't know how to be anything else," Warren explained.

What Warren had said was true. They'd been best friends for years and although the thought had occurred to India from time to time, it had been only that: a fleeting thought. It would have been convenient as they got along so well together, but she wasn't attracted to Warren that way and she was pretty certain he felt the same way.

But Petey wouldn't let it go. "If you guys got married, Warren could help me with my math."

"I already help you with your math," Warren pointed out.

"Oh yeah, that's right," Petey said. "Forget it then." He disappeared from the kitchen.

Once India had the kitchen cleaned up, she joined Warren in the living room to get started.

He looked up from his phone. "Hey what happened with work? You said you'd quit your job?"

She plopped down on the sofa next to him and nodded. "I did."

"Why?" he asked. A troubled look cast a shadow over his expression.

She looked down at her hands, folded in her lap. "Because he accused me of stealing his watch."

Warren was outraged. "He did what? Of all the lowdown—"

India gently laid her hand on his arm. "It's all right, Warren."

He protested. "But it's not all right. He can't just go around making false accusations about you with no basis in fact." He pushed his glasses further up on his nose.

"Maybe he can't, but he did," she said.

"That's despicable behavior. I mean, who does he think he is?" Warren asked.

India shrugged. "You can see why I had to quit."

Warren looked at her. "Of course you did, India. I mean, I know it kind of leaves you in the lurch financially but it's the principle of the matter. If that doesn't just fry my socks!"

India had to laugh. That was only one of Warren's endearing expressions among many.

"Shall we get to work?" she asked.

He nodded. "Good idea. Okay, first, I want you to watch this video. I thought we could do something like this. A foxtrot."

India paled. "That seems ambitious."

"Not really. It's just some basic steps," he said.

What India had discovered with their practices was that they were stiff and awkward and couldn't get their steps coordinated. She was an optimist but Warren could run circles around her with that stuff.

"It's easy."

India chuckled. "You always say that and it never is."

He regarded her and replied, "It's only hard if you think it is."

"Whatever, come on, Arthur Murray, turn the video on," she said.

MRS. WITTNER, THE OWNER of the dry-cleaning place, threw up her hands in surprise. "Mr. Laurencelli! It has been a long time indeed!"

He greeted her with a smile and enquired after her health.

Mrs. Wittner's smile disappeared. "Is everything all right? Is there a problem?"

He shook his head. "Not at all. Everything is fine. I'm just without a personal assistant at the moment."

"Oh, didn't it work out with that nice young girl who was in here last week? She was lovely. So warm and friendly," Mrs. Wittner twittered on.

"She no longer works for me."

"That's too bad," she said. "But I'm glad you stopped. I have something for you. Hold on." She disappeared into the back room and returned, carrying a gold envelope. "I found this in the breast pocket of your suit coat." She opened the envelope and his watch fell out into her hand.

John closed his eyes and his face reddened with shame.

"You shouldn't be so careless. That's an expensive watch," she scolded. "Always check your pockets." She handed him the watch and said, "I'll get your dry cleaning."

John looked at the watch and thought of all the trouble he had caused because of it. He knew what he had to do and it involved swallowing his pride, which he rarely had to do. But still, right was right.

INDIA PARKED HER CAR in the lot and pulled her backpack off the seat next to her. Today was hump day. Almost there. Two more days until Friday. The positive thing about quitting her job had been the fact that she had had all that extra time to study, which she did, and more free time in general. It had bothered her that Mr. Laurencelli thought she was nothing more than an opportunistic crook. She was surprised at how wounded she was. Despite a poor night's sleep, she'd gotten up early that morning to go over her notes and reading. There were no more clinicals, just lectures, and for the most part, classes this week would be all about review. When Stella and Petey came downstairs that morning, she had surprised them with a hot breakfast of French toast and sausages. Afterward, she'd driven them both to school to give them a break from the bus, then headed to the college.

She locked her car and began cutting through the parking lot on foot. It was a crisp winter morning, cold but brisk, a beautiful mid-

December day with the sun shining brightly and the white snow that blanketed the landscape practically glittering. She saw a Mercedes approach but paid no attention to it. It pulled into an empty spot ahead of her and she still took no notice. She was too busy reviewing her notes in her mind. When John Laurencelli stepped out the car and turned toward her, she stiffened and halted in her tracks.

She didn't acknowledge him and although he could have arrived at the college for other business, she knew he was here to see her. She didn't move, waiting to see what he did.

She regarded him with a wary eye as he approached her. He looked as if he had just stepped off the pages of GQ magazine. He wore a cashmere coat over his suit and a pair of black leather gloves that looked as soft as butter.

"Ms. Ramone, I hoped I'd find you here," he said.

What could he want now? Frowning at him, she remained silent.

"I know you're heading to class so I won't detain you for long," he started.

He pulled something out of his pocket and showed her: his watch. The one that had gone missing. The one he had accused her of stealing.

"I found my watch," he said.

"Where was it?" she asked, curiosity getting the better of her.

"In my suit pocket," he replied.

"I'm happy for you," she said blandly, and she started to walk away.

"Wait, Ms. Ramone," he said. Closing the gap between them, he stepped closer until he stood in front of her.

India stopped and sighed. She hated confrontations of any kind. She hated scenes. The bright morning sunshine made his eyes blaze even more strongly than usual. And he had such beautiful cheekbones . . . But she couldn't let his looks diminish her resolve. She stood her ground and looked him in the eye.

"I wanted to apologize," he said. "The way I treated you was utterly wrong and I am ashamed of myself. I hope you can forgive me."

"Apology accepted," she said. "Have a nice day." She stepped away but he laid his hand gently on her arm. His touch was electric and she regarded him with alarm. There was no way she wanted to have that kind of reaction to him.

"Ms. Ramone, please," he appealed. "This isn't easy for me."

"Really? You should see how not easy it is when you're falsely accused of something," she said, the anger rising within her. "Like stealing."

He grimaced. "I know, and again, I am truly sorry."

"All right, fine. Now goodbye."

"I want you to come back to work for me," he said.

A bitter laugh escaped her. "I don't think so."

"Please, Ms. Ramone," he said.

She shook her head. "I may be broke, but I'm not desperate." She thought she saw him flinch but she didn't care. "Who do you think you are? Lord of the manor? No, it wouldn't work." She took a step closer to him. "You don't trust me. Every time something was misplaced you'd think I stole it to get my hands on some cash."

"I wouldn't," he said softly.

She felt sad. She was determined not to budge from her stance. Other students and faculty passed by them, some giving them curious stares and some recognizing Mr. Laurencelli. She had to get out of there.

"Look, I'm going to be late for my class," she said.

"Ms. Ramone, I'm going to appeal to your sense of decency," he said. "Don't you believe in second chances?"

She squinted at him, remembering she had thrown those same words at him not too long ago when he had fired her on that first day.

"Do you remember when you asked me to give you a second chance? How you said there were people depending on you? I'm in the same boat. There are a lot of people depending on me," he said. "For me to be able to run my business properly, I need someone to make sure my personal life is running smoothly."

She looked at him and thought, Oh boy, you are dangerous. He was not only appealing to her sense of decency but also fair play and quid pro quo. He was ruthless.

"Look, it's only for a couple more weeks," he said. "And then you'll never see me again." He paused. "I'm asking you to give me a second chance."

Against her better judgment, she said, "With reservation, I'll agree. But no more false accusations."

"I promise. Thank you," he said, smiling. It was hard to resist that smile and those blue eyes. "Now Ms. Ramone, have tonight off and I'll see you in the morning. You'll get paid for the full week."

"That isn't necessary," she said.

"Oh, but it is," he said, walking back to his car. He paused, turned back to her, and called out, "You better get a move on or you'll be late for your class." And then he disappeared into his car.

She stood there staring after him for a moment and when he pulled out of the parking space, he gave her a slight wave.

Becky sidled up beside her. "Was that John Laurencelli?"

"Yes."

Becky peered at her. "What does he want with you?"

"He wants to make my life difficult," India said with a sigh.

CHAPTER TEN

India immediately settled back into her routine the following morning. It felt as if she had never been gone. She plated up Mr. Laurencelli's breakfast.

"How are you this morning, Ms. Ramone?" he asked as he sat down. She wanted to roll her eyes. He was going to try and make small talk.

"I'm fine," she answered politely.

"Exams next week?"

She nodded.

"What's the first one?" he asked, sipping his grapefruit juice.

She peered at him. "Mr. Laurencelli, you don't have to make small talk with me."

A look of discomfort flitted across his face. "Maybe if I'd gotten to know you a bit better, I wouldn't have jumped to conclusions," he said soberly.

India sighed. "Don't beat yourself up over it, please. You apologized—let's put it behind us."

"Are you always this forgiving?"

She smiled. "I find it difficult to hold a grudge."

They looked at each other for a minute and India smiled at him. "Your breakfast is getting cold."

She retreated to the safety of the kitchen, glad for all her tasks. They distracted her from the meaning of the subtle shift in their employer-employee relationship. He didn't attempt to engage her in any more conversation before he left.

HE HADN'T BEEN GONE that long when the doorbell to his apartment rang. Initially, India wondered if he had forgotten something, but then he would have just used his key to let himself back in. She put the dish towel down on the kitchen counter and went to answer the door. She hoped it wasn't the doorman.

She opened the door to find a tall, dark-haired woman standing there. It was the bright blue eyes framed with dark lashes and brows that made India suspect this woman may be a relative of Mr. Laurencelli's.

"Yes?" she asked.

"Hi, I'm Bridget, John's sister," the woman said.

India held the door open for her. "Come in. But he's already left for work," India told her.

"I figured as much." She sailed past India and removed her coat.

"Will I call him and let him know you're here?" India asked, unsure what to do with his guest. Marta hadn't covered that on the cheat sheet she'd given her.

The woman winked at India and said, "No, I'd like to surprise him."

India wondered if that was a good idea. She wasn't sure of much but she doubted Mr. Laurencelli treasured surprises.

"Can I get you coffee or tea?" India asked.

Bridget shook her head and smiled at her. "Can I ask who you are? A girlfriend?"

India was alarmed and sputtered, "Oh, God no!"

Bridget burst out laughing. "Tell me how you really feel about him."

"Oh, I am so sorry, Ms. Laurencelli. I'm India Ramone. I'm filling in for Marta," India said, extending her hand.

Bridget shook it. "Oh right. He had mentioned she broke her wrist. How is she?"

"Good."

"Look, call me Bridget. I know my brother likes a lot of formality with his staff but you're not my staff, so first names, please."

"All right," India smiled.

Bridget camped out on the couch. She looked around the place. "It's been a while since I've been here."

India wondered about that but decided it was none of her business.

"Are you sure I can't get you any tea or coffee?"

"Only if you join me," Bridget said.

India shook her head. "Actually, I need to finish up here and get to school." The truth was she wouldn't feel comfortable sitting and socializing in Mr. Laurencelli's home. She'd expect his voice to boom in from somewhere calling her out on it. It'd be a cup of tea or coffee she surely wouldn't enjoy.

"What are you going to college for?" Bridget asked.

"Nursing," India said proudly.

"Good for you," Bridget said.

India looked around. As lovely as his sister was, she had to finish her work so she could leave on time.

Bridget's face softened. "India, you don't need to entertain me. I'll stay out of your way. Go ahead with what you were doing."

"Are you sure?" she asked.

"Yes, I am. I'm going to hang around until John gets home."

India finished her morning tasks and called out goodbye to Bridget. "I'll be back this afternoon."

"Okay, India, it was nice meeting you."

ANGELA RAPPED ON JOHN'S office door and walked in.

He looked up from the mountain of paperwork on his desk.

"Brenda's coming in at four this afternoon." She sank down into the chair across from his desk. "Can you meet with her?"

John glanced at his schedule, which Janice had left on his desk. "I've got a few minutes. Why, where will you be?"

She slid a piece of paper across his desk. It had been ripped out of a magazine. He unfolded it, curious. It was a high-gloss ad for a diamond necklace. The necklace itself was brilliant against the blacks and grays of a silhouetted neck. John estimated it had to cost five figures.

"It's going to be my Christmas present to myself."

"Very nice." He hoped she wouldn't bring up that other matter.

But she must have been reading his mind, because she crossed her legs, fiddled with the hem on her skirt and asked, "Have you given any thought to what I asked you?"

Sighing, he sat back in his chair, not wanting to have this conversation but deciding it was better to get it all out in the open.

"Angela, I can't do it. I can't bring a child into this world and not be a part of his or her life."

"But it isn't necessary, John," Angela said.

"For you, it isn't necessary, but for me it is," he said. "It would really put a strain on our relationship if we were to have a baby together."

"If the actual deed, or doing the deed with me, turns you off—" she started, clearly offended.

"I didn't say that. Please don't put words in my mouth," he said.

"Instead of the old-fashioned way, we could do it in a clinical setting," she suggested.

He shook his head. "Thank you for thinking of me, but this proposition is not for me."

She drew in a deep breath. "Even for a friend?"

"Even more so because you're a friend," he said. "We run a business together. I can't believe you think I'd be comfortable with you talking about your son or daughter, posting photos in your office and there I am, knowing the child is mine."

"Do I look like the type to bore people with stories of what my child was up to? You know I can't stand that in other people," she said with a hint of annoyance.

"I'd hope you would with your child, Angela," he said quietly.

Abruptly, she stood up. "This is your final answer?"

He nodded. "Yes, it is."

"Thanks for helping me out, John," she said bitterly.

"Angela, I hope this doesn't affect our friendship."

"It already has."

AFTER JOHN ARRIVED home from work, hung up his coat, and set his briefcase on the floor of the hall closet, he strode into the living room, loosening his tie. He stopped in his tracks when he saw his sister, Bridget, sitting on his sofa. There were overflowing shopping bags piled next to the couch. There was also the smell of baking in the area. He glanced toward the kitchen and saw snickerdoodles laid out on baking racks. He had hoped to avoid her altogether until after the holidays. That had always been the trickiest part of his plan every December: bypassing her and her ideas of a family holiday.

"Hello, brother," Bridget said cheerily.

"Bridget, what brings you here?" he asked as if he didn't know.

"Hmm, funny you should mention it," she said, looking up toward the ceiling and resting her index finger against her lip. "Since you weren't returning my calls, I figured I'd drop by. India was kind enough to let me in," she said.

"I must remember to thank her for that," John said with sarcasm.

As if on cue, India popped her head out of the kitchen and asked, "Will I serve your dinner now?"

"Can you give me five minutes, Ms. Ramone?" he asked.

"Of course," she said. "I took the liberty of preparing a plate for your sister, too."

He nodded but thought, Just terrific. He went into the sanctuary of his room and closed the door behind him, grateful for the privacy. The last person he wanted to see was Bridget, not this month. Not any December, for that matter.

He stripped down to his boxers and T-shirt and splashed cold water on his face to brace himself for the inevitable conversation that was coming. Why was it he could handle anything that was thrown at him businesswise but he couldn't seem to manage his own sister? Irritation flooded him. Why couldn't she leave him in peace this one month? He was at her disposal and willing to be involved with her and her kids for the other eleven months. He was already prickly from his encounter with Angela earlier. Then in a fit of pique, Angela had gone and canceled the meeting with Brenda Boker and told her that their company was no longer interested in her beach glass magazine.

No sense in delaying the inevitable, he thought wearily as he pulled on a pair of jeans and a fresh shirt and headed back to the dining room. He'd let her have her say and then he would send her on her way. And tell her he'd see her in January.

Bridget was already seated and sipping at a glass of wine. India set the dinner down on the table.

"India, it looks lovely," Bridget said.

"Thank you," she said.

"Why don't you join us?" Bridget asked. "It's a shame for you not to enjoy your own efforts."

Ms. Ramone had a look of horror on her face that John suspected matched his own expression. To her credit, she respected the employer/employee boundary just as much as he did.

"I really have to get home," India said.

"Thank you, Ms. Ramone, that will be all," John told her. "I'll see you in the morning?"

"Goodnight, Mr. Laurencelli. Goodnight, Bridget, it was nice meeting you."

Bridget raised her glass to her. "And you too, India. Thank you for all this." She spread her hand out at the dinner laid out on the table.

"No problem."

"And if my brother gives you any trouble, let me know," she said, staring at John evenly. "No matter how old he gets, he's still my baby brother."

John was mortified at his sister's lack of propriety with his employee. He decided it didn't deserve a comment.

He sat down and dug in. It was chicken cordon bleu, green beans almandine and roasted baby potatoes. He took a few bites and decided it was delicious. He said nothing. He was not going to engage with his sister while Ms. Ramone was present. No sense in giving her anything to gossip over.

Bridget ate her dinner and sipped her wine, staring straight ahead and not looking at him. He poured himself a generous amount of wine, figuring he was going to need it.

They heard India gather her things, walk down the hall, open the door and then close it quietly behind her.

It was several minutes before either one of them spoke.

Bridget put down her fork. John braced himself for what was coming.

"If you'd return my calls, I wouldn't have to ambush you like this in your own home," she said softly, the bravado gone.

He didn't look at her. He stared at the food on his plate. "I've been busy. We're in the middle of buying out another company."

She sighed. "No one is that busy, John. Besides, that's what your company does, buy out other companies. It's nothing out of the ordinary for you."

He decided to cut to the chase. "Is there a purpose to your visit?"

She looked at him in anger. "Does there have to be? You're my brother."

There was tense silence again. John opted for the safe topic.

"How are Terrence and the kids?" he asked. Bridget had three children: two boys and a girl. He liked Terrence a lot; he felt he didn't have to worry about Bridget.

"They're all good. They're all fine," she said. He didn't miss the exasperation in her voice. "But the kids wonder why Uncle John, who they see all year round, won't be around for Christmas."

He shrugged. "Tell them I'm busy. Tell them I'm out of town."

"Okay, they're all under the age of eight, so they won't understand that concept."

"Did they not like the presents I sent them last year?"

She rolled her eyes. "Of course they did. But they like spending time with you. Although why I don't know, when you're so stubborn."

"I'll take that as a compliment," he said with a wry smile.

"It wasn't intended as one," she snapped. "Seriously, John, you can't act like this every December. It's not healthy."

"I don't know what you're talking about," he said, turning his attention back to his dinner. The chicken was very good. Ms. Ramone certainly could cook.

"Stop it, John," Bridget said sternly as if he were a recalcitrant child.

He decided again that silence was his best option.

She decided otherwise. "You can't shut yourself away every December and not celebrate Christmas. It just isn't right. It isn't healthy," she said.

"I don't know about that. I've been doing fine all these years," he said.

"It depends on what your definition of 'fine' is," she said. She speared a piece of chicken. "And you're not doing fine."

He sat up straighter, offended, and stared at her. "Says who?" he demanded.

"Says me, your big sister, who knows you better than anyone," she said. "Are you happy?"

He drew in a long breath. The meal would have been almost perfect if it wasn't for the present company's nagging.

"I never gave it much thought, to be honest,"

"You should examine your conscience," she suggested.

"Now you're a priest?" he asked.

"You can't keep doing this to yourself," she cried.

He knew where this was leading and he decided to just ignore her and let her get her rant out.

"Mom has been dead for more than twenty years. It's more than time for you to rejoin the land of the living. You need to move on with your life."

"I have," he protested.

"No, you haven't," she said softly. "Because if you had, you'd be happy and you wouldn't be so difficult and trying to control every little thing. And most of all, you'd be able to celebrate Christmas. Yes, it sucked that Mom died around Christmas. I agree with you there but you can't lock yourself away for the whole month of December. You still have me and Terrence and the kids. We're your family and you need to move on and share Christmas with us. The kids would love it." She paused, took a liberal sip of wine and added softly, "Most of all, I would love it."

He remained silent.

"Mom would never have wanted this."

His anger flared. "Don't you dare do that to me. Don't you ever presume to know what Mom would have wanted."

"I can presume because as a mother I know for a fact that no mother would ever want to see her child suffering. That is universal!" She stood up and threw her napkin on the table. He could see her chin quivering and he hated himself for letting her goad him into this kind of response. Although she acted tough, he knew her to be very sensitive.

"I give up on you. All this money and you're still a lost cause," she said. She walked past him and he allowed her to have this parting shot without snapping back at her. She grabbed her coat, purse, and shopping bags and stormed out the door, slamming it behind her.

He knew deep down that everything she said was true but he just wasn't ready to deal with it. Or even admit it.

INDIA SANK DOWN ON the couch next to Petey. All the lights were out and he was bathed in the bluish glow of the television as well as the multi-colored Christmas lights lining the front window.

She glanced at the TV screen. "Not zombies again! How about a nice Christmas movie? We could watch It's a Wonderful Life. That's a great movie."

He looked at her with a scowl. "Nah. Been there, done that. Too long, and the movie is in black and white."

"That's part of its charm," India pointed out.

"No thanks."

They settled in and India steeled herself against the zombie on-slaught.

Petey paused the TV and turned to India. "Can I ask you a question?"

India wondered briefly if he was going to ask her about the facts of life. She braced herself. "Sure, go ahead."

"What was Dad like?" he asked.

India had not expected this and it caught her off guard. Their father had been killed in a car accident when India was just barely in her teens and Petey was still a baby.

"Dad was nice," she started, realizing how lame it sounded and how it didn't do their father justice. "He was a musician, you know. He played in a band. They played most every weekend. It was nice because he was always home during the week to take me to school. To make my lunch. To pick me up after school," India laughed. "Dad was pretty straightforward and such a creature of habit!"

"What do you mean?" Petey asked, interested.

"When I was in school, he made me a bologna-and-mustard sandwich every single day of the third grade."

Petey laughed but there was a wistful look in his eyes. "I bet that got old fast."

"You have no idea." India laughed. "To this day I can't stand bologna!"

"What else do you remember?"

India was thoughtful. What could she impart to Petey about their father? "He was always singing around the house. He had a nice voice."

She fell back into those years. It wasn't that long ago but it felt like a lifetime. So much had happened since his death. Some of it good—Stella came to mind—and some of it horrible. The memory of Mom's sickness and death assailed her.

"He always used to sing 'Sweet Caroline,'" she said, and she swallowed hard to disguise the tremor in her voice.

"Because Mom's name was Caroline?"

"You got it!"

They were quiet for a moment, each lost in their own thoughts.

"You look like him, you know," India said quietly. "And your love of music and your ability to play instruments also comes from Dad. He was a great musician. He was always strumming his guitar or playing the drums out in our garage. The neighbors used to complain." She laughed at the long-forgotten memory.

"Do you still have his guitar and drums?" he asked, his eyes lighting up.

"We do," she said. "Somewhere around here."

"I'd like to see them sometime," he said.

"All right," she said. An idea began to form in her mind. She smiled at him. Gramps would shake his head from time to time and say Petey got the short end of the stick, having lost both his parents before he was ten. India made a solemn vow to herself that wherever she and Stella lived, Petey would be there also. The three of them were a package deal.

"Is his band still around?" Petey asked.

"I think so," she said, unsure. "After Dad died, they kind of fell apart, but I heard a few years ago that they were back together doing the circuit—bars, weddings, oldies nights and that sort of thing."

"What was the name of the band?" Petey asked.

"Stereo Components," she said.

Petey laughed. "How did they come up with that name?"

It was India's turn to laugh. "I have no idea."

CHAPTER ELEVEN

India walked out of her first exam on Monday breathing a sigh of relief. Microbiology was over. It was her hardest class and the exam had been difficult, but she thought she'd done okay. She'd need a C or better or she'd have to repeat it. But at least, for now, it was behind her. She was beginning to see the light at the end of the tunnel, and the good news was that it wasn't that of an oncoming train.

She said goodnight to Mr. Laurencelli after her shift that evening, gathered her belongings, and left his apartment, anxious to do some final studying before her exam on Tuesday. There'd be no practicing with Warren tonight, despite the fact that they only had this week and next to get their routine down. The way things were looking, she highly doubted they could pull it off. She pushed that out of her mind; she couldn't dwell on it now, not with more exams to get through.

She waved goodbye to Martin on her way out. It was snowing heavily. She walked quickly to her car, her mind racing with all the things she had to do when she got home: study, give Stella her bath and wash her hair, help Petey with any homework, catch up on the laundry, make the lunches, and then study some more. She'd be lucky if she got into bed by midnight.

To distract herself, she thought of the things she was going to do this weekend to get ready for Christmas. She wanted to pull the plastic bins and boxes of decorations down from the attic and finish putting them up with help from Petey and Stella. She wanted to make some holiday cookies and she was going to try her hand at her mother's recipe for fudge. Again. Hopefully, this time she wouldn't burn the sugar like she did last year.

She slid in behind the wheel of her car, shivering. The interior was cold from sitting there for a few hours and the windshield was covered in a thick blanket of snow. She'd get the car started to let it warm up while she brushed off the snow. She hoped the weather wouldn't add extra time to her drive home. But somehow, she knew she wouldn't get that lucky.

She turned the key in the ignition. Nothing. She turned it again and still nothing.

"Oh, come on Betsey," she said. "Don't fail me now. Just get me home, girlie."

But the car still didn't respond when she tried for a third time. It didn't even make that weak whine it usually did. The image of a car repair bill came into her mind, causing her to groan. Just when she was getting ahead. So much for possibly finishing the Christmas shopping this weekend. She almost wanted to cry but she pulled herself together. Just get home for now, she told herself.

After the fourth and final attempt, India gave up, leaned back against the seat, looked up and sighed. Not even enough juice to light up the dashboard to see if there were any warning lights on. Frustrated, she took the key out of the ignition and dug through her purse for her phone. She was going to call Warren to see if he could pick her up. She didn't want to drag Gramps out in this. But one look at her phone told her it was dead, too. She had meant to charge it when she arrived earlier at Mr. Laurencelli's but had forgotten.

Grabbing her purse and backpack, she locked up the car and trekked through the heavy snow back to the lobby, thinking maybe she could use Martin's phone. But when she arrived in the lobby, he was nowhere to be found. She waited for a few minutes and when there was still no sign of him, she headed toward the elevator. She hated the thought of having to ask, but she was really left with no choice. She'd have to use Mr. Laurencelli's phone to call Warren.

Mr. Laurencelli had a look of surprise on his face when he answered the door. "Did you forget something, Ms. Ramone?"

She smiled guiltily. "No, I was wondering if I could use your phone. Both my car and my phone are dead."

"Please, come in," he said, holding the door open for her. She followed him inside and he closed the door behind her.

"Thank you. I'll just call my friend and ask him for a ride home and then I'll leave you in peace."

"Don't worry about that—I'll take you home myself," he said. "Let me get my shoes."

India was not prepared for that solution. She stammered. "Oh, Mr. Laurencelli, that isn't necessary at all. I certainly didn't mean that you should do it."

"I know, but it doesn't make sense to drag your friend all the way here when I'm perfectly capable of driving you home myself."

She hesitated, opened her mouth, then closed it.

"Unless of course, you don't want me to," he said.

"No, no, not all," India said in a rush. "I just don't want to trouble you."

"It's no trouble at all," he said. "Give me two minutes." He disappeared into the other room, then reappeared and pulled his coat out of the hall closet. "Maybe it's time to get yourself a more reliable vehicle," he suggested as he checked his pocket for his wallet and keys.

"Gee, why hadn't I thought of that," India said dryly. What did he think? That she liked riding around in an undependable car? That she had access to that kind of money, to just go out and purchase a newer one? There was a serious disconnect between the real world and Mr. Laurencelli.

THEY TOOK THE ELEVATOR down to the underground parking garage, and India followed Mr. Laurencelli to his car. He pressed a button on the remote on his key chain and the lights on his Mercedes flashed, accompanied by a beeping sound. He took her backpack from her to set it on the floor of the backseat, caught off-guard by the weight of it.

"What on earth do you have in here? A dead body?"

"Nursing textbooks," she answered with a laugh. He opened the front passenger side door for India and waited for her to get in before closing it.

"Thank you," she murmured.

"Now, what's your address?" he asked.

She rattled it off her address and he typed it into the GPS on the dashboard. "All right, we're on our way."

When he pulled out of the garage, he was surprised at the amount of snow that had accumulated since he'd arrived home an hour ago. It continued to fall. He was glad of the garage and the fact that he didn't have to brush off his car or warm it up. He saw one car, an older, beat-up model, in the outdoor parking lot.

"Is that your car over there?" he asked.

"It is," she said, staring straight ahead out the windshield, her brow furrowed.

"Ms. Ramone, are you all right?" he asked. He maneuvered his car smoothly through the freshly fallen, greasy snow.

"Yes, I'm fine." Her voice sounded a little more high-pitched than normal.

"You seem a little tense," he put forward.

"Nope," she answered quickly. "I'm fine."

He sighed. She wasn't fine but he wasn't in the mood to play guessing games so he said nothing.

"It's just . . ." India started.

He glanced over at her, eyebrows raised, waiting for her to finish her sentence.

She squirmed in her seat. "It's just that my rear end feels like it's on fire," she said.

He chuckled. "I'm sorry. It's the heated seats. I'll turn them down."

"Thanks," she said. After a few minutes of quiet, she spoke again. "Can I ask you a question, Mr. Laurencelli?"

"Yes," he said, hoping it wasn't a personal one. He liked boundaries, especially boundaries with employees. Rules and boundaries made him feel secure.

"What is it you do for a living?" she asked, peering at him.

He hadn't expected that. He was more than happy to discuss his business. He was proud of the way he'd built it from the ground up right out of college.

"I own a company that buys other companies, smaller companies," he said. "I like to help them reach their potential and then I either keep them or sell them."

She was thoughtful for a moment. "Can you give me an example?"

"Of what?" he asked. He kept his eyes on the road. They were slick.

"Of the types of companies of you buy or own," she clarified.

"Well, we're in the process of buying a small-operation whiskey distillery in Scotland, for one," he said.

She raised her eyebrows again. "What, like Jameson?"

He laughed. "No, it's not on that scale. It's a smaller, mom-and-pop operation. But they've won several awards. And I like their whiskey."

"Is that important?" she asked.

"It is. I have to be as passionate about the product as they are."

"Okay, what else?"

"We're in the process of purchasing—at least I hope we still are—a magazine devoted to beach-glass enthusiasts," he said.

"Beach glass?" she repeated.

He nodded. "I was surprised, too, but apparently the beach-glass community in the US is large. It's a very successful venture. The magazine is less than five years old and the woman who started it up has taught herself everything there is to know about magazine publishing."

"Is that important?" she asked.

"No, not so much magazine publishing, but I admire her drive and determination to get it done. She's a force to be reckoned with," he said.

"Do you have a business partner?" she asked. "Because you often say 'we.'"

He nodded. "Yes, you've met Angela. We've been together since our college days. But I consider everyone who works for me as part of the team."

India nodded.

Mr. Laurencelli reached over to turn on the radio but switched it off quickly when he recognized the sound of Christmas music. "Ugh!"

India searched his face questioningly but said nothing.

In an attempt to straddle the silence, he remarked after a few moments, "I recognize the name of your street. I know that neighborhood. Have you lived there long?" He felt compelled to make conversation although he was at a loss as to why.

"No," she said softly. "I live with my grandfather. We all do. When Mom died, we had to move in with him."

"Oh. I'm sorry, Ms. Ramone." He could certainly relate to that. "When did your mother pass away?" he asked gently.

"She died two years ago," she answered, staring out the window.

They both went quiet. He suspected she didn't want to elaborate on the subject and he respected that more than she could ever imagine.

When they got close to India's house, she pointed ahead. "The next street is mine. But you can just drop me off at the corner."

He looked at the calf-deep snow on her street and said, "I don't think so. I'll take you right to your house." He wasn't going to have her trudging through all this snow with her purse and a backpack that weighed a ton when he was perfectly willing to take her right to her door.

He turned left onto her street and slowed down a bit.

"It's that two-story red brick house over there," she said pointing to it.

Although it was a street of older homes, it was a nice area. A lot like the one he grew up in. He pulled into her driveway, wondering if he had made a mistake as it hadn't been shoveled and the snow was halfway up the wheels of his Merc.

He idled the car, wondering how long it would take him to get home.

"There you are, Ms. Ramone," he said. He looked at the house. It was in some need of mild repair. A porch light over the side door illuminated the driveway and the El Camino parked there. He hadn't seen one of those cars in a long time. Didn't think there were any still on the road. There were multi-colored Christmas lights twinkling in the front window. A lone blow-up snowman lay on its side in the yard, deflated and covered in snow.

"Thanks, Mr. Laurencelli, I really appreciate it," she said. Her hand was on the door handle.

"Look, Ms. Ramone, if the weather is as bad as this, please stay home tomorrow morning," he said. No job was worth risking your life.

"Oh, I'm sure it will be clear by morning," she said. "After all, this is Buffalo and we do snow."

He chuckled. "Yes, we do 'do' snow. But if the roads aren't clear by morning, it's okay not to come to work," he said. He didn't want any one of his employees putting their life in danger. It was only a job after all.

She seemed to hesitate before getting out. "Mr. Laurencelli, would you like to come inside for a minute?" she asked, biting her lip.

He could tell she was nervous about inviting him in. Was she afraid he'd say no or was she afraid he'd say yes? "Yes, I'll come in for a minute. I'd like to meet your family."

"You would?" she asked, unable to mask her surprise.

"Yes." He laughed. "Unless you don't want me to meet them."

"No, no, no," she said. "It's not that at all."

He put the car into park and turned off the engine. He followed her into the house through the side door, into the small hallway, and up three steps. He noted the winter boots parked on newspapers by the inside door. There was a small pink pair lined with white fur, a bigger navy fleece-lined pair for an older kid, and a pair of old-fashioned black galoshes, the kind his own grandfather used to wear.

She opened the door and called out, "I'm home."

What happened next surprised him. All at once, they all came out of nowhere and mobbed her.

A little girl who was the image of India wrapped her arms around her waist and yelled, "Mommy!"

A preteen boy with slightly lighter-colored hair than India appeared and asked, "Do you think we'll have the day off school tomorrow?"

"I don't know, Petey, let's hope so!" she answered.

"India, I've saved you a plate," said an older man. This must be her grandfather.

The boy whispered to India, "Give it a pass. It was a meatloaf again."

All three soon realized that India wasn't alone. They looked over her shoulder and stared at him, and then looked back at India.

India introduced him. "This is my boss, Mr. Laurencelli."

"Oh, the billionaire!"

"Petey, don't be rude," India scolded. "This is my grandfather, Mr. Miller, my brother, Petey, and my daughter, Stella."

Stella stood in front of her mother and India wrapped her arms around her.

"Mr. Laurencelli was kind enough to give me a ride home," she explained. "My car died."

"Again?" her grandfather asked.

"Yes," India said wearily. She turned to John. "Come in, come in."

He followed her as they stepped from the kitchen into the open area that served as a combination dining room and living room. John admired these older houses: the higher ceilings; the heavy, ornate woodwork; and the overall general charm.

From behind him, he heard it before he saw it, or rather felt it.

"Woof!" A deep bark.

"Jumbo! No!" India warned.

What kind of dog had a bark like that? John turned around to see and came face to face with what he thought was a dog. The shaggy white beast bounded toward him, rose up on his hind legs, and jumped on John with such force that the dog knocked him down onto his back.

The dog lay on top of him with his paws on John's chest. A big pink tongue emerged from the dog's mouth and licked John's face.

"Oh, my God, I am so sorry!" India exclaimed. "Jumbo, get off!" John felt the dog being dragged off of him.

The boy was laughing in the background. "If that isn't a sackable offense, I don't know what is!"

John Laurencelli couldn't help but agree.

CHAPTER TWELVE

From his position on the floor, John looked up to the sea of faces that surrounded him. There was India, with an expression that looked like she was afraid she was going to get fired again. Gramps looked concerned as if he was wondering if John was injured and whether his homeowner's insurance would cover it. The little girl, who was missing her two front teeth and had a constellation of freckles across her nose, said nothing but just continued to stare at him mildly as if it was a normal occurrence for a grown man to be lying on their floor. And India's brother, Petey, had a wicked grin on his face. John turned his head and came face to face with the grandfather's ankles, or more specifically, his maroon-and-navy argyle socks.

"Are you hurt?" India asked. A deep frown was etched between her eyebrows.

"No, I'm fine," he said curtly.

They all helped him up. He brushed off his cashmere coat, now covered in dog hair. India came at him with a lint brush that had seen better days.

He turned to the grandfather. "While I was on the floor, I was admiring your socks."

Gramps beamed. "Thank you. I like them myself. I got them off of Mr. Bannon."

John frowned and looked at India, confused.

Gramps explained. "When the neighbor died, his wife gave me his socks and shoes. We wore the same size. And he had some nice Florsheims, let me tell you."

The proud owner of a dead man's socks and shoes. John decided to let it go.

"What on earth was that?" he asked, looking around to see if the creature was anywhere in the vicinity and whether there might be a repeat performance.

"That was Jumbo, our dog," India said. "I am so sorry, Mr. Laurencelli."

John glanced around him, afraid the dog might come bounding out of nowhere again. "A dog? He looks more like a yeti."

Petey laughed. "A yeti. That's a good one."

Is it? John wondered. He'd never been noted for his humor.

"So, I hear you've got more money than God," Petey said, folding his arms across his chest. The incident with the dog was clearly behind the boy as he went on to ask questions that demanded answers.

"Petey!" India said, horrified.

"I don't know," John answered him. "How much money does God have?"

Petey continued. "They say you're a billionaire."

John shook his head. "Not really."

"Millionaire?" Petey asked.

"Stop it!" India admonished. "Mr. Laurencelli, I am so—"

John raised his hand. The boy's frankness was refreshing. You always knew where you stood with people like him. "A mere multimillionaire, I'm afraid."

Petey shrugged. "I guess you can't have everything."

John let out a bark of laughter that surprised even him. "The papers insist on overstating my net worth."

"Don't worry, your secret's safe with me," Petey said.

"Thanks, I appreciate that," John said. He was about to say something but was distracted by signs of movement in the hood of Stella's jacket. He frowned. The head of a tiny ginger cat peeked out from the safety of Stella's hood. The cat sized John up and retreated into the safety of the fleece hoodie.

"Do you realize you have a cat in your hood?" John asked Stella.

She giggled, revealing her gap-toothed smile. "That's Mr. Pickles. That's where he hangs out. My hood."

"It must get awfully hot in the summer," John remarked.

The little girl shrugged and smiled. "Mommy cuts the arms off an old hoodie so I can carry him around during the summer."

"What about swimming?" John asked.

Stella giggled. "Mr. Pickles doesn't go swimming, silly! He's a cat."

"No, of course not."

India put her arm around her daughter and herded her away. "Come on, little lady, get upstairs and get ready for bed. You too, Petey."

"Aw, do I have to?" Petey moaned.

"Yes, please," India answered. "Take Stella with you."

Once they'd disappeared, India said, "Mr. Laurencelli, I don't know where to start. Jumbo usually doesn't behave like this. I don't know what came over him."

The offending creature reappeared in the doorway, wagging his tail. He was a massive dog covered in white and gray curly hair. John suspected he was some kind of English sheepdog mix. He braced himself for another lunge but the dog remained still. He thought the beast was eyeing him up but as his face was covered with hair, John couldn't be sure.

"Offer the man some tea or coffee," Gramps suggested. He looked at the dog and then back at John and added, "Or maybe something stronger."

"Of course! Where are my manners?" India said. "Would you like tea or coffee?"

John shook his head. He sensed that India was uncomfortable with him being in her home. He looked around. The kitchen was small and cluttered, not from mess but from the sheer lack of space. The refrigerator was covered in artwork he surmised belonged to Stella. At the end of the counter, on the side of the cabinet, was a calendar with just about every daily block filled in with something: appointments, reminders, school issues. Although small and cramped, the room was clean. There were no dirty dishes in the sink, no crumbs or empty wrappers on the countertop.

"It isn't necessary but thank you anyway."

She seemed almost relieved that he was leaving as if she didn't want her personal life mixing with her work life. He could respect that. He felt the same way.

"It was nice meeting you, Mr. Miller," he said to Gramps.

"You, too," the old man answered.

India walked him to the side door. When he reached the bottom step, he paused with his hand on the door handle. "What about your car? Do you need it towed somewhere?"

She shook her head. "No, thank you. I'll get that taken care of. I can use Gramps's car if the roads are clear enough for driving in the morning."

He nodded. "If there's any doubt, please don't take any chances. Stay home with your family."

She gave him a small smile. "We'll see."

"Okay, well if I don't see you tomorrow, I'll see you Wednesday, Ms. Ramone."

She was behind him now at the foot of the stairs. He became very aware of her in the small space they both presently occupied. She barely came up to his shoulder. She smelled lovely, but not like any of the expensive women's fragrances he knew. Something light and flowery. Her dark hair fell over her shoulders and her complexion was flawless, with the exception of the dark shadows beneath her eyes. Her pretty face looked tired.

"Good night, Mr. Laurencelli," she said. "Thank you for bringing me home. I'm sorry for all the trouble."

"It was no trouble at all, Ms. Ramone," he said. He slipped outside, and as he walked back to his car he heard her close and lock the door it behind him.

John climbed into his car and started it up. Wow, he thought. That is certainly one interesting household. Ms. Ramone certainly had her hands full. He eased out of the driveway, the snow obscuring his view. There was no sign of a plow yet; the snow in the street was now up to the top of his tires. He frowned when the car chugged and sputtered. If he could just get to the stop sign at the bottom of the street, Abbott Road had been plowed. As the car inched along he began to rethink the wisdom of trying to drive through this much snow at all. He was almost at the stop sign when the car stalled.

He tried to start it up again, several times, with no success. Finally, he conceded defeat and pulled out his phone to dial his emergency roadside service. Due to the inclement weather and the large volume of requests for assistance, he was told there would be a minimum two-hour wait. After verifying his cell number and his location with the call center representative, he sat there and tried to decide what to do next.

He was peeved for two reasons: his own stupidity and the inconvenience of having to wait two hours for a tow truck. He thought of his briefcase at home in the hallway and all the paperwork inside of it that needed to be done. He sighed. He certainly couldn't sit here for two hours in the cold, waiting for a tow truck. It might even be longer than that. The snow continued to fall. Calling his driver, Frank, came to mind but he dismissed it. How could he drag him out here, away from his sick wife?

Resigning himself to his fate, he got out of the car, locked it up, and abandoned it in the middle of the street. Walking in the path his tires had created, he headed back to India Ramone's house.

INDIA HAD CHANGED INTO her fleecy pajamas and heavy robe the minute Mr. Laurencelli had left. After throwing a load into the washing machine, she went back upstairs, plopped herself onto her bed, closed her eyes, and sighed. What a day. She opened her eyes and stared at the Christmas lights that hung from her ceiling. Her room was done up in pastels and florals and the headboard and foot-board of her double bed was a white iron frame that she had rescued from a flea market and lovingly restored. There were framed movie posters on the walls: Pillow Talk, Charade, and Rear Window. On her nightstand was a framed photo of her and Petey with their Mom and Dad. It was taken a long time ago. She touched it and smiled. Next to it was a picture of Stella taken at one of those shops in the mall when she was a baby.

The moment Jumbo knocked John Laurencelli to the ground played over and over in her mind like some terrible flashback. If he had been upset, he had contained himself. He had been a little stunned but had recovered quickly. Then Petey asking him all those questions about how much he was worth—she had wanted to die.

It was getting late and she still had to go over her notes one more time before calling it a night. She was hoping for a snow day tomorrow but she didn't want to bank on it. By the looks of things outside Petey and Stella would be off, but she didn't hold out much hope for the college canceling exams. She would love a snow day right about now, just to hang out all day at the house with Stella, Petey, and Gramps. She'd make them a big breakfast and she'd stay in her pajamas all day. She could bake Christmas cookies with Stella. She smiled to herself. Yes, that would be a dream day.

She needed to get out of bed and get that studying done for her exam. Just a few more days and then she'd have a nice break until the third week in January when she'd return for her final semester. She thought of all the things they were going to do while they were on Christmas break. And although she still had the morning and evening shift with Mr. Laurencelli, she'd have all that time during the day with them. She'd take them to the movies, out for pizza, and they could go ice skating and sledding. She was going to do all the things with Petey and Stella that she hadn't been able to do for the last few months because of lack of money or the pressure of school and clinicals. Now school was finished for this semester and the job was winding down at Mr. Laurencelli's. Marta would be back after New Year's. She was going to miss taking care of Mr. Laurencelli. She had to admit she had enjoyed it for the most part. Earlier, she'd been a little nervous about him coming into her home but he seemed comfortable with it and even took the incident with the dog in stride. For all the rumors that persisted about him being difficult and overbearing, India—with the exception of the missing watch debacle—couldn't validate them with her own experience.

As tired as she was, she forced herself out of her bed to get everything done so she could call it a night.

JOHN WATCHED AS INDIA descended the stairs in her pajamas and robe. They were so thick and fluffy looking she resembled a pink confectionary. He did not miss the look of surprise on her face when she saw him standing in her living room talking to her grandfather. He found it amusing when she pulled her robe closed at her throat.

Her grandfather spoke up. "Mr. Laurencelli's car broke down at the end of the street. He came back here to wait for his tow truck."

"Of course," she said. "I'm sorry for all the trouble I've caused you this evening," she said. She was little, but John thought the nightwear made her look like the Michelin man standing in front of him.

"India, if you don't mind, I'm going to bed," Gramps said.

"No problem, Gramps," she said. "I'll see you in the morning."

"Thank you for bringing my granddaughter home," Gramps said. "Just make yourself at home."

"Thank you, Mr. Miller," John said.

"Call me 'Gramps,' everyone does."

Gramps disappeared down the back hall. John and India stood there awkwardly for a moment. Not for the first time, he had the distinct impression that she was uncomfortable with him being there.

"Look, Ms. Ramone, don't let me get in your way," he said.

She looked mortified. "Oh, Mr. Laurencelli, it isn't that at all. I just feel bad that you're stuck here."

He laughed. "I'll survive."

At her invitation, he removed his hat and gloves and put them on the dining room chair.

"What can I get you to drink?" she asked. "Tea? Coffee? Soda? Or if you prefer, Gramps always has a bottle of whiskey on hand. You know. Just in case."

Jumbo lumbered into the kitchen and John eyed him warily. Having a bottle of whiskey on hand in this house was probably a prudent decision.

"Coffee is fine," he said.

She put the kettle on. "I only have instant."

"That's fine," he said. How bad could it possibly be?

"Sit down," she said. She cleared the newspaper off the table.

"Actually, do you mind if I look at the paper?"

"Not at all." India looked almost relieved that she didn't have to entertain him. She handed it back to him.

He sat down and unfolded *The Buffalo News* with a flourish. He saw her raise her eyebrows and he did it again just for effect. She rolled her eyes and he laughed, shaking his head. He focused on reading the paper but he also watched her out of the corner of his eye as she scurried around the kitchen.

India lifted her backpack from the floor and set it on a kitchen chair. She dug through it, removing textbooks and notebooks and laying them on the table.

The kettle whistled and she poured the water into a mug. "Milk and sugar?"

He nodded. "Just one each."

"Would you like a snack?" She blushed then, probably realizing he wasn't eight years old.

"The coffee is fine, Ms. Ramone," he said. "Thank you."

She handed it to him.

She filled the dog's water bowl and gave the beast a cookie from the box in a bottom cupboard. John thought the dog was plenty big enough and that they should probably lay off the treats but he kept his mouth shut. Over the top of the paper, he watched as she took hold of the dog's collar and wrestled him outside. She left the kitchen door open and a cool draft blew in from the back hall. He heard her run down the basement steps and soon heard a dryer rumbling and a washing machine starting. He listened as she ran back up the stairs and opened the outside door, calling the dog's name.

"Let me wipe your feet, Jumbo, you're all covered in snow," he heard her say. "That's a good boy."

He rolled his eyes.

India and the dog appeared in the kitchen and India closed the door behind her, locking it.

She started to unload the dishwasher. The dog sat next to the table, staring at John. At least, John thought he was staring at him. He couldn't tell for sure with all that fur.

"Do you think your dog needs a haircut?" he asked.

She looked over at them, smiling. "Oh, he does for sure. It's on the list with a lot of other things that need to be done."

He could only imagine.

"Jumbo, leave Mr. Laurencelli alone. Go on to bed," she said, trying to shoo him away.

The dog didn't budge. He continued to stare at John. John wanted to laugh but he didn't want to encourage that kind of behavior. It was obvious the dog had some discipline issues and a dog that size needed to be disciplined. He reminded himself again that the goings-on in her household were none of his business.

When the dog still wouldn't move despite India's coaxing, she grabbed a broom from the closet, stepped into the dining room, and banged on the ceiling.

Interesting, John thought.

From upstairs came the boy's shout. "What?"

"Call the dog," India shouted back.

"Jumbo!" called the boy. "Come on, Jumbo!"

The dog took off like a flash, scrabbling up the staircase.

John frowned and tried to concentrate on his newspaper. He looked at his watch. He eyed the textbooks on the table and wondered if she'd ever get to them.

She began loading the few dishes on the counter into the dishwasher, now that she had unloaded it.

Finally, he put his paper down. "Ms. Ramone, is there anything I can do to help?"

She looked at him, startled. "What?"

"I'm concerned about your career," he said with a nod toward her unopened books on the opposite side of the table. "It seems like you have plenty of tasks to do yet and it's getting late. You do plan on going to bed tonight, don't you?"

"Of course. Besides, I'm almost finished," she said brightly.

"Tell me what you have left to do," he said.

"I have to make the lunches for Stella and Petey. I have to put Gramps's pills out for the morning. I have to set the table for to-morrow's breakfast. I have to put out clothes for Stella. I need to go through Stella's backpack to make sure there are no notes—"

He stood up from the table. "Ms. Ramone, please let me help. Watching you run around trying to get everything done is making me nervous," he said.

There was a faint flicker of a smile on her face. "It was never my intention to make you nervous, Mr. Laurencelli."

He sighed. "Well, here we are. Look, I can set the table and make the lunches if you just tell me what to put in them."

She raised an eyebrow at him. "You'd make their lunches?"

"Sure," he said. "Just because I pay someone to do everything for me doesn't mean I'm incapable. I think I can manage to make a few sandwiches." He looked thoughtful for a moment. "Don't you think they'll have the day off due to the snow?"

"More than likely. But in the event that they don't, I won't have to scramble around in the morning to make their sandwiches. And should they get a snow day, then it's one less thing Gramps would have to do."

"All right, then, who takes what?"

"Okay," she said, still unconvinced. "Stella gets a peanut butter and jelly sandwich, cut into four squares. Strawberry jam. Petey gets a turkey and lettuce sandwich with a little bit of mayonnaise. He also gets a bag of ten grapes and Stella gets a tangerine, but you have to peel it for her and put it in a baggie. And they both get two cookies in a baggie."

"Got it. Leave it to me."

CHAPTER THIRTEEN

The snow had stopped falling during the night and the roads had been cleared by the time India's alarm sounded in the morning. Local grammar, middle, and high schools had all been closed, but the colleges remained open. In a way, India was relieved. Had her school been closed, it would only have postponed the inevitable. Better to get the exams over with and move on with her life. She decided she could get into work.

Gramps had started his El Camino ten minutes before India's departure. When she got in the car, the heater blasted out warmth. As much as she hated taking Gramps's car, as it then tied him to the house for the rest of the day, she was grateful for it. The El Camino was a smooth ride and handled better in the snow than she could have imagined.

Last night when Mr. Laurencelli had been stranded at their house, she had been very nervous, especially when she'd come downstairs in her pink, fluffy nightwear. The truth was, in his environment, she had her role and as long as she stuck to it, she felt secure. Nothing else was expected of her, not even small talk. There was no deviation from the plan. And her own environment, her own life, felt distinctly separate from her role as his personal assistant. Which is perhaps why he'd looked so out of place in her home last night. It felt as if the tables had been turned, the game changed, and no one had given her the rules. She hadn't known how to play.

To be fair, he had made it easy on her. When he'd offered to help, she'd been caught off guard. John Laurencelli? Making lunches and setting the table for breakfast? Wonders never ceased. He himself had suggested that he could be difficult, back when she'd first started working for him. And it was true that he was demanding and wanted things done a certain way. But he wasn't obnoxious about it. Like Marta had said, he just wanted things done the way he wanted them done. But didn't we all? she wondered. And then there was Marta. Marta had been with him for years, as had his driver, Frank, and his secretary, Janice. If he was so bad, why wasn't the turnover in the employees who had the most interaction with him, higher? She thought of him last night, standing at the kitchen counter, sleeves rolled up, spreading jam over a slice of bread. A billionaire making a PB&J. She smiled to herself. It was a nice thing for him to do, helping her like that. And when Stella had appeared, as she usually did, looking for a glass of water, it was Mr. Laurencelli who had gotten it for her. When the dryer had buzzed down in the basement, she'd stood up but he had held up his hand. "Let me run down and get it." It wasn't long before he returned with a basket full of warm laundry.

She had definitely seen him in a different light. A better light. It had been easier to ignore his deadly good looks when she thought he was a bit of a jerk. But her mind drifted again to him standing at that kitchen counter, and that's when she realized she found her boss very attractive.

Oh, no. Developing a crush on her boss was not a good idea. Especially since he had Angela, who was far more suited to him. There was no way. She couldn't allow his moment of kindness last night to be her undoing. She just had to hang in there a few more weeks and then she'd never see him again.

When she pulled into the parking lot of Mr. Laurencelli's apartment, she saw her own car covered in snow. She was disheartened at the sight of it. She'd have to pay someone to tow it, and then pay to get it fixed. She tried not to let it discourage her. Her nice pay packet was becoming smaller and smaller by the minute.

"MS. RAMONE." JOHN NODDED in greeting when he sat down to his breakfast.

"Thank you for your help last night," she said, setting his plate down on the table.

He looked up at her. She was dressed in her usual outfit: an over-sized white blouse with the sleeves rolled up and black pants. Her dark hair was pulled back into a loose ponytail. He'd begun to think of it as her uniform. Around her waist was tied another one of her vintage aprons, this one white with a red and green holly print. A Christmas motif. He wondered why she covered up her figure. He had seen her in that red velvet dress—it was a figure worth showcasing.

"I should be thanking you and your grandfather for letting me stay while I waited for my tow," he said. "Making a peanut butter and jelly sandwich was the least I could do."

"What about your car?" she asked.

"It was taken to the dealer," he explained. She winced and he said quickly, "It'll probably be ready by the end of the day." He turned his attention to his breakfast, taking a sip of his grapefruit juice.

India continued to stand there. He looked up at her. She appeared to be struggling with something.

"I would like to offer to pay for your car," she said.

Alarmed, he turned his body in the chair to give her his undivided attention. "As appreciative as I am of your offer, I'm going to have to decline."

She protested. "But if you hadn't driven me home, your car wouldn't be in the shop today."

He shrugged, studying her, his breakfast forgotten. "Please, Ms. Ramone, compensation isn't necessary."

"You're very kind," she said quietly.

He laughed. "Whatever you do, don't spread that rumor around."

She giggled and he said, "All right?"

She nodded. "I'll let you get back to your breakfast."

JOHN SAID GOOD MORNING to Frank as he climbed into the back of the car and explained how the Mercedes had been towed the previous night. Glancing around the parking lot, he spotted Ms. Ramone's snow-covered car. He sighed and pulled out his cell phone. Within thirty seconds of walking into her house, he had seen what the deal was. He knew the reason she hadn't had it towed. She could easily have come to him for help but he knew he wasn't the most approachable or accessible person on the planet. There was also that other little thing: her pride.

He scrolled through the contacts on his phone until he found the number of his own personal mechanic and dialed.

"Tommy? It's John Laurencelli," he started. "Look, I need a favor."

THERE HAD BEEN ONLY one exam Tuesday and she was finished by eleven. After Friday, she'd be able to do anything she liked. Other than work and that charity dance next Friday night, her time would be her own for a few weeks. She could read any book she wanted, something other than a textbook. She could binge-watch holiday movies on the Hallmark channel. She smiled to herself. It was going to be a wonderful Christmas this year.

With no more classes, she was able to dash home before heading back to Mr. Laurencelli's. She had lunch with Gramps, making them grilled cheese sandwiches with a salad on the side.

She cocked her head and studied Gramps across the table. "Gramps, are you feeling all right? You look a little pale."

He shrugged. "I feel fine as far as I know." He picked up one half of his grilled cheese sandwich. India shrugged. Maybe it was just the light.

"Gramps, where did we store all of Dad's stuff?" she asked.

"All the stuff you brought from your house is up in the attic."

"Even Dad's guitar? Drums?"

Gramps nodded. "Yes, everything went up there. Why?"

"Petey was asking me some questions about Dad the other night."

Gramps shook his head. "Poor kid, he got the short end of the stick," he said like he often did when they talked about Petey.

"I was thinking of giving him Dad's guitar for Christmas, and maybe the drums."

Gramps grimaced. "Maybe we could hold off on the drums for a bit."

India laughed. "Maybe you're right."

INDIA HAD AN HOUR BEFORE Stella and Petey would be home from school. She went to the second floor and from there took the staircase to the attic. The door sprang open after she unlocked it, a blast of cool air hitting her in the face. India reached around for the string that hung from the ceiling. When she pulled it, a bare bulb illuminated the vast space.

It was packed. There was furniture, boxes, and trunks all over the place. Mostly things Gramps and Gram had accumulated during their marriage. Gram had died when India was a little girl and she didn't really have too many memories of her, just impressions.

She trawled through the attic, lifting some of the old white bed-sheets that covered everything. In the corner of the attic, she found the boxes from their previous home and pulled off all the coverings. There were boxes and plastic bins stacked up against the eaves of the house. She swallowed hard. This is what her parents' life had been reduced to. Her bottom lip quivered. She was not going to cry. She didn't want to get sucked into the vortex of the past when her parents had been alive and they had all been happy. She wouldn't do that.

With the first box she opened, she came into contact with her mother's favorite blanket. Gram had knitted the afghan for Mom when she had first gotten married. And it was this blanket that Mom had used during her last months as she lay dying in her bed from cancer. India hadn't laid eyes on it since her mother's death. It caught her off guard and she cradled it to her chest, tears stinging her eyes. In the beginning, the loss was so overwhelming she'd wondered if she'd ever stop crying. There was still the occasional outburst at times when her grief snuck up on her and took her by surprise. She had realized that you never finish grieving. The grief was always there, like a constant companion. Life moved on building up around it, but it was always there. There wasn't a day that went by that she didn't think of her mom or her dad. But then she'd look for something to do—there was always something that needed to be done—and she'd distract herself from her feelings. It had worked so far.

After digging around in a few more boxes, she finally found her dad's guitar in a dust-covered case behind an old trunk. Pulling it out, she noticed that two strings were missing. She sank down into an old rocking chair with the guitar in her lap, rubbing her hand along the grain of it as memories of her father came at her, one after another.

She tried to remember the sound of his voice and it was like a distant echo in the past. The tears came and she found she could not stop them. She sat there in the dim, cold shadows of the attic, hugging her father's guitar and crying over all she had lost.

Eventually, she pulled herself together, closed the lids on the boxes and the trunks and covered everything with the sheets once more. She pulled the string to the bulb, extinguishing the light and carefully descended the staircase with the guitar and blanket in her hands

"I found Dad's guitar," she said proudly, showing Gramps. "It just needs a few new strings."

Gramps held out his hand. "Let me do that. I'll take it down to the music shop and have it restrung properly and cleaned up. You've got enough to do."

"Thanks, Gramps," she said.

"I'll put it in my bedroom closet for now so Petey doesn't see it."

She held up the blanket and announced, "I'm going to give this a wash and put it on my bed." She did not miss the melancholy expression on Gramps's face.

AFTER HER SHOWER, SHE was getting ready to go back to Mr. Laurencelli's to get his dinner ready when Gramps shouted to her. "India, there's someone at the door for you."

India ran down the stairs, her wet hair wrapped in a towel. She frowned at Gramps.

"Who is it?"

Gramps shrugged and said, "I don't know, but whoever it is, they've brought your car back."

"Really?" she asked, surprised.

"Look for yourself," Gramps said.

India went out into the side hall. A man stood there, wearing a knitted hat and a heavy jacket over navy-blue mechanic's overalls.

The stranger looked at India and then at the piece of paper in his hand. "Are you India Ramone?"

"I am," she said.

"I'm Tommy from the Mercedes dealer in Amherst. Your car is fixed," he said. "I've towed it for you."

"You what?" she asked. "Hold on." She grabbed her winter coat and threw it on, then went outside, followed by the mechanic.

Sure enough, there was her ten-year-old car. Parked in the driveway.

"The ignition coil was shot," he explained. "It should be all set now. He pulled out a computer-generated list and read it to her. "Four new all-season tires put on and aligned, an oil change, general service, and valet."

India swallowed hard. She had not authorized new tires or an oil change. And definitely not valet service. "How much do I owe you?" she asked. She braced herself for the answer as she saw her pay packet flying out the window and then some.

"Owe me?" the mechanic repeated, confused. "You don't owe anything. Mr. Laurencelli paid for this work."

India's heart sank. She didn't want to be indebted to Mr. Laurencelli. Or to anyone, for that matter. "Oh, I didn't want him to do this," she said, more to herself than to anyone else.

The mechanic chuckled. "That's Mr. Laurencelli for you. It's not the first time he's done this."

"But why?" she asked.

He shrugged. "Just generous, I guess. He once said to me that it was important for him to help people get where they wanted to go. I guess this is what he meant."

India was speechless.

The mechanic was still talking. "Over the years, I've lost count of how many cars I've fixed for him. I fixed his secretary's car so many times, he finally just bought her a brand-new one. The one she had was a real lemon."

"He bought his secretary a new car?" she asked, not sure she'd heard correctly.

He nodded. "Mr. Laurencelli is one of the most generous men I know."

HER CAR HAD STARTED on the first go and had been running like a dream ever since. It had never been so clean and the heat blasted out of the vents instead of the usual wispy puffs of slightly warmed air. The thought of her clunker at the Mercedes dealer getting the spa treatment made India laugh.

Feeling grateful for all Mr. Laurencelli had done for her with her car, she took it upon herself to reciprocate the gesture.

It had not gone unnoticed by her that Mr. Laurencelli had not put up one Christmas decoration in his home. She figured he was just too busy to be bothered with it. She'd hunted around the apartment that morning, in all the closets, looking for any box or plastic bin marked 'Christmas,' but there was nothing. Maybe the tenants had storage units in the building; that was the most likely scenario. She'd ask him about it, but in the meantime, she'd decided to indulge in a little shopping and pick up a few things to cheer the place up a bit.

She chose three things to decorate his house: a luxurious wreath for his front door that she wouldn't mind having for herself, a scented candle that smelled of gingerbread, and a small, artificial Christmas tree complete with lights, ornaments, and tinsel. She loved tinsel; it reminded her of Christmases years ago when tinsel was much more popular. That evening, as she went about cooking his dinner, she played some Christmas music on her phone.

Deciding to be brave, she'd ignored his menu and cooked something different for him: Coquilles St. Jacques. She hoped he'd appreciate her efforts, which were borne of her gratitude.

JOHN STEPPED OFF THE elevator to his floor, exhausted. It had been a trying day. One of the companies they'd been in the process of taking over had decided, at the last minute, to try to out-negotiate him. The contracts had already been drawn up but the owner of the business had decided he wanted more money. Usually, John would just drop the deal and move on but he had his heart set on this company for personal reasons. The aggravation was in the owner's idea that he could manipulate John. He was in for a rude awakening.

And then there was Angela. She wasn't returning his calls or texts and when he saw her at the office, she barely acknowledged him. Something was going to have to be done about that. Their business would begin to suffer if they carried on like that. Frankly, he was disappointed in her. He'd mistakenly thought she wouldn't let her personal life interfere with the running of their business. He was still doing a slow burn over the fact that she'd sabotaged their intent to buy the beach-glass magazine. Operating from the back foot, he had called Brenda Boker himself to tell her he was still interested.

He was looking forward to a quiet night, maybe a glass of whiskey later on. Most of all, he was looking forward to tonight's dinner.

As he approached the door to his apartment, he frowned. Hanging on the outside of it was a big Christmas wreath with gold and silver baubles and burgundy velvet ribbons. Annoyed, he pulled it off its hook before unlocking the door. When he stepped inside his foyer, he was greeted by the smell of gingerbread and the sound of Christmas music. Both caused an immediate flashback to happier times as a child, and memories overwhelmed him.

Not bothering to remove his coat, he marched through the apartment with the wreath on his arm and his briefcase in his other hand. He came to a standstill when he saw the Christmas tree in his living room. John Laurencelli had never had a Christmas tree in any home he had occupied in his entire adult life.

India appeared from the kitchen, wearing that silly vintage Christmas apron of hers and a bright smile.

He turned on her. Holding up the wreath, he demanded, "What is this?"

India looked confused. "It's a wreath."

He rolled his eyes. "I know what it is. I want to know what it's doing on my front door."

"I thought it would look nice," she said brightly.

"And what is that smell? And that music?" he asked.

She smiled. "That's a gingerbread-scented candle. And that's Christmas music with all the great voices. Peggy Lee. Connie Francis. Judy Garland—"

"I don't need the liner notes."

Her eyes grew wide.

It was too much. He could feel himself losing control. He needed to get out of the room before he said something mean or hurtful. He had to remind himself that she didn't know. It wasn't her fault.

"I do not want any decorations up," he said, gritting his teeth. "Get everything out of here."

"I thought it might cheer the place up," she said.

"I'm not interested in cheering the place up," he said tightly, managing to control his temper.

She didn't say anything. She just looked awkwardly around.

"Is my dinner ready?" he asked.

She nodded.

He headed toward the bedroom. "By the time I come out of the bedroom, please have the candle, the wreath, the music, and most of all, that stupid tree, out of my sight."

CHAPTER FOURTEEN

Once Mr. Laurencelli had shut the door behind him, India grabbed a large black garbage bag from the utility room. She threw the small Christmas tree, fully decorated, into it, followed by the wreath and the CD. She blew out the candle, wet the wick, and placed that inside, as well, then set the bag by the front door.

She couldn't understand why he was so mad. Her plan to thank him had backfired tremendously. In her wildest dreams, she would never have imagined he'd be so angry.

Hurriedly, she served up the dish of Coquilles St. Jacques. It was a dish she had been longing to make for herself, but fresh scallops were expensive so it had never happened. But she'd decided to make it for him. There was also a salad, and she'd paired the meal with an expensive white wine. She'd uncorked the bottle to let it breathe. Now, she wondered if it had been such a good idea at all. Fortunately, she hadn't used his grocery money; she had paid for it herself.

He appeared just as she was setting the dish down on the table. He approached, pulled out his chair, and scowled at the meal she had laid out.

"What is this?" He glared at her. "Isn't it supposed to be steak tonight?"

India tried to control the tremor in her voice but failed. "I thought you'd like something different for a change."

"And I thought I had made it very clear that I don't like to deviate from the script," he said. He sat down, resigned.

Immediately, she removed the offending dish, her hands shaking.

"Wait," he said. "What is it?"

"Coquilles St. Jacques," she said. She laid the plate back down and took a step back.

Mr. Laurencelli picked up his fork, sighed, and took a bite of the seafood dish. He raised his eyebrows in surprise. India breathed a sigh of relief.

INDIA HAD RETREATED to the kitchen. John glanced at her from time to time but she kept her back to him as she went about cleaning up the dinner mess.

He downed two glasses of wine and felt the edge wearing off his bad humor. He hated himself for being so awful toward her; she certainly didn't deserve that but he had been careful all these years about getting through Christmas unscathed. He could not change now. It had been too long and it was now too late.

Despite his anger at her full throttle deviation from the plan, he had to admit the meal had been delicious. He wiped his mouth on his napkin and sat back in the chair.

India soon appeared to clear the table. He noticed her hand shaking as she lifted the plate. He looked up at her and saw that her eyes and her nose were red. He looked away, ashamed. What did that say about him—a man who made a woman cry? Especially after said woman had gone to a lot of trouble. He sighed. Money certainly didn't buy class.

"Ms. Ramone," he said. His voice in the silence startled her and she dropped the plate, including the remains of his dinner, on the carpet.

"Oh no!" she said, dropping to her knees to mop up the mess with his napkin.

He bent down beside her. "Ms. Ramone, it's all right. Please."

She nodded but said nothing. He realized it was because she was crying. He pressed his lips together. It took all his self-control not to reach out and touch her.

He picked up the silverware from the floor and carried his wine glass into the kitchen. She laid the plate on the counter and disappeared into the utility room. She reappeared with a damp cloth and a bottle of carpet cleaner in her hand.

While she worked at the spot on the rug, he cleared the rest of the table. By the time she finished, he had corked the bottle of wine and loaded the dishwasher.

Without looking at him, she wiped down the counters and rinsed out the dish cloth. He stood there and watched her.

Still avoiding eye contact, she said, "I'll see you in the morning. Have a nice evening."

"Ms. Ramone," he said.

She stared steadily at the floor.

"Again, I have to apologize for my appalling behavior," he started.

She nodded.

"This is in no way a justification for my behavior today, but please let me try to explain."

She finally lifted her head and eyed him with uncertainty.

"When I was a teenager, my mother died unexpectedly a few days before Christmas," he said. "Since then, I don't celebrate the holiday. I don't like any reminders of that awful time. I realize how many people love Christmas and everything associated with it, but I don't. I just try to get through the season as best I can."

She looked thoughtful. "I'm sorry. Had I known I would never have put up all those decorations."

"I know you wouldn't have," he said. "And I appreciate the fact that you must have gone to a fair bit of effort organizing it all. A fair bit of expense, too, I'm guessing."

Her posture stiffened but she said nothing.

"You have enough financial responsibility at home," he pressed on.

Her face reddened. "I don't want your pity, Mr. Laurencelli. I am well aware of my financial situation. Recently, you took it upon yourself to have my car fixed, for which I am truly grateful. All of this—the decorations, the meal—was my way of showing that gratitude."

He closed his eyes. "It was never my intention to insult you." He paused and tried to dig himself out of his hole. "I just don't want you spending your money on me, because I—"

"Because you have plenty and I don't," she said, finishing his sentence. Her eyes widened in anger. "It wasn't about the money. Yes, my family is in a rough financial situation. And there are many people who have been generous to us, especially in the last few years since my mother's death. But here's the thing—I'm very conscious of always being on the receiving end of charity and it's hard not to become resentful. Why do you, simply by your bank balance, always get to be the giver and someone like me, the taker? It's hardly equitable," she managed to say. "Just for a change, I would have liked to be the giver. All I wanted was to do something nice for you in return for what you had done for me."

Feeling like a complete and utter jerk, he followed her out to the entryway, where she pulled on her coat. She picked up her backpack and lifted the bag of unwanted decorations but he asked her to leave it. She set it back down and opened the door.

He sighed. "I don't know what to say."

"Don't worry about it," she said wearily. "It doesn't matter."

She closed the door behind her and he spoke softly into the empty space. "It does to me."

THE FOLLOWING MORNING, India was surprised to see the wreath back on the door of Mr. Laurencelli's apartment. Unfortunately, it didn't bring her much joy seeing it there. Too much had transpired between them the previous evening. After last night's confrontation, she could add 'volatile' to the list of his unique qualities. Just when she'd become convinced that he was a decent human being, capable of kindness, he'd proved otherwise. She couldn't wait for this job to be over with. Despite it being a free country, there was a clear divide between them. He had certainly highlighted that.

She let herself in and set about getting his breakfast ready. He emerged from his bedroom earlier than usual.

"I don't have your breakfast ready yet," she said, looking at the clock. Had she missed something? "Are you leaving early or something?"

He shook his head, doing up his cuff link. "No, I wanted to make sure everything was all right between us." The bright white business shirt combined with the blue eyes and black hair was a heady combo. India chastised herself, warning herself not to be lulled by his luminous blue eyes. Or anything else. Even the quiet sadness that flickered behind those eyes.

"I'm certainly not going to quit at this point," she huffed.

"I'm relieved to hear that," he said.

They both stood there awkwardly for a moment.

He spoke first, adjusting the shirt sleeves beneath his coat. "I wanted to run something by you."

"All right." She waited.

"Despite going off the menu last night, I really enjoyed the dinner. I wanted you to know that."

A little smile formed on her lips. "Thank you," she said. She wanted to add, 'I told you so,' but refrained.

"I'd like you to have free rein with the menu during your last few weeks here," he said. He paused, then added somewhat dangerously, "Surprise me."

She broke into a wide grin. "Seriously? You're not just doing this to be nice?"

He frowned at her. "I assure you, I don't do anything to be nice."

"All right then." She smiled broadly.

"If you need me to leave extra grocery money to cover the cost, just let me know."

"Thank you."

"But there is one condition," he said. He eyed her intently and India tried not to melt under his gaze.

Hesitantly, she asked, "Yes?"

"I'd like you to join me for dinner twice a week," he said. "You choose the days."

"Oh," she said. She hadn't expected this and she wasn't sure how she felt about it.

"I'm tired of eating alone."

She tried to process what he'd just said.

An alarm went off somewhere. "Oh! Your egg is ready."

"Wait," he said, reaching out and laying his hand on her arm. Her senses became heightened and every nerve end on her body tingled. "Is it a deal?"

She nodded, curious about how this pushing of the boundaries between them would play out. She hurried back to the kitchen, prepared his breakfast, and set it on the table in front of him.

"Um, Mr. Laurencelli, may I say something?" she asked as he started in on his meal.

"I probably can't stop you, so go ahead," he said.

She stepped up to the table so he wouldn't have to look over his shoulder.

"It's about your not wanting to celebrate Christmas," she blurted out. She ignored his scowl and continued. "You see, I gave it a lot of thought last night."

"That wasn't necessary," he said tightly. He glanced up at her with what she perceived to be a 'tread carefully' look, but she chose to ignore it.

"It seems as if maybe you have some unresolved grief issues surrounding your mother's death," she suggested quietly.

"I asked you to share dinner with me, Ms. Ramone, not psychoanalyze me. There is nothing unresolved in my life."

She blundered on. "It may seem that way to you but I think you might be wrong."

She could tell he was irritated with her but she didn't care; she wanted to help him.

"Is it your intention to try to fix me?" he asked.

She shook her head. "There's nothing to fix," she assured him. "Just some tweaking."

"Tweaking?" he repeated. She thought there was a glimmer of a smile there but she couldn't be sure.

"Can I ask you another question?"

"If I said no, would you ask anyway?"

"Yes," she replied.

"Why does this not surprise me?" He sipped his grapefruit juice.

"Before your mother passed away, did you enjoy Christmas?"

"Of course I did, I was a kid," he answered before finishing his poached egg and laying his knife and fork on his plate.

"Are you happy?" she asked.

He looked up at her. "What do you mean?"

"Are you happy with not celebrating Christmas? With this self-imposed exile from the holiday season?"

When he didn't answer, she removed his plate and glass and said, "Just something to think about."

JOHN DROVE INTO WORK, replaying the conversation with India in his head. Was he happy? He didn't know the answer to that. He had never really thought about it. He supposed he was happy with his work. He liked what he did and he looked forward to going into the office every day.

Christmas as a kid had been wonderful. His mother had loved the holiday season. She was always laughing, always smiling. There was always music playing in the house. Every year, she purchased a new Christmas album for her collection. She had definitely been the heart of their family. His father had been a quiet man, never affectionate, but enthralled with his vivacious wife. She would drop herself into his lap and wrap her arms around him, or if a song came on the radio that she liked, she'd grab him and start to dance. Either way, John reflected, his father always looked secretly delighted.

On Christmas day, after all the gifts were opened and he'd played with his new toys, his mother would cook the turkey and the ham and she would lay all the Christmas goodies out on a cake stand in the center of the dining room table. There were cookies, bars, and fudge. He could still hear her saying, "Today is a special day, so just help yourself whenever you want," winking at him as if it was a secret between them.

When he was fourteen years old, on the morning of December twenty-first, his mother had appeared at breakfast complaining of a terrible headache. No one took any notice, including his mother. In fact, she had actually laughed about it, saying she had so much to do to get ready for the big day, she didn't have time to be sick. By lunchtime, she was dead from a brain aneurysm.

The wake and the funeral in the days that followed had been a blur of shock, disbelief, and a lot of wearing of black—a stark contrast to the excess of Christmas lights, the boxes of red candy canes on the kitchen counter and the two trees in the house. John had had a hard time reconciling the two. His mother had been buried on Christmas Eve.

Within a year, his sister had gone off to college and John was left at home with his father, who spent most of his time in his study with the door closed. From then on, John had despised change, especially drastic change. He'd spent his adult life maintaining careful control of his environment, his surroundings, so as never to experience that kind of abrupt pain again.

Even hanging the wreath back on the door had made him slightly uncomfortable.

As he pulled into the parking garage at his company, he focused on what really bothered him: India Ramone. He had been anxious for her arrival that morning. He had wanted to set things right with her. When he complimented her on the dinner she had cooked for him, she had given him a little smile and he had felt a weight lift from his shoulders. When she agreed to share dinner with him, he could feel himself breathe a sigh of relief. He wondered why her being happy meant something to him. He knew these to be dangerous thoughts.

INDIA'S PHONE RANG as she unlocked the door to Mr. Laurencelli's apartment that afternoon. Scrambling to answer it, she saw Warren's name flash across her screen. She set her bag down on the foyer floor and answered his call.

She'd barely said hello when Warren rushed through the reason for his call.

"I know, Warren, but there's nothing I can do about it," India argued. "I can't leave work early." Definitely not, she thought. "If you have to go to your rotary club meeting tonight, we'll just have to skip practice. I can see no other way around it."

"But we need to practice," Warren wailed. "It's next Friday, you know. And I'm going out of town tomorrow."

"I know. And I know we need more practice, but it is what it is. We've still got next week," she said.

"What if I came there?" he said.

Alarm bells went off in her head. "Where?"

"There, at your place of work. You said you had some down time," he said.

"Uh, I don't think that would be a good idea," she sputtered. Actually, it was an awful idea.

"Just for an hour. Look, give me the address and call your boss and tell him what we're up to," Warren suggested brightly.

"I don't know," India mumbled.

"Look, we don't want to make fools of ourselves next Friday night," he said.

She sighed, relenting. "All right, be here at five, but you have to be out by six. And I mean it, Warren." She tried to sound stern but Warren laughed.

"I'll be there," he said.

She gave him the address and hung up, then dialed Mr. Laurencelli's number, but it went to voicemail. She'd at least run the idea by him before Warren got there. And if Mr. Laurencelli was totally against it, she'd have to figure something else out or she and Warren were going to end up looking like nitwits at this charity dance.

AFTER THE CONFERENCE call with the owners of the Scottish whiskey company and his own team, John returned to his desk and picked up his cell phone and saw there were two missed calls from India. He listened to his voicemail and heard India's voice.

"Mr. Laurencelli, this is Indi—uh, Ms. Ramone. This is not an emergency, I just need to run something by you. If you could call me when you get a chance, I'd appreciate it."

John decided there was nothing that important that couldn't wait until he got home. Besides, he could feel himself coming down with something. He'd felt shivery since this morning when he left home. Since lunch, a headache had loomed large. As much as he hated the idea, he was thinking of leaving early and going home to bed. Whatever she needed to 'run by' him could surely wait until later.

He glanced at the clock. One more meeting and then he would go home. He pocketed his phone, stood up from his desk, and left his office.

INDIA ANSWERED THE door when Warren arrived.

"You're late, and you have to leave by six."

"I know, but that doorman stopped me, asking me all sorts of questions," Warren explained.

"Pay no attention to him, he's kind of a busybody," she said, anxious to get going.

"I noticed. He wanted to know what business I had going to Mr. Laurencelli's apartment," Warren said.

India rolled her eyes. She hoped Martin wouldn't say anything to Mr. Laurencelli before she had a chance to explain things to him but a small part of her doubted it.

"I told him I was here to make a delivery." Warren laughed. He held up his wireless speaker

"Whatever," she said. She was glad he'd remembered to bring it as she hadn't thought about the music component. And she certainly didn't want to use Mr. Laurencelli's sound system, if he even had one. Not after yesterday.

She glanced at the clock, calculating how much time they had before she needed to start getting Mr. Laurencelli's dinner ready. The pressure was immense. She wanted to clock Patti for talking her into this charity dance-off thing. As if she didn't have enough to do.

"Are you all right?" Warren asked.

"Just a lot on my mind," she said with a dismissive shrug. "We'd better get started."

"Just a minute, India, I wanted to talk to you," he said, laughing amiably.

"Okay, but we really need to hurry," she said, looking over at the clock again.

"I've met someone," he said.

She looked at him strangely. "You met someone?" she repeated, taken aback. What, like on the bus? she wondered. At the grocery store? At a Rotary Club meeting?

He nodded.

"Tell me," she prompted. It made sense—he'd been in an even better mood than usual lately.

"Her name is Penny. She works in my department. We've been friendly for a while and I asked her out a few weeks ago and she said yes." He set the wireless speaker down on the coffee table. "We've gone out a few times."

"Oh, Warren," she said softly. Warren had always been, well, available. And although she wasn't interested in him in that way, and she knew he wasn't interested in her that way—they had had that talk years ago before Stella was born—it still seemed strange. She had always thought he would be perfect for someone.

Although this was a surprise, it was good news. She couldn't help but wonder how the addition of a third person would affect their friendship. Then she felt a little pang of envy. She hoped someday to say the same thing to Warren: I've met someone. Immediately, she pushed those thoughts out of her mind.

"I am so happy for you," she said, stepping closer to him. "No one, and I mean no one, deserves it more." She hugged him and he hugged her back.

"When will I be able to meet her?" she asked. She wanted to meet the girl that had captured Warren's heart.

"Soon. Soon. She's anxious to meet you, too. I've told her all about you," he enthused.

She grimaced a little, wondering what he had told her.

This time it was Warren who looked at his watch. "India, we'd better get a move on. The clock is ticking. We've got exactly forty-two minutes."

"Let's go."

Warren pressed the 'start' button and music flowed out into the room. India turned the volume down. She gave him an apologetic smile. "I don't want to disturb the neighbors."

"Oh, sure."

He pulled out his diagrams. "Actually, I had an inspired idea."

"Let's hear it," she said.

"I know we're not the best dancers—"

"That's an understatement," India added, giggling.

"—and I thought if we added a lift or two, it might distract from our woeful footwork."

"A lift or two?" she asked, uncertain.

"Yeah, you know, a lift—me lifting you up," he said. "In the air."

India frowned. "Oh, I don't know about lifts, Warren. That sounds dicey to me. I think we should just stick to the dancing and forget about the gymnastics. It's ballroom dancing, not pairs at the Olympics," she said. She bit her lip. She certainly appreciated Warren's enthusiasm in wanting to add another dimension to their dance routine but what did it say about their dancing ability if they had to add a distraction? It only served to confirm what she already knew: they were terrible dancers.

"India, have I ever let you down in the past?" he asked.

She didn't even have to think about it. "Of course not."

"Then will you humor me?"

She relented. "All right then."

"Okay, let's start at the beginning. Let's practice what we know."

"Such as it is," she said, laughing.

He waved a finger at her. "Don't be negative. We got this."

They stumbled through their dance routine, looking at their feet and counting under their breath. India felt they were almost hopeless and most likely would have to add more than just mid-air lifts. Like maybe two better dancers, for instance.

Warren stopped and cocked his ear to listen to the music. "At this juncture is where I'm going to lift you."

"Okay," India said tentatively. "How are you going to do this?"

"Don't worry," he reassured her. "I've been studying videos. I'm pretty confident."

That did not reassure India.

He walked her through the steps he proposed to do, three times. India didn't feel any better by the final time.

She glanced at the clock, starting to get anxious. "Come on, Warren, we don't have much time left."

Warren looked at the clock, too. "Oh right." He clapped his hands and said, "Okay then, let's do this."

He verbally reviewed his plan one more time and India nodded, crossing her fingers behind her back and hoping it would all work out in the end. "Just remember to jump as I go to lift you, to give yourself momentum."

India scowled. She certainly didn't want to end up being catapulted out the window and into the lake.

They went through the steps of the routine and when they got to the part with the lift, India awkwardly leapt up on cue. Warren lifted her into the air with an 'oomph,' then quickly and somewhat clumsily put her back down.

A fine sheen of perspiration ran along Warren's forehead.

"Not as easy as you thought," India said with a giggle.

"And you're not as light as you look," he countered. "A few more tries and we should have it down pat."

"I don't know, Warren," India started. "With less than a week left, maybe we should just concentrate on the dancing and try to get better at that rather than practice these lifts." She didn't know how much more she could take of being suspended in the air, teetering on Warren's hands.

"Come on, keep up," he said. "We've got this."

She wasn't so sure about that.

CHAPTER FIFTEEN

J ohn wrapped his scarf around his neck and shrugged his coat on. Despite being bundled up, he shivered. He planned to go home, shut off his phone, and go to bed for the rest of the night.

Exiting his office, he paused at his secretary's desk. Janice frowned at him.

"I'm heading out," he said.

She nodded, looking worried. "Are you all right, Mr. Laurencelli?"

He waved away her concern. "I'm fine." But even he couldn't remember the last time he had left early. He pulled a handkerchief from his breast pocket and sneezed into it.

"Good night, Janice," he said, walking out without waiting for a reply.

Despite the heat blasting out of the vents in his car and the warmed seats, John shook with cold all the way home. He pulled into the underground parking garage and got out, pulling his briefcase out of the backseat. With a click, he locked up his car. He had a charity dinner scheduled for tomorrow night but if he felt as he did now, he doubted he'd make it. He hated to cancel as he was their main benefactor, but he could hardly go into a crowd of people with a cold or a flu.

He could barely contain his impatience when Martin greeted him in the lobby.

"Mr. Laurencelli, you're home early," he observed.

John nodded and wiped his nose with his handkerchief. He walked by the doorman and headed toward the elevator.

"Oh, Mr. Laurencelli—" Martin called out.

Not wanting to, he stopped.

"Look, I should prepare you—Ms. Ramone is not alone up there in your apartment," Martin started.

"What?" John asked.

Martin shrugged, trying to appear casual, but John could see he reveled in delivering this bit of news. "A man arrived an hour ago and went up to your apartment." He raised his eyebrows. "I haven't left my post so I would have seen him leave."

Now what? John thought. He said nothing but stepped into the elevator.

Martin called out after him. "Forewarned is forearmed!"

John barred the closing of the elevators with his arm. He spoke directly to Martin. "Whatever Ms. Ramone is doing in my apartment is absolutely none of your business."

As he dropped his arm the elevator closed shut, but he did not miss the look of tension on the doorman's face.

On the ride up, he wondered what she was up to this time. He knew there was a perfectly good explanation for her having a man in his home. He couldn't wait to hear it. If he had learned anything about India Ramone over the last few weeks, it was that she was beyond reproach. And he was pretty sure the voicemail she'd left had something to do with this. Unfortunately, he just wasn't up to dealing with it tonight.

He strode down the hall towards his apartment and put his key in the lock. He opened the door and set his briefcase down on the hall table. He could hear music coming from the living room. Without removing his coat or scarf, he strode down the hall to see what was going on.

"Come on, India, let's do it one more time," said a distinctly male voice.

"No, Warren, that's enough," India pleaded.

"Come on," he said.

"All right, one more time but then you have to go!"

John picked up his pace and entered the living room to see something he hadn't quite envisioned: there was his personal assistant, being held up in the air by some man he didn't recognize. He looked from one to the other, then back to India. Neither had noticed him standing there.

"What is going on here?" he questioned.

Warren, startled, lost his grip, and India came tumbling down on top of him as they landed in a heap on the floor.

India jumped up immediately, her face flushed. "Oh, Mr. Laurencelli, I can explain everything."

"Please do," he said. He looked to her companion, who remained on the floor. "Would you please get up off my floor?"

Warren looked up at John with a pained expression on his face. "I can't. I think my leg is broken."

THE PARAMEDICS WHEELED Warren out of Mr. Laurencelli's apartment on a stretcher.

India leaned over him. "I'll follow in my car to the hospital, Warren. I'll meet you in the emergency room."

"It's not necessary, India," Warren protested, but then added, "Will you call my mother? Let her know I won't be home for dinner."

India smiled at him. "I will."

After Warren was carted off, India went back into the apartment and closed the door. She ran around gathering Warren's things as well as her own coat and purse.

Before she left, she rounded on her boss. "Did you have to come in here all gangbusters and everything? You scared the life out of us!"

"It's my fault now that he broke his leg?" John was still in his overcoat, but he was shivering.

"Just forget it," she muttered. She stopped and looked at him. "I suppose you'll fire me now."

He shrugged, feeling a bit lightheaded. "Do you want me to?" He hoped her answer would be no.

She laid her coat over her arm. "I am sorry. Again. But I tried to reach you twice today." Exasperated, she added, "I even left a message for you to call me."

"I thought it could wait until I came home," he replied. "Can I ask what your boyfriend was doing in my home lifting you up in the air?"

"First, he's not my boyfriend. Second, we were practicing for a charity dance next Friday night," she explained. "We were supposed to take part in it." She peered at him. "But since you've broken his leg—"

"Me?" he asked, incredulous. He sneezed. He wondered if he had any lemons in the house. Or honey for that matter.

She barreled on. "Yes, you were the indirect cause of my best friend breaking his leg."

He decided not to argue with her. He didn't have the energy for it.

"Mr. Laurencelli, can you dance?" she asked, looping her purse onto her shoulder.

He looked at her, alarmed. "Right now?"

"No, not right now. But since you took Warren out of commission, you'll have to step in and take his place."

A coughing jag prevented him from responding.

India frowned at him. "What's wrong? Oh my goodness, you're sick."

"I think I'm coming down with something. That's why I came home early."

"By the sounds of it, you've already come down with it," she said, concern flooding her face. She laid her coat and purse down on the sofa. "Here, give me your coat and scarf." She held out her hand and would not take no for an answer. Reluctantly, he shed his overcoat and unwound his scarf.

"Now go get changed into something more comfortable and get into bed," she commanded.

"I hadn't realized before how bossy you are," he said, relieved that someone else was taking over. If just for a bit. "But I don't want to get into bed yet." The thought of climbing into bed so early depressed him, sick or not.

"Would you rather come back out here to the sofa after you get changed?"

He nodded, and she put her arm around him and led him to the bedroom.

"You know, Ms. Ramone, I am hardly an invalid," he said, but he was in no hurry to disengage himself from her arm. There was something tender and protective about the gesture. It was something he wouldn't mind getting used to.

"All right, then," she said. "I suppose you're not in the mood for dinner?"

He shook his head. She placed her hand on his forehead. Her hand was cool to the touch and he found it soothing. "Mr. Laurencelli, you're burning up!"

He didn't say anything.

"All right, get changed. I'll fix you something to drink," she said.

"Not necessary. Go after Warren," he said.

"Not yet, not until you're settled."

"Wow, you really are bossy," he remarked.

"I heard you the first time," India said, lifting one eyebrow.

He closed the door behind him and leaned against it. Every muscle in his body ached. He removed his suit, tie, and shirt and put them in the dry-cleaning bag for Monday. He pulled on pajama bottoms and a T-shirt. He then took his bathrobe off the hook and got into it, still feeling cold.

INDIA RAN TO THE KITCHEN. She opened the refrigerator, took stock of the contents, and decided that a simple meal of tea and toast would be enough. There were two fresh lemons in the fruit bowl on the counter. Once the kettle was on, she took a tea bag out of the canister and dropped it into a cup. She searched the cupboards for honey but found none, adding it to her mental grocery list. She made the tea, added some sugar, and squeezed some lemon into it. Mr. Laurencelli reappeared from the bedroom wearing a gray bathrobe over pajama pants and a T-shirt, just as she was carrying in a tray of tea and toast. Momentarily, she was disconcerted by the sight of him in pajamas. He was an altogether different beast. She was used to seeing him only in suits. And expensive ones at that. But he looked just as good in leisure wear.

He sat down on the couch, back amongst the cushions. He pressed a button on a remote and a cabinet opened up, revealing a television on a swivel shelf. India blinked. She hadn't even known that was there.

She had seen blankets in the hall closet and headed in that direction. She opened up the double doors, surveying the folded stacks of linens and towels and blankets. On the top shelf was a lovely, soft Sherpa blanket. She carried it over to him and spread it out over his legs. He was sitting up and sipping her tea.

"I hate to leave you here alone," she said, chewing her bottom lip.

"Not the first time I've been alone," he muttered.

"I can stay if you'd like," she suggested.

He shook his head. "There's no need. I'm a big boy now."

She made a 'tsk' sound and he looked up. "I know that, but you're sick. You need someone to look after you. Will I call Angela?" she suggested tentatively.

He gave a short bark of laughter. "Angela? What for? She really doesn't do sick."

Some girlfriend, she thought. "Can I call you later?" she asked. "To check up on you."

He raised his eyebrows. "To check up on me?"

"Yes."

"I'll probably be sleeping." He paused. "I hope I'll be sleeping."

"Will you call me?" she asked.

"No," he said. "Now go home."

"All right," she said, but she wasn't convinced. "I'll be here in the morning before my last exam."

He shook his head. "It's not necessary. I don't know if I'll be going into the office and there'll be no need for you to come over."

"No, I'll be here, whether you go into work or not. I'll want to see how you're doing."

She pulled her coat on. Conflict filled her. She wanted to get to the hospital to check on Warren and yet a part of her wanted to stay here and look after Mr. Laurencelli.

"Will you call me if you need anything?"

"I won't need anything," he assured her.

"But if you do . . ." Her voice trailed off.

He sipped more of the tea. "I promise I will."

"Do you have Tylenol?" she asked.

"Somewhere around here," he said.

"Where is it?" she asked.

He looked at her as if he was wrestling with something. Finally, he sighed. "In the medicine cabinet in my bathroom."

India hurried to the ensuite off the master bedroom. Opening the medicine cabinet felt oddly intimate to her. There wasn't much there: Tylenol. Motrin. Dental floss. Antibiotic ointment. No prescription medicines. She grabbed the bottle, then closed the cabinet door and headed back to the living room, setting it down on the coffee table. She went to the kitchen and poured a glass of water. This she set down next to the bottle of Tylenol.

"Goodnight, Ms. Ramone. I'll see you tomorrow."

"Can I get you anything else before I leave?" she asked.

He waved her away. "Go see to your friend."

"I'll see you in the morning."

India was halfway down the hall when he called out to her.

"Ms. Ramone, will you bring me my briefcase from the front hall?"

She picked it up, surprised by the weight of it. Breathing in the smell of leather, she carried it back to him and set it down on the floor by the couch.

"Goodnight, then," she said.

IT BOTHERED INDIA THAT Mr. Laurencelli was so sick and home alone. All that money and no one close to take care of him. That just wasn't right. And where was his girlfriend, Ms. Preston? She rang Gramps before she left the parking lot and relayed to him the disaster involving Warren. She'd go over to the hospital and then head home.

"I'll be home as soon as I can," she told Gramps. She hoped to be there before Stella went to bed but it was looking doubtful. Thank goodness, school was almost over. It was always something, she thought. When were the quiet, boring days coming? She wanted to try quiet and boring, just for something different.

"Don't worry, India, I'll hold down the fort."

She made her way to the city hospital and parked her car in the accompanying lot. She went through the emergency room doors and looked around for a member of Warren's family. Not seeing anyone she recognized, she approached the desk.

"I'm here for Warren Scott," she said.

"Are you family?" asked the disinterested receptionist. She never took her eyes off her computer screen.

"Well no, but—" India started.

"Then take a seat, please."

India sat down on a hard, plastic seat. Her stomach growled and she realized she'd missed dinner and had only had half a peanut-butter-and-jelly sandwich for lunch. They had run out of bread at home and she only had just enough for their lunches. She went to the vending machine and chose two candy bars and a bottle of soda. It would have to do for now.

Once she finished her snack, she threw her garbage in the bin. It had been an hour and no sign of anyone. She leaned back and watched all the people sitting there in the emergency-room waiting area.

She must have dozed off because the next thing she knew was she was being shaken gently and her name was being called.

"India? India?"

India woke up quickly and looked around, remembering where she was. In front of her was Warren's mother.

"Oh, Mrs. Scott, how is Warren?" she asked, standing up immediately.

Warren's mother nodded. "He's all right. It was a clean break, so all they had to do was set it."

"He didn't need surgery?" she asked.

"No, thank God, he'll be discharged in a bit. He won't have to stay overnight," Mrs. Scott said. "Warren sent me out here. He said you'd be here."

"Can I see him?" India asked.

Mrs. Scott hesitated and then shook her head. "Warren told me to tell you that it's getting late and you're to go home to Petey and Stella."

"I could just pop back there for a few minutes," India suggested. She'd feel better if she could lay eyes on him herself. She felt awful about what had happened.

Warren's mother shook her head again. "No, it won't be a few minutes once you two start gabbing. Go home and stop by to see him over the next few days."

"I will," India promised.

WHEN INDIA ARRIVED home, Petey was up watching television with a bag of chips and a bottle of soda in front of him.

India plopped on the sofa beside him, exhausted.

"Is Stella asleep?" she asked. She leaned back against the cushions and began to feel drowsy.

"I think so," Petey said. Then he burst into a shout of laughter at something inane that was being said on the TV, startling India out of her sleepy state.

"Where's Gramps?" India asked, looking around.

"I dunno," Petey said, digging into the bag of chips. He looked briefly down the back hallway. "I think he went to bed."

"But it isn't even ten," India pointed out.

Petey shrugged.

Gramps usually stayed up until midnight watching old black-and-white movies and television shows. He was fond of *Perry Mason* and *Murder, She Wrote*.

India stood up to check on him. She walked down the hall towards the back of the house and the two bedrooms that were located there. She, Petey, and Stella were in the three bedrooms upstairs.

No light shone from under the bottom of Gramps's bedroom door.

"Gramps?" she asked, rapping lightly.

"Come in," said a small voice from the other side.

She opened the door and the hall light cast a yellow beam into the room, illuminating Gramps in his pajamas, under the blankets in his bed.

"Are you all right? You never go to bed this early," she said, worried.

"I'm just tired, that's all," he said.

"Gramps, now that the semester is almost over, I'll be home more and you can take a break."

"Oh, India, don't worry about it. I'm happy I can help."

"All right, then, goodnight," India said, shutting the door. She hoped Gramps was all right.

"Don't stay up too late, Petey."

He only nodded.

In the kitchen, she made herself a cup of tea. From her backpack, she pulled out her pathophysiology book and notebook. It was her last exam on Friday and she wanted to study before she went up to bed. It had been her favorite subject so she wasn't too worried over the final. Biting her lip, she pulled her phone out and dashed a text off to Mr. Laurencelli.

How are you feeling?

Within seconds, a reply came back. *The same.*

I'll be there in the morning. She expected him to tell her it wasn't necessary. It was a few minutes before he replied.

Ok but no need to be here so early. Will work from home tomorrow. How about 8?

See you then, she sent back.

CHAPTER SIXTEEN

Despite being able to sleep in a little longer, India was awake well before the alarm went off. She stared at the ceiling for a long time, thinking of all she had to do that day, and finally, she gave up and climbed out of bed. Her plan was to get Stella and Petey ready for school and head on over to Mr. Laurencelli's. She'd pick up a few groceries on her way in.

After she showered, she put on a little makeup and pulled her hair up into a messy bun. She wondered how Mr. Laurencelli's night had gone.

She rapped on Petey's door. "Time to get up, Petey."

There was a groggy response from the other side of the door.

Anxious to get breakfast on the table, she dashed down the stairs.

Within minutes, Stella appeared in the kitchen, her hair a mess. She wore a pink bathrobe with Mr. Pickles nice and snug in the hood of it.

"Good morning, honey," India said. "I'm going to make us chocolate-chip pancakes with whipped cream for breakfast."

"Yummy. My favorite."

Jumbo pushed past Stella, knocking her into the doorframe. "Jumbo! Be careful," she whined.

"Come on, Jumbo, you probably need to go out," India said. She flew down the hall steps and opened the side door for the over-large dog, who bounded joyfully out into the snow. What was it with dogs and snow?

India went about making breakfast. Once the bacon starting cooking, Petey and Gramps both staggered in at the same time.

"Something smells good," Gramps said.

"Breakfast in five, Gramps, just pull up a chair. I'm making your coffee now," she said.

"I'm hungry," Petey said, bleary-eyed.

"Sit down, Petey, I'm just about to serve it up," she said, indicating toward the table with her spatula. He slid into a chair next to Gramps and put his head in his hands. She looked at him, worried. He had stayed up too late again last night.

India served up the pancakes on the plates and put a handful of chocolate chips over Stella's and Petey's, along with a good dollop of whipped cream. She set a platter of crisp bacon in the middle of the table. Gramps and Petey each reached for a piece.

"It's been awhile since we've had pancakes," Gramps said, taking his plate from India.

"We were due," she said. "Jumbo!" She'd forgotten about him. "Petey, go let Jumbo in, please."

"Why do I always have to let him in and out?" he asked, muttering under his breath.

India ignored him and sat down to eat her own breakfast. She dipped her finger in her whipped cream and dotted it on Stella's nose. The little girl laughed in response.

Petey returned. "I don't know where he is. I called for him but he didn't come."

"Oh, Jumbo!" India groaned. The last thing she needed was Jumbo on the loose in the neighborhood. He was as gentle as a lamb but people who didn't know him could be intimidated by his size. Luckily, they knew him well enough down at the precinct house. She half expected a patrol car to roll up in front of the house with Jumbo in the backseat. It had happened before.

"Just open the window. Once he smells breakfast he'll be back in a flash," Gramps suggested. He glanced at the clock on the wall. "You're going to be late for work, India."

She shook her head, scooping up pieces of pancake, chips, and whipped cream with her fork. "Mr. Laurencelli is under the weather, so he isn't going in to work. I don't need to be there until later."

"That's too bad," Gramps remarked.

"I was thinking of making him a pot of chicken soup," she said, thinking out loud. There was plenty of time today.

"That's a kind thing to do. Especially after he had your car fixed."

"That's what I thought, too," she added. She didn't comment on Mr. Laurencelli being home alone with no one to check in on him. She felt protective of his privacy; no one needed to know that.

"Leave the cleanup to me," Gramps said.

"Does anyone want any more pancakes?" she asked, looking at the three of them seated around the table. "Last call." It warmed her heart to see them all together eating a big, hot breakfast.

"I'll have one more," Petey said.

"Me, too," Gramps said.

"Very good. Stella?"

Stella shook her head. India could see she was struggling to finish what was on her plate.

She made a few more pancakes and served them up.

"Okay, eat up and start getting ready for school."

When she was finished, she stood and began to bundle up for the frigid weather outside. As she went out the side door, she bumped into Jumbo, who was coming into the house.

"Jumbo, where have you been?" she asked. "Come on, get inside."

The dog didn't move and kept his head down. India noticed he had something in his mouth. "What have you got there?"

When he didn't budge, she lifted his chin with her gloved hand and saw he was holding a puppy by the scruff of its neck.

"Jumbo! Where did you find him?" she asked. She took the pup from his mouth, just a little brown ball of fur who shivered in India's hands. "Oh, boy, this little guy is freezing."

She brought the puppy into the kitchen with Jumbo following her, wagging his tail.

The puppy lifted his head slightly and gave his tail a little wag.

"Look what Jumbo brought home," she announced.

Gramps rolled his eyes. "This dog has to stop bringing home strays. We're running out of room."

"I'm sure he belongs to someone. We'll call the vet and see if anyone is missing a pup. In the meantime, he needs to be warmed up and given a little water and a tiny bit of food."

Stella perked up and jumped down off her chair. "I've got a blanket for him. Hold on."

She disappeared but soon returned with a pink doll's blanket.

"Not pink!" Petey said.

It's all right for now, we just need to get him warm," India said. She took the blanket from Stella, wrapped the pup in it and handed him back to her. "It's your job to keep him warm until you leave for school."

"Okay, Mommy." Stella smiled her toothless smile.

"Good job. All right, I'm leaving for a second time."

JOHN WOKE TO THE SOUND of knocking at his front door. He wondered why Ms. Ramone didn't just use her key. And why was she here so early? It took him a moment to realize that he had fallen asleep on the couch. He sat up, feeling only marginally better than yesterday. He'd woken up drenched in the middle of the night when his fever had broken, but it felt back on the rise today. He wanted a shower and some clean clothes. But the knocking at the door persisted. He headed out to the front hall to answer it.

He was both surprised and dismayed to find Angela standing there. He really wasn't in the mood for a confrontation.

"I've been knocking for a while," she said, breezing past him and entering his home. "Janice said you weren't feeling well. Thought I'd better check on you and make sure you're all right."

He sighed. "I'm fine."

She noted his pajamas. "Not going in to work, then? You must be sick," She regarded him with an expression he couldn't read.

"No, I'm staying home today. I have the flu or something," he said. "Don't want to spread it around."

"You better come sit down," she said, leading the way back into his living room. "I hope it isn't catchy. Christmas is coming and the last thing I need is to get sick."

"Better not hang around then," he suggested.

She ignored him, removing her coat and laying it on the back of the sofa. She regarded the box of tissues and unkempt couch with a slight moue of distaste.

"You slept on your couch?"

"I fell asleep . . ." he said with a hint of annoyance. Why did he have to explain anything to her? She was his business partner, not his parent. Or his wife.

They both sat down on the sofa. He looked at the clock, wondering whether it was too soon to ask her to leave.

"I've got a dinner coming up on Friday the twenty-second. I was hoping you'd go with me," she said.

He remembered India saying something about needing a dance partner for a charity benefit. He figured he'd better keep his calendar clear. Besides, it was about time he and Angela stopped using each other as a crutch on the social scene. "I'm going to have to take a rain check on that, Angela."

"What? You can't! I bought a brand-new dress just for the occasion," she said, clearly peeved.

"You can still go without me," he said. He was tired and weak and he didn't have the energy to argue with her. "In fact, you should go without me."

"Where is this coming from?" she asked. "Is this because I asked you to father my baby?"

He hesitated, definitely not wanting to have a follow-up conversation to that. "You can't say that the nature of our friendship hasn't changed since I declined your proposition."

She pressed her lips together. "Since your refusal to help a friend in need, I would say our friendship is teetering on the brink of nonexistent."

He shrugged. "That's unfortunate, but that would be your choice at the end of the day."

"Yes, it would be!" she said.

He felt parched and reached for his water bottle on the coffee table, taking a few gulps from it. The remnants of last night's cup of tea were still on the table, as well.

He heard the front door open and knew it was India. He heard her walk down the hall.

"Mr. Laurencelli," she called out quietly. "Mr. Laurencelli?"

INDIA CALLED HIS NAME quietly in case he was sleeping. In both hands, she carried canvas bags filled with groceries. She entered the living room but pulled up short when she spotted Angela Preston seated on the sofa next to John.

"I'm sorry, I didn't know you had company," she stammered. "I've brought you some things."

"How nice," Angela said, sounding less than sincere.

India wasn't sure what to make of her tone. "Let me put these away." She carried the bags into the kitchen and set them on the countertop. Once she'd unloaded the groceries, she laid out the ingredients for homemade chicken noodle soup. She pulled out a stock pot from one of the cabinets below.

When she returned to the living room, Angela was pulling on her coat.

"Don't leave on my account," India said.

"I'm not," Angela said tightly.

India, puzzled, turned her attention to John. "How are you feeling?"

"About the same."

"Have you had anything to eat or drink?" she asked.

He shook his head. "No."

"Will I make you some tea and something light, maybe toast?"

"That would be nice."

She headed toward the kitchen and she heard Angela say in hushed but clipped tones, "For help, she's on pretty familiar terms with you, John. Is that why you turned me down?"

"She's got nothing to do with it, Angela. It's not like that," John said. India could hear the weariness in his voice.

"Then what is it like?" she asked. "Never mind, don't bother."

India could hear her stalking down the hall with the click-clack of her boots. That was followed by a slamming door.

She busied herself in the kitchen, then carried Mr. Laurencelli's breakfast out to him. "Will you eat it there or will I set the table?"

"I'll just eat it here. I don't have the energy to walk over to the table."

She walked over and set everything down on the coffee table, lining up the silverware per his preference.

"I've picked up a thermometer and some vitamin C," she said. She went around the living room, straightening up. She folded the blanket he had used and laid it over the back of the sofa. She removed yesterday's teacup and the empty water bottle and took them to the kitchen.

He ate the toast and drank some of the tea and then pushed the plate away.

When she emerged from the kitchen, she found him lying on the couch.

"I'm beat again. I don't know what I've picked up but it's knocked me out," he said.

"It's that time of year. It's going around," she said. She stood behind the couch and looked down at him. She placed her hand on his forehead and she became acutely aware that his eyes were on her. "You still feel warm. Let me take your temp."

The thermometer was one of the newer scanner models. She slid it across his forehead and when it blinked, she read out the number. "One-oh-one point five. Have you taken any Tylenol today?"

He shook his head.

India removed two from the bottle and got him a fresh glass of water.

"I'm sure you have better things to do than tend to me," he said, putting his feet back up.

"I've got a few things to do here and I'm going to make you a pot of chicken noodle soup," she explained.

"You don't have to do that," he protested.

"It's no trouble at all."

"Chicken soup would be nice, though," he said.

"That's what I figured," He probably couldn't handle much more than that, she thought; he looked quite ill. He'd gone pale and had dark circles under his eyes. "Look, Mr. Laurencelli, I'll be as quiet as I can but if you need something, just let me know."

"I will," he said, lying back down on the sofa. He reached for the blanket but India was closer so she unfolded it and laid it out over him.

"Thank you, Ms. Ramone," he said.

She returned to the kitchen and placed the whole chicken in the stockpot. After she cut up onions, celery, and carrots she added them to the pot, covered everything with water, and turned the burner on high. For extra measure, she added a bay leaf, salt, pepper, thyme, rosemary, and parsley.

She spent the rest of the morning doing her usual tasks, all the while keeping an eye on Mr. Laurencelli. After she'd checked on the chicken and turned the heat down, she crept in to find him with his eyes closed. She turned to go.

"No need to tiptoe, I'm not asleep," he said.

"You should be," she said. "It's important to get your rest. I've got the soup on simmer, and it's going to need a few hours. I'll be back after I finish my exam. You don't need to do anything with it, it's fine," she said.

"All right," he answered. "It smells great."

"Is there anything else? Anything you need done?"

He shook his head. "Good luck with your exam. I'll see you later."

She left him there on the couch and quietly let herself out of the apartment.

JOHN SAT THERE, NOT having the energy to do anything else. He flicked on the TV remote and put on the financial news, watching the stock ticker scroll past the bottom of the screen. He started to shiver again. Suddenly, he felt very tired and decided to move to the bedroom. He collapsed on the bed and pressed a button on the remote control on the nightstand. The drapes glided closed electrically along the rod, plunging the room into darkness.

He pulled the down comforter up around his shoulders and closed his eyes. Sleep would come easily and he was surprised when he found his thoughts wandering toward India Ramone. India was still on his mind when he drifted off to sleep.

INDIA ARRIVED BACK at John's apartment after her exam. The place was quiet and she noticed he was no longer on the couch and the door to his bedroom was closed. She hoped he was sleeping. A person needed plenty of rest and fluids to get through viruses, flus, and colds.

She turned her attention to the pot on the stove. It smelled marvelous. She pulled out a platter and used a large knife and fork to remove the chicken from the pot, noting with satisfaction the meat falling off the bone. She drained the liquid through a strainer and some cheesecloth and then poured it back into the pot. Pulling the breast meat off the carcass, she shredded it and added it to the soup, along with a whole bag's worth of wide egg noodles. She turned the burner back up to high, to bring the mixture back to a boil.

A noise from behind made her turn around. Mr. Laurencelli had emerged from his bedroom with a look of sleep around his eyes.

"I didn't hear you come in," he said.

"Good, you need your sleep," she said.

"That smells good. I'm hungry," he announced, scratching the back of his head.

"That's a good sign," she said. "It'll be ready in a few minutes."

"Do I have time to take a shower?" he asked.

"You do."

"All right then, I'll be out in a few minutes."

"I'll have it ready."

He strode back toward his bedroom but stopped and turned around. "Ms. Ramone, would you join me for lunch?"

She didn't hesitate. "I will."

"THAT FEELS BETTER," John said as he emerged from his bedroom. India was setting the bowls of soup on the dining table. His stomach growled in response and he had to agree with her that it was a good sign.

Once she had everything laid out—bowls of soup, a water pitcher with slices of lemon, and a crusty loaf of bread—she stood back.

"Will we eat?" he asked.

She nodded. He pulled out her chair for her and she sat down.

"You've gone to a lot of trouble making homemade soup," he noted as he took his own seat.

She smiled at him. "It was no trouble at all."

He picked up his soup spoon, gathered some soup and lightly blew on it before tasting it. "This is delicious," he said.

"It was my mother's recipe," she said.

"It's important to carry those things on," he added.

"It is." She nodded as she sliced up the loaf with a bread knife. Crumbs littered the table. She handed him a plate with one slice of bread on it. "See how one piece goes."

He buttered it and asked, "What made you choose nursing?"

She put her spoon down. "Two things, I suppose. My favorite subject in high school was biology, and I like taking care of people. I had the privilege of taking care of my mother during her sickness and after she died, I thought I'd like to take care of more people," she explained.

"Your mother was lucky to have you at her side," he said.

She cast her eyes downward briefly, then appeared to soldier on, continuing to eat her soup.

"I don't think I could do it," he said. He tried to picture himself giving shots and doing whatever else nurses did in relation to people's bodily functions. He laughed.

"What's so funny?" she asked. She lifted a piece of bread to her mouth and he noticed how delicate her hands were.

"I was trying to picture myself as a nurse," he said.

Even she had to laugh at that. "I'm sorry, I don't mean to be rude, but I can't picture you in scrubs."

"Don't apologize because I can't, either."

"But you do take care of other people," she observed. She regarded his empty bowl. "More soup?"

"Please," he said.

When she returned from the kitchen with his bowl refilled, he asked, "What do you mean when you say I take care of people?"

She shrugged. "You warned me the first day I came to work for you that you can be difficult. Other people have said it, too."

He suppressed a grin.

"But you're not like that at all," she said.

"Why would you say that? And how would you know?" he asked.

"One of the first things they teach us in nursing school is to observe."

He was almost afraid to ask but he couldn't help himself. "All right, what have you observed about me?"

She looked thoughtfully out the window at the lake. "You do like things a certain way. But you're fair," she mused. "And you must be kind because your employees are long term and they seem loyal to you—and I'm judging that by Marta."

"Tell me more," he insisted, suddenly and inexplicably fascinated by her take on him.

She eyed him up with an intensity. "And, I think you prefer to be labeled as 'difficult'—mean, even—because maybe you think it gives you an edge in business."

He stared at the contents of his bowl and wondered briefly if she should be running her own company. "You're very intuitive."

"That was another thing I learned in nursing school, to always trust your gut. Your intuition."

"Good advice."

"How did I do?" she asked.

"Pretty well." He hoped she'd ask him what he thought about her. Suddenly, he had the urge to tell her that she was all that was noble and good and worthy. That he admired her more than he admired most people. That her genuine care of people was a very attractive quality. That he wanted to know more than anything who took care of India Ramone while she was busy taking care of everyone else. And if there was no one to look after her, could he apply for the position? He longed to tell her that she had his undivided attention in a way no one else ever had. It took all his self-control not to lean over and place his hand over hers.

But she didn't ask. And he regretted that. He also wondered if these runaway thoughts were the result of his fever. In a few days, when his head was clear and his body temperature back to normal, would he go back to seeing her as just his employee?

Somehow, he doubted it.

CHAPTER
SEVENTEEN

India arrived home before Petey and Stella were back from school. The house was quiet and Gramps was nowhere to be found. His car was in the driveway, still covered in snow, which meant he hadn't even gone out that morning.

The only one who came to greet her was Jumbo. In his mouth, he carried the puppy by the scruff of the neck. Again. The puppy didn't seem to mind. India bent down, nuzzled Jumbo's furry head, and the dog wagged his tail furiously in response. Gently she removed the puppy from Jumbo's mouth and cradled it to her chest. "Where's Gramps, Jumbo?"

Carrying the puppy, she walked back to Gramps's bedroom. The dog trailed behind her. She knocked on the door, then peeked her head inside and found Gramps lying on his bed. Jumbo scrabbled beneath her, trying to push through the doorway, but she held him back with her knee.

"Are you all right, Gramps?" she asked.

"Just tired," he said.

She gave up the losing battle with the dog and opened the door, and Jumbo blew in and landed at the side of the bed. Gramps looked at her holding the stray. "I meant to call around to the vets to see if anyone was missing a puppy, but I forgot." He sighed.

"Don't worry about that, I can do it now. I've got plenty of time."

Gramps eyed her. "It'll probably be a nice break to be off from school for a while."

"It will be. Only one more exam! I can't wait. And other than hanging out with the three of you, my plan is to just kick back and put my feet up."

"That sounds like a good plan," he agreed. "I'm real proud of you, India. You've carried on like a champ after your mother's death."

"Thanks, Gramps. I just wish Mom could have lived to see it," she said wistfully.

"On some level, I'm sure she does."

India hoped so. She moved closer to the side of the bed. Holding the puppy in the crook of her arm, she reached out with the other and felt Gramps's forehead. "There's a lot of stuff going around. But you don't feel warm."

The dog jumped up on the bed, rocking it.

"Jumbo!" she scolded. The puppy licked her face.

"He's all right," Gramps said, reaching over and petting the dog.

"I'm going to make you an appointment with the doctor," she said.

Gramps didn't protest and that worried India more than anything.

INDIA CARRIED THE PUPPY back into the kitchen and picked up the phone. Gramps's doctor didn't have any openings until Tuesday morning, but that would work out fine because Petey and Stella would be at school and she'd be able to accompany him.

Then she called a few of the vets in the area and the local precinct house to see if anyone had reported a puppy missing. The fact that he wasn't wearing a collar concerned her; she hoped someone hadn't dumped him.

She held him up and looked at his little face. "You're too cute to be dumped."

In response, he wagged his tail and licked her face with his warm puppy tongue.

She put him down and gave him some fresh water and a bit of kibble. She'd have Petey make some posters later to plaster on the telephone poles on their street and up and down Abbott Road. Surely, someone must be missing him.

MR. LAURENCELLI HAD sent India a text stating there was no need for her to come back in the evening as there was plenty of soup for him to have for dinner. He also told her he was going back to work on Friday morning and would see her at the regular time. She frowned at his text. She would have told him to stay home one more day just to be sure, but she had a feeling that Mr. Laurencelli wouldn't take kindly to being bossed around anymore. Especially if he was on the mend.

Lunch with him earlier had been an eye opener. He had seemed interested in her and what she was doing and why she was doing it. She didn't think he was just being polite; he seemed genuinely interested in her answers. In the past, she wouldn't have thought he'd give someone like her the time of day. They were at opposite ends of the social and economic strata, that was for sure. But today, she didn't feel nervous or intimidated and had enjoyed lunch with him. It had been companionable.

AFTER STELLA AND PETEY came home and they each had a snack of hot chocolate and Christmas cookies, she bundled Stella up to go over and visit Warren.

"Are you sure you won't join us?" India asked Petey.

"No, thanks. Why? Can I write my name on his cast?" he asked.

"Petey, that isn't nice," India said. "Think of all the times he's helped you with your math homework."

"Whatever," he said.

Petey could sometimes turn surly for no apparent reason and India had concluded that it was most likely due to the fact that they'd lost both their parents. He never vocalized it but sometimes there was acting out. She didn't know if it was the onset of puberty, grief, or all of the above.

She decided his refusal to join them was not a hill she was going to die on. "All right then. Please keep an eye on Jumbo and the puppy. They'll need to go out in half an hour. And keep the noise level down—Gramps is resting."

"Yeah, okay," he said, not lifting his head up from his homework.

India helped Stella put on her boots and secured her hat underneath her chin. The two of them headed out, similarly bundled up. She held Stella's hand. Warren only lived over on the next block. They walked to the corner of their street, then swung right and headed north on Abbott Road. Stella chatted the entire way over. She told India about things that had gone on in class and at the rehearsal for her upcoming Christmas pageant. She and Gramps had decided that India would go to Stella's pageant and he would go with Petey to his parent luncheon. She hoped he would be up for it.

She and Stella walked up the cleared path to the side door of the house Warren shared with his mother. She noticed an unfamiliar car in the driveway and wondered who was there visiting him. She opened the storm door at the side for Stella, rapping on it to announce their arrival.

Once inside, she pulled off Stella's boots. Mrs. Scott came out into the hall. "Oh, India, there you are. And is that Miss Stella?"

Stella gave her a shy smile in response.

"Go on in, Warren's in the living room," she said. She took their coats from them. Clasping Stella's hand, India went through, surprised to see Warren wasn't alone. His company was a young woman with long blonde hair and glasses. Ah, this must be Penny, she thought.

"Hey, Warren, how are you?" India asked, indicating to his casted right leg which was propped up on an ottoman.

"I've been better," he said. He cleared his throat and announced, "India, this is Penny, my, um . . . girlfriend." He smiled to himself as if he liked the way that sounded and he looked up to the girl sitting on the arm of the sofa next to him. She gave him a warm, encouraging smile.

"And Penny, this is my friend, India, and her daughter, Stella."

India extended her hand as Penny stood up from the sofa. "It's nice to finally meet you. Warren has told me so much about you. I feel as if I know you already."

Warren looked up to Penny with what could only be described as a look of adoration. India wondered if anyone would ever look at her that way.

"Stella, would you like to be the first one to write or draw something on my cast?" Warren asked. Stella nodded. "Go out to the kitchen and ask my mother for some markers."

The three of them settled down comfortably and after enquiring about his leg, they made small talk. Stella drew flowers on Warren's cast and he didn't seem to mind. Penny was a nice girl and India immediately took a shine to her. By the time she left an hour later, she was satisfied that Warren was happy, but she wondered if she'd ever find that kind of happiness for herself.

ON FRIDAY MORNING, India arrived to find Mr. Laurencelli up and about and ready to go to work.

"Are you sure you're ready to go back?" she asked, studying him. He looked so much better than he had yesterday. His color was back and there was that light in his eyes.

He nodded, doing up his tie. "I feel much better, thank you." He pulled the knot tighter and adjusted it under the tips of his collar. "I think it was the chicken noodle soup."

"All right, if you're sure," she said. She knew she sounded like a mother hen, but someone had to look after him.

After breakfast, he shrugged on his coat. "You'll be here tonight? At dinner?"

She nodded. "I plan to be."

"I suppose we should practice some dancing," he said.

He hadn't forgotten. She had not mentioned it again, not wanting to force him. The other day, when she'd insisted in the heat of the moment that he would have to take Warren's place, she hadn't actually believed he would accommodate her.

"Oh, Mr. Laurencelli, you don't have to," she said. "I may have spoken out of turn during all the chaos."

"I don't mind, Ms. Ramone. Besides, it's the least I can do to make up for breaking your friend's leg," he said, wrapping his scarf around his neck and tucking it into his coat.

She was mortified. "You didn't break his leg—I don't really think that. It was just an accident."

"Still, I feel responsible," he said, adding, "It'd be a shame to drop out now. What charity are we dancing for?"

His enthusiasm caught her off guard. "Um, the neonatal unit at Children's Hospital." She hoped his skill on the dance floor matched his willingness.

"A worthy cause, so will we practice after dinner?" he asked.

"All right," she conceded, her voice tinged with uncertainty.

———— ✧ ————

BEEF WELLINGTON WITH roasted potatoes was on the menu that evening. The Wellington was a tricky and time-consuming dish but it had turned out beautifully. Glancing at the kitchen clock, India noted the time, expecting Mr. Laurencelli in half an hour. She turned the oven down to low.

He arrived just as she was setting the table.

"Ms. Ramone, how was your day?" he asked, setting down his briefcase and removing his coat.

She smiled. "It was good. Productive." And it had been. She had finished her last exam, and then she'd finished up her Christmas shopping and begun wrapping everything. Then she had made a batch of her mother's fudge and had just about squealed when she dropped a bit of the mixture into a glass of water and it passed the test, forming a little ball. It had set perfectly.

"We can't ask more than that," he said. "Are you ready to dance?"

"I should warn you that I'm not very good," she said.

"Not a problem." He looked toward the kitchen. "Something smells good."

"Beef Wellington. It's ready if you're ready."

"Ambitious—I am impressed," he said. "Let's eat, I'm starving."

She served it up and hesitated before she sat down. It still felt awkward to her to be sharing a meal with him. Thank God he hadn't insisted on lighting candles, as that would have been over-the-top intimate. Sensing her hesitation, Mr. Laurencelli pulled out her chair and then she had no choice but to sit down.

"So, what's expected of us at this charity dance?" he asked.

"We have to do three dances. They can be any three, even the same three. If you wanted to waltz around for all of them that would be fine," she explained. "The rules aren't that strict." Patti had said she liked things fast and loose, which hadn't surprised India.

"What did you have in mind?" he asked. He put a forkful of food into his mouth and regarded her thoughtfully. He indicated to his meal and said, "This is beautiful, by the way."

India sipped from her water glass, hiding her smile. She was happy with the way the main dish had turned out, with the pastry nice and flaky. "Sorry—what did I have in mind in regards to what?" she asked.

"In regards to your three dances. Have you and Warren chosen? Fox-trot? Waltz? Tango?"

India frowned. "No, we were just dancing. And then Warren got the idea to add lifts. As a distraction."

He grinned. "That bad?"

"I'm afraid so."

She tentatively asked, "Can you dance, Mr. Laurencelli?"

He nodded. "Actually, I'm a pretty good dancer."

She breathed a sigh of relief. All was not lost.

He laughed. "You can't possibly be that bad."

"Oh, but I am," she countered.

There was silence between them before India took a deep breath and spoke. "Are you sure your girlfriend won't mind us dancing together?"

"My girlfriend?" he asked, confused.

India nodded. "Ms. Preston."

He laughed. "She's not my girlfriend, she's my work partner." He paused, his fork mid-air. "What about you? Do you have a boyfriend?"

She shook her head. "No. Too busy."

Both went quiet, each lost in their own thoughts.

She had made strawberry parfait for dessert but Mr. Laurencelli declined. "I'll save it for later or I won't feel like dancing," he explained.

Together they cleaned up, working side by side, carrying every-thing back to the kitchen, loading the dishwasher, and scrubbing the pots.

"We'd better get started," Mr. Laurencelli announced.

India nervously followed him to the living room. As he put on some music on his sound system, she pulled the diagram that Warren had sketched out of her purse and unfolded it.

Mr. Laurencelli clapped his hands. "Okay, let's do this."

She showed him the diagram. "Warren drew this up for us."

He took it from her, looked at it, and then crumpled it into a ball and tossed it aside. "Not needed."

She raised her eyebrows.

"Let's try some basic steps," he said.

Up close and personal, India began to feel flustered. He was very masculine and his short dark hair, piercing blue eyes, and sculpted cheekbones were just about to enter her personal space. She'd never realized before how his biceps strained against his shirtsleeves.

He demonstrated a basic one-two, one-two pattern. She watched but she didn't remember. She began to feel dizzy. Mr. Laurencelli stepped forward and placed his hand on her waist. India began to melt. She blushed and hoped he wouldn't notice.

"Your hands go here and here," he said, taking her hands in his, placing one on his shoulder and clasping the other one. Her hands felt dainty and small in his large ones.

Looking for a reprieve, she stared at her feet and swallowed hard. She reminded herself over and over again that he was a billionaire and she was just a girl from South Buffalo. It was just a dance.

"Ms. Ramone, I can't have you looking at your feet while we dance," he said.

"Of course not," she stammered, looking up to him. His face was mere inches from hers. This was never going to work.

"I would take it as a personal insult if you stared at your feet the whole time," he said, cocking an eyebrow.

"Sure, okay," she mumbled.

"That was my attempt at levity," he prompted.

Her eyes widened. "Oh right, of course, it was." She let out a feeble laugh. She didn't feel like laughing. What she felt like doing was kissing him. Oh no, she thought miserably. I can't possibly fall for him. No good will come of it!

Mr. Laurencelli frowned at her. "Are you all right? You seem pretty tense."

She gave him a quick smile. "Just trying to concentrate."

"Very good. Shall we dance?" he asked.

She could only nod, her speech having left her. What was this? What were these new feelings that assailed her? And when on earth did she start to respond to John Laurencelli's swoon-worthy looks? When? She wondered. She knew the answer. As soon as he'd placed his hand on her waist.

She was doomed.

ALL WEEKEND, INDIA could not get John Laurencelli out of her mind. They'd practiced for an hour before she'd gone home and she didn't remember any of the dancing but she remembered with acute clarity things about her boss. She came up to his chin and was able to tuck right into the corner of his shoulder. She liked the way she felt in his arms. He had a small mole on his neck that was only visible up close. She had to fight the urge to kiss it. And most of all, he smelled wonderful. A combination of soap and aftershave, a citrusy, woodsy scent. It was all too much.

She reminded herself that her time with him was drawing to a close. Marta would be back after the New Year. Before, she had thought she'd miss the pay packet, but now she realized she was going to miss something even more: him. And all of this was ridiculous. She wasn't even in the same league as he was. To him, she would always be 'Ms. Ramone.' She doubted he even remembered her first name. These thoughts were dangerous and not practical. After all these years of keeping to herself, of not getting involved with anyone, of closing herself off to anyone that might be of interest, she had to go and fall for her boss. And a billionaire to boot!

India decided that as soon as Christmas was done with and this job was over, she was going to get her head examined.

JOHN HAD DIFFICULTY concentrating at work Monday. He wondered what he had gotten himself into by agreeing to be India Ramone's dance partner. Over the weekend, thoughts of his assistant had kept him up at night. He had always thought her attractive but up close, with his hands on her, she was absolutely ethereal. More than once, he'd felt dumbstruck. He had had to force himself to focus on the dancing and not on her. It had proved just about impossible.

Marta would be back soon and then he'd have no reason to see India ever again. He couldn't fire Marta; that would hardly be right. And he supposed he could find a place for Ms. Ramone here with his company but there weren't any existing jobs that matched her skill set. The company didn't need a nurse, but he did.

The most painful thing was that Ms. Ramone had never given him any indication that she was interested in him. He knew the signs; he'd been chased by women all his adult life. But she signaled nothing to him but the boss/employee relationship. There was no flirting, no secret looks or staring. It was clear to him that she wasn't interested in him at all.

He sighed, discouraged by the impossibility of it all.

And yet, he looked forward to dancing with her again tonight. In fact, he couldn't wait. It was his only excuse to take her in his arms.

INDIA PUT THE FINISHING touches on the chicken marsala. Mr. Laurencelli was due soon. They would sit down to dinner and then they would dance. She started shaking just at the thought of it. The dance contest couldn't come soon enough.

As she set the dining room table, she heard her phone ringing in the kitchen. She picked it up and saw 'home' come up on her screen. She frowned. They knew not to call her unless it was an absolute emergency. With apprehension, she answered.

"India!" Petey shouted. "You need to come home!" He was practically hysterical.

"Petey, what's wrong?" she asked, dread filling her stomach. "Calm down."

"It's Gramps," he said.

Something in India sank to the bottom of her knees. She grabbed hold of the edge of the countertop. "What do you mean?" she asked with a calmness she didn't feel.

Petey was hyper. "I came home from school and Gramps was out cold on the kitchen floor."

"What?" It was India's turn to get agitated. When she'd left, he had been fine. He'd been sitting in the living room with a cup of Sanka, watching Murder, She Wrote.

"I can't wake him up!" Petey wailed.

"I'll be right home. In the meantime, call 9-1-1!"

"I already did that," he said. "India, what if he's dead!"

"I'm on my way. Be on the lookout for the ambulance."

"They're here," he shouted and hung up.

India rang Mr. Laurencelli to tell him she was leaving but it just kept ringing and ringing and didn't even go to voicemail. She grabbed her purse and coat but paused, setting her purse on the counter and digging through it for a piece of paper. Nothing, except an envelope marked for the North Pole. "Gaahh!" she cried in frustration. She pulled it out; she'd have to use that. Furiously, she scribbled a note about what had happened. She trusted him to understand why she had left early. She was sorry to leave dirty dishes in his kitchen but her family needed her. She flew out of the apartment, pulling on her coat as she went.

CHAPTER EIGHTEEN

John walked up from the parking garage to the main lobby and sighed with resignation at the sight that greeted him. Martin had been busy that day. The marble-and-brass lobby was all done up in expensive gold and red ornaments. There was a fully decorated Christmas tree in the corner near the front desk with elaborately wrapped gift boxes beneath it.

Martin was busy affixing a luxury wrap of garland to the brass banister of the marble staircase. When he saw Mr. Laurencelli coming, he gave him a big artificial smile.

"Women's work, I know," Martin started.

John rolled his eyes. He decided no response was the best answer.

Martin stopped what he was doing and headed toward the elevator. John put his hand up. "No need. I can manage myself."

"Hey, not to cause trouble or anything—"

John turned to look at him.

"I noticed your girl left about twenty minutes ago," Martin said. He added quickly, "I like to keep my eye out for my tenants."

The elevator doors slid open and John stepped inside, pressing the button for his floor. "I was aware of that," John lied. It irritated him to no end that Martin felt it was his duty to report on the comings and goings of his assistant. "But thanks for your spying."

The elevator doors swooshed closed before the doorman could respond.

INDIA DIDN'T REMEMBER much about the ride home. She pulled wildly into the driveway, parked the car and ran into the house. Mrs. Bannon from next door was in the kitchen. She had known Gramps longer than India had. They'd been neighbors for over fifty years.

"When I saw the ambulance, I came right over," she explained.

"How is Gramps?" India asked. There was a tremor in her voice.

Mrs. Bannon spoke softly. "He's alive but they couldn't wake him up," she said. "They've taken him to Mercy Hospital."

"Okay," India acknowledged. Mercy was right up the road. "Where are Stella and Petey?"

"In the living room." Mrs. Bannon lowered her voice further. "Petey is very upset."

India could only nod. She was sure he was. The boy had already experienced a lot of loss in his young life. She whispered some quick, anxious prayers.

Petey sat on couch with his head in his hands. Stella jumped up at the sight of India.

"Mommy, where's Gramps?"

"Honey, Gramps is sick and he's gone to the hospital," she explained. She was worried about Petey and sat next to him on the couch. She put her arm on his back. "You all right, bud?"

Petey broke down sobbing.

In response, India started crying, too. Pretty soon the three of them were huddled up on the couch in tears. Finally, she said, "Look, I have to go up to the hospital and see what's going on with Gramps. I'll ask Mrs. Bannon to stay with you."

She gave them both a hug and stood up. Back in the kitchen, Mrs. Bannon stood with her back to the sink.

"Mrs. Bannon—" India started.

Mrs. Bannon put her hand up. "I'll stay until you get home. I've got a nice pot roast on next door. I'll make sure they get their dinner."

"Thank you so much," India said. Before her neighbor could respond, India was out the door and on her way to the hospital.

JOHN OPENED THE DOOR to a darkened apartment. Something smelled good—his dinner, no doubt. He hung up his coat and headed toward the kitchen with his briefcase in his hand. Dirty dishes littered the sink. There was a pot and pan on the stove. He lifted the lid on the pan and peered inside at the chicken marsala. Something must have happened for India to leave everything like this. He saw the note on the counter and picked it up.

Something had happened to India's grandfather.

What could he do for her? He pulled his cell phone out of his breast pocket and dialed her number. Not surprisingly, it went to voicemail. He went and changed out of his suit, then plated his dinner and sat down with it at the table. It was delicious but given the circumstances, he couldn't enjoy it and gave up after a few bites. He went about cleaning his kitchen, his thoughts on India all the while. When he was finished, he took a look around, trying to figure out what he should do next.

"Damn!" he said out loud. He went to the hall closet and grabbed a jacket. He'd go to India's house and see if she needed help with Petey and Stella, or anything. Anything at all.

INDIA MANAGED TO FIND a parking space on the ground level of the parking ramp. Hurriedly, she ran through the doors marked 'emergency' and went up to the desk.

"My grandfather was brought in by ambulance," India said.

"His name?" asked the woman behind the desk.

"Robert Miller."

"Okay, have a seat and someone will be out shortly."

"Can I see him?"

"Soon. Someone will be out shortly."

India let out a big sigh of relief. That fact that she could see him soon meant that he was still alive. She took a seat in the waiting room, but she'd no sooner sat down than a door opened on the other side of the room.

"Family of Robert Miller," said a male nurse.

India stood up and held tightly onto her purse strap as if it were a safety line. She followed the nurse inside. He had a neatly trimmed beard and mustache and wore a set of blue scrubs.

"Are you the next of kin?" he asked, pulling open a curtain to admit her.

She nodded and looked at Gramps, lying awake on the emergency-room gurney. Gramps, with his white hair and blue eyes, looked small and helpless in the hospital gown. Tears filled her eyes as she realized how old he looked. He looked frail and every day of his eighty years. It occurred to her how even though she'd lost both her parents, she'd taken for granted the fact that Gramps would always be there. He had always been there. When Dad died, he had helped Mom out. And then when Mom had gotten sick, he had driven her to her radiation and chemo treatments. He'd been there for all of them. And now here he was, sick himself.

India went to his side. "Gramps, are you all right?"

"The doctor will be in shortly to talk to you," the nurse said. He disappeared before India could ask him any questions.

India took Gramps's hand. It was cool. She brushed away a tear from her face.

"Now, now India," he said. "Don't cry. Because then I'll cry, too." His own eyes filled up in response to her tears.

She nodded and bit her lip, stemming the flow of tears. She promised herself a good cry later in her room. When she was alone.

"What happened?" she asked.

"I don't know, to be honest. I haven't been feeling too good lately," he started. "After you left, I was waiting for the kids to come home from school when I suddenly felt very tired and everything went black."

India shuddered. "Oh, Gramps! I should have got you in to see the doctor sooner!" Guilt assailed her.

"You have enough on your plate," he countered.

"Gramps, in the future, I don't care how much is on my plate," India said. "You need to tell me these things."

He gave her a dismissive wave. "I don't need babysitting. I can take care of myself."

"I know you can. But still . . ."

"I didn't feel bad enough where I felt I needed to go to the doctor," he said. "I've just been feeling different."

"Okay, but in the future, promise you'll tell me," she said. "Even if it's something like your arthritis in your knees is acting up and you think it's going to rain."

He laughed.

"We'll just wait and see what the doctor says."

It was two hours before a doctor pulled the curtain aside and said, "Good evening!" He was middle-aged, balding with glasses, and wore a white coat over scrubs with the words 'Dr. Patel' embroidered over the jacket pocket. He had a young, college-aged man with him who worked on his laptop. India figured he must be a medical scribe.

"Mr. Miller, how are you feeling now?" the doctor asked.

"All right, I guess," Gramps said. India looked at him, concerned. She thought his voice sounded shaky.

"There are a couple of things going on," Dr. Patel explained. "First, your blood glucose level was very low when you came in. In layman's terms, sugar."

"I've never had a problem with sugar. I'm not going to lose my toes or anything?" Gramps asked, his voice full of panic. India knew he was thinking of his friend, Chester, a lifelong diabetic who had recently lost the toes on one of his feet.

The doctor smiled. "Your toes are fine, Mr. Miller. We'll start you on some medication and we'll monitor you. We'll also refer you to a nutritionist to make some dietary changes. But when we did the EKG, there were some cardiac irregularities noted."

India's ears perked up at this. Hypoglycemia and cardiac issues? Definitely not sounding good.

"My granddaughter here is going to be a nurse," Gramps said proudly.

The doctor smiled at India.

"We'd like to keep you for a few days and do some more tests," the doctor explained. "As soon as we get a bed on a floor, we'll move you up there."

"But I need to be home by Friday morning," Gramps protested. "I've promised my grandson I'd take him to his Christmas luncheon."

"Gramps, don't worry about that," India said. "I'll take care of that."

He turned his head and looked at her. "But how can you be in two places at the same time?"

"It's okay. It's more important that you stay here and get better," she said.

Gramps looked to the doctor. "What are the chances I could be home by Friday?"

The doctor shrugged. "I can't make any promises."

India spoke up. "He will stay. It's not a problem." She looked at Gramps and nodded.

IT WAS AFTER MIDNIGHT when India finally left the hospital. She had wanted to wait until Gramps was settled in a hospital room and not stuck down in the emergency department. She would have given anything for someone to carry her to her car. She was anxious to get home to Stella and Petey. Poor Mrs. Bannon! She was no spring chicken herself.

She drove home, thinking about how nice it was going to be to get into her fleecy pajamas and climb into bed. She couldn't wait. As soon as she got Petey and Stella off to school tomorrow, she'd run back up and see how Gramps was doing. Thank goodness her own classes were finished for this semester. She worried about Friday morning and the conflicting events. How was she going to sort it all out? There was Stella's Christmas pageant, her first school one. And then there was Petey's Christmas luncheon. Biting her lip, she wracked her brain, trying to come up with a solution. If they were both in the same school, it would have been doable. Tricky but doable. But Petey was over at the middle school now and Stella was still at the grammar school. Then there was the charity dance Friday night. Ugh. She was sorry she had ever agreed to that. What had she been thinking? That was the problem; she hadn't been thinking. As soon as she was told, 'it's for charity,' she'd been sold. She wondered if it was too late to get out of it.

She turned onto her street and Gramps's house came into view. The Christmas lights twinkled merrily in the front window and there was a bluish cast of light in the front window, which meant Petey was still up watching television.

Her mouth fell open when she saw Mr. Laurencelli's car parked in their driveway.

JUMBO GREETED INDIA with a wagging tail when she entered the house. He whined, seeking her attention, clearly aware that something was amiss. She nuzzled the dog and petted him until he calmed down. From the living room, she could hear the muted sounds of the television. The kitchen was clean: there were no dishes in the sink and the table and the counters had been wiped down. She was grateful for that. The last thing she needed was a sink full of dirty dishes.

She laid her coat and purse on one of the kitchen chairs. She peeped through the door to the living room and saw Petey and Mr. Laurencelli camped out on the couch. On the coffee table was an empty pizza box and two cans of soda.

"Oh, did you see that?" Mr. Laurencelli asked Petey.

Petey looked up at him, smiling. "Pure class!"

India could almost guarantee it was some kind of zombie film.

"Hello there."

When Mr. Laurencelli caught sight of her, he immediately stood up.

"How's Gramps?" Petey asked.

"He's okay. He's going to have to stay in the hospital for a few days," she explained.

Petey's face betrayed no emotion. She couldn't tell how he was handling it. He may have been putting on a brave face because Mr. Laurencelli was there.

"But he's going to be okay, right?" Petey asked. This time, India did not miss the anxiety in his voice.

"Yes, he is. Just needs some new medications is all," she said. She looked over to Mr. Laurencelli, aware of his eyes on her face. "What are you doing here?" she stammered. "I'm sorry, I didn't mean for that to sound so rude."

"I figured you had your hands full and I thought I'd come over and see if there was anything I could do."

"I appreciate that," she said. It was thoughtful. She almost wished he hadn't; good looks were one thing but coupled with kindness it became an intoxicating mixture that was difficult to resist.

He gave her a slight nod.

"What about Stella?" she asked.

"Your neighbor put her to bed before she left," John explained.

"Oh good."

"John ordered pizza for the movie," Petey said. "We should do that sometime. Order takeout while we're watching TV."

India nodded. She looked at the empty box with its grease stains, her stomach growling.

"We saved two slices for you," John said. "They're on a plate in the fridge."

"Thank you," she said, biting her lip. For the second time that night, she felt like bursting into tears.

"Are you hungry?" he asked.

"I'm starving," she said.

"Let me heat it up for you," he offered, moving toward the kitchen.

"That's not necessary," she said, mortified at the thought of Mr. Laurencelli waiting on her. "Besides, you probably want to get home."

"I don't mind," he said. "Why don't you go upstairs and check on Stella and by the time you come back down, it'll be ready."

Too tired to protest, she did as he suggested and climbed the stairs, realizing how weary she truly was. She peeked in on Stella, who was sound asleep with Mr. Pickles and the puppy curled up together in the doll crib next to her bed. Thoughtfully, Stella had covered them with a little blanket. India crept into the room and pulled the covers up around Stella's shoulders. She leaned over and placed a kiss on her forehead. The cat opened his eyes and peered at India. The puppy did not move.

"Good night, Mr. Pickles," she said softly.

JOHN REHEATED THE PLATE of pizza in the microwave. He set it down on the table and looked around the kitchen.

"Any napkins?" he asked Petey.

The boy shook his head. "Nah. We just use paper towels."

He took one off the roll, folded it lengthwise, and laid it next to the plated pizza. He poured soda over ice cubes in a tall glass for India.

She arrived in the kitchen and he thought she looked tired.

"Sit down and have something to eat," he said.

"Thank you, I'm starved!" She looked at Jumbo sleeping under the kitchen table. "Has Jumbo been out tonight?" She looked at Petey.

"I let him out about an hour ago," John told her.

"Thank you," she said. To her brother, she said, "Did you and Stella eat all your dinner?"

Petey nodded. "Mrs. Bannon gave us pot roast. It was pretty good. Much better than Gramps's meatloaf."

John wondered if India ever stopped taking care of people. If she ever stopped looking out for everyone.

INDIA SCARFED DOWN the pizza and guzzled the soda, suppressing a burp afterward. When she was through, she felt sated and wiped her mouth with the paper towel. She sent Petey to bed. Twice. He protested vehemently but when she said nothing the second time and just glared at him with that look, the same one her mother used to give her, he went, although he did drag his feet.

"India, is there anything I can do for you?" Mr. Laurencelli asked, picking up his coat off the kitchen chair.

"No, we're good," she said, trying to convince herself as much as she was trying to convince him.

"Are you sure?" he asked. He put on his coat and picked up his car keys off the counter.

She stood up and loaded her plate and glass into the dishwasher. She shook her head.

"No, really, Mr. Laurencelli, we'll be fine," she said.

"Are you certain?" he asked. He had one hand on the doorknob.

She nodded. She walked over and stood at the door with him. "I'll see you in the morning."

He hesitated. "About that. Look, why don't you take the morning off? I can manage."

"Oh, no, I'll be there," she said.

"I'd prefer if you weren't," he said.

The look of shock on her face must have betrayed her because he said hurriedly, "I didn't mean it like that, Ms. Ramone. What I meant is that you've got a lot to deal with right now and your time would be better spent with your daughter and your brother."

She was so grateful for his kindness that she started crying.

He reached out and put his arm on hers. "Hey, hey, it's all right. Would you like the rest of the week off? Or at least until your grandfather comes home?"

"Thank you so much—I do appreciate it, but it isn't necessary," she said.

"Please, at the very least, stay home tomorrow morning. You've got to be exhausted," he insisted.

She frowned, wiping away her tears. "Only if you're sure."

"I am positive," he said, then added with a grin, "Besides, weren't you the one who said I needed to shake things up a bit?"

She gave him a faint smile in response.

He stepped outside and she called out to him. "Mr. Laurencelli, wait a minute. I was thinking of bowing out of the charity dance."

"Why?" he asked.

She gave a nervous laugh. "There just seems to be too much going on right now." And although she would miss dancing with him—if ever there was a heaven then that was it—the truth was she was tired. And what time was left in the run-up to Christmas, she wanted to enjoy. She didn't want to end up frazzled and exhausted by the time Christmas Eve rolled around, like last year.

"I'm disappointed," he said.

"Really?" she asked, unable to hide her surprise.

"Yes, really, Ms. Ramone. I've been looking forward to it," he confessed.

"Really?" she repeated. What did it say about his social life if he looked forward to dancing with her, she of the two-left-feet club?

"Have you not enjoyed it?" he asked, studying her.

"Oh, I have!" she said a little too enthusiastically. She dialed it down and added, "Although I'm not a good dancer."

He started to protest but she cut him off. "I wasn't fishing for compliments, honest!"

He laughed. "Maybe you're not the best dancer, but you're perfect for me."

Oh.

"Anyway, will we practice tomorrow night?" he asked.

She nodded but then said, "Wait—would you mind coming here? I wouldn't be able to leave the kids here alone at night. And I can't keep asking Mrs. Bannon to watch them. She might be able to manage them until I get home from work but I couldn't ask her to stay all evening."

"Not a problem," he said. "Look, take tomorrow night off, too. There's no sense in you coming down to cook my dinner and then driving back home."

"I couldn't do that!" she protested. She thought for a moment. "Would you like to join us for dinner here tomorrow night?"

"I'd love to." He smiled and there was something inside her that melted, as if that smile was meant just for her.

SNOW FELL LIGHTLY AS John made his way home. The roads were quiet at this time of night. He'd been glad he'd trusted his intuition and gone over to give India a hand. Stella had been shy with him and Mrs. Bannon had been kind enough to stay until it was her bedtime. He and Petey had spent the night watching zombie shows and John had enjoyed his company; the boy was really funny. But it was India who had made his heart do a quiet leap. There was something about her that he admired—just about everything, really. The way she took care of everyone and dealt with everything by herself, without complaint, was the definition of grace.

He unlocked the door to his apartment and flipped on the lights. It was late and he was tired and he was going to head to bed soon. He pulled a bottle of water out of the fridge and uncapped it. Standing at the counter drinking it, he spied India's note lying there. He set the bottle down and picked up the envelope. Ms. Ramone had delicate, feminine handwriting. He studied it for a moment, smiling at the North Pole address. He pulled out the sheet of paper, thinking it was Stella's. What did five-year-old girls want from Santa Claus these days? Was it still dolls or had technology completely taken over?

He unfolded the lined notebook paper and began reading. First, he was confused, and then he scanned to the end of the letter and saw that it was India who had signed it.

Deciding he wasn't ready for bed, after all, he poured himself a tumbler of Macallan 25 and sat down on his sofa to ponder India's letter.

1. *To give Stella, Petey, and Gramps a great Christmas.*

2. *To do well on my nursing finals.*

3. *To meet the love of my life and have him accept all of us as a package deal.*

He fingered the letter. There was nothing he could do about number two and he hoped she had done well. In fact, he didn't doubt it. She was organized, responsible, and intelligent. But he wondered about numbers one and three.

It would be very easy to buy his way into her Christmas. Send the kids the latest technology and the latest gadgets and get Gramps whatever he needed. But he suspected that wasn't the way to India's heart. She'd see right through it and it would spectacularly backfire. If he had learned anything about her, it was that she was fiercely independent. He respected that.

As for number three, that was the most difficult one of all. Not her conditions but the reality that she hadn't appeared to be the least bit interested in him. He would give his fortune to be the love of her life.

CHAPTER
NINETEEN

"Mommy, I like it when you're home in the morning," Stella said to India.

Despite being tired, India had gotten up early to make them French toast for breakfast. She put a plate in front of Stella and put a pat of butter on it with a bit of warmed pancake syrup. She loved to make them a hot breakfast on a cold, snowy morning, the way her mother used to do a long time ago.

Petey entered the kitchen and India plated up his breakfast for him.

"French toast! Sweet," he said, pulling up a chair to the table.

"Since I'm home this morning, I'll drive you both to school," India said.

"Okay," Petey said, loading up pieces of French toast onto his fork.

"Why can't you drive us every day?" Stella whined.

"I will this week," India promised. She bit her lip, thinking about how she was going to manage the school mornings. There was work and there was Gramps ... She exhaled loudly and decided she'd think about it later.

Marta was due back at the first of the year and India was going to miss her job with Mr. Laurencelli. She'd miss the job and she'd miss him, but there was no point in thinking thoughts like those. This time of year always made her feel more lonely than usual and she supposed as Mr. Laurencelli was the only eligible male on her horizon it was only natural that she'd zero in on him. But she had to admit, he had surprised her on more than one occasion with his thoughtfulness and consideration. Despite all those rumors circulating about him being difficult, she had also seen some kindness. Good looks and thoughtfulness were heady combo. Again, she knew this was dangerous thinking. They traveled in different circles altogether. She was so far out of his league that she might as well have been on a different planet.

AFTER SHE DROPPED STELLA and Petey off at school, she headed over to the hospital to see how Gramps was doing. He had had a good night but the doctors were still no closer to deciding when he could be discharged.

This seemed to upset Gramps. He fidgeted in the bed, fooling with the edge of the hospital blanket. Then he looked back and forth between the window and the door as if he were waiting for something to happen. When he reached for the sheet a third time to straighten it out, India leaned over and placed her hand over his.

"Gramps, what is it? You seem anxious."

"I want to go home," he said.

"I know, but you're in the best place right now until they get you sorted out," she said.

"But you need me at home, helping out," he said. "You've got enough to do as it is."

"No, I—we—need you here, getting better," she said. "Everything is under control at home. Don't even worry about it."

"But what about your job?" he asked. There was a sense of agitation about him that concerned India. It was obvious he worried about the three of them a lot more than he let on. She wasn't leaving until he was calm and reassured.

"Mr. Laurencelli has been very accommodating," she explained. "He is aware that you're in the hospital and told me to take the day off."

"That was kind of him," he said.

"Yes, it was," she agreed.

"You wouldn't think he'd be like that, the way they depict him in the newspapers," Gramps said. He shook his head. "It's a shame, really."

"It is."

"India, I promise I will get home as soon as I can," he said.

"You're going to stay in here as long as necessary. You're not going home a day earlier than you need to. Now, I want you to rest up for the day," she said.

"Harry and Cal called and said they'd be up in the afternoon," he said.

India nodded. "That's fine, but don't let them tire you out."

"I can hardly ask them to leave—it would be rude."

She bent in close. "Just close your eyes and pretend you're sleeping and you won't have to say anything."

"I'll make a note of that."

"Good."

India stayed until after Gramps finished his lunch, making sure he ate enough. Once the tray was removed, she kissed him goodbye and told him she'd see him in the morning. She promised that Petey and Stella would call him after dinner.

INDIA WAS VERY NERVOUS about John coming for dinner. She was more anxious over this than she'd been on her first day of nursing clinical when she'd had to give her first intramuscular injection. Her hands had been shaking that day and they were shaking now. After she'd left the hospital, she'd stopped at the grocery store and picked up a few things. She knew John was used to fussier, fancier meals but this was Naragansett Street and they didn't do fussy. It was hard to cook for three different people with three different palates. Luckily, she wasn't fussy at all. There was plenty of time to prepare a pot of sauce and a pan of lasagna. As a backup, she made a tossed salad and had a loaf of garlic bread on hand.

He arrived a little after six.

"You didn't say John was coming for dinner," Petey said, looking from his sister to John Laurencelli.

"Well, he is," India said. She sliced up the lasagna. The cheese was melted and gooey. She turned to her boss and wiped a stray hair away from her face.

"Mr. Laurencelli, take a seat anywhere." She smiled. "Petey, take his coat, please, and go put it over the dining room chair."

Petey did as he was told without comment, which India found refreshing.

Mr. Laurencelli sat down and looked around the table. He greeted Stella and asked her about her day at school. Stella shyly smiled at him in response.

Jumbo came barreling in and Mr. Laurencelli eyed him warily. The dog circled the table and John raised his eyebrows.

"Pay no attention to him, Mr. Laurencelli. He'll settle down in a minute. Just don't feed him from the table or he won't leave you alone," she said.

"You don't have to worry about that," he said.

He looked up at her as she placed a plate of lasagna with a small portion of spaghetti in front of him. "Are you all ready to dance?"

Petey's head snapped up. "Dance? What do you mean?"

"Since Warren broke his leg, Mr. Laurencelli has been gracious enough to replace him and be my partner for the Christmas charity dance," India explained. She looked around the table to make sure they all had everything they needed before sitting down herself.

Petey shook his head. "How did she rope you into that?"

John shrugged. "I don't mind, really."

"She made me dance with her once at a wedding and that was enough for me," Petey grumbled. He twirled a bit of spaghetti onto his fork.

"Let me tell you a secret," John said, leaning forward. "Girls love to dance. So, it goes without saying that if you can dance . . ."

"Give me a break," Petey said. "I haven't even gone through puberty yet."

They all laughed.

"Will you be smooching when you dance?" Stella asked, her mouth circled with a stain of tomato sauce.

John looked at her and raised his eyebrows. Embarrassed, India blushed. "Oh no, this is strictly dancing."

"Yeah, right," Petey said, not looking at either one of them and helping himself to a piece of garlic bread.

JOHN INSISTED ON HELPING India clear the supper dishes. No matter how much she protested, he wouldn't take no for an answer. He eyed the big sauce pot on the stove and the big pan of lasagna. She was a great cook. He was beginning to wonder if there was anything she couldn't do. Besides, with all that pasta sitting in his stomach he had to move around or there'd be no dancing. Maybe napping, but no dancing.

Petey went upstairs to do his homework and India occupied Stella at the kitchen table with a box of crayons, then set about clearing the living room. John helped her push the sofa up against the window. There was nothing to be done about the big Christmas tree.

India opened up the lid of the old record player. She removed an album from its sleeve and laid it on the turntable. It began to spin, and she lowered the needle onto the vinyl record. The music floated around the room.

John swallowed hard. He was transported back in time to his childhood living room decades ago and he could hear his mother's laugh as clearly as if she were beside him now. It blindsided him. He had forgotten about her record player, her serious love for music, and her even more serious love of collecting albums. His father had built her a special case so she could store them all. He wondered briefly where it had gone.

India turned around and asked, "Are you ready?"

He nodded but said nothing. She looked lovely standing there with her hair held back with a headband and her bangs in desperate need of a trim. His mind drifted to thoughts he'd never really given serious consideration before. This was how it would be to come home to someone who cared enough about you to cook you a home-made meal, to gather around a table with your family and share your day, and afterwards, to relax together. He was beginning to realize what he had been missing. To spend some alone time with that one person who connected you to life. And to living.

He smiled and held out his arms for her.

INDIA WAS LOST IN JOHN'S embrace, grateful for the excuse of dancing to be there as he twirled her expertly around the tight confines of the living room on Naragansett Street. So she was startled when she heard the thud from above and saw the chandelier with the missing prisms that hung over the dining room table shaking in response. She glanced at John. "Excuse me."

She dashed up the stairs and made a beeline for Petey's room. She threw open the door and caught Petey in the middle of tearing apart his room. Her mouth hung open. He had ripped down his posters, and the Christmas lights they had fastened to the wall above his bed now hung precariously by one tack. One of the window panels hung crookedly off several of the curtain hooks. He hadn't seen her yet. He had his back to her as he approached his desk and with one great heave of his arms, swept everything off of it. His math textbook went to the floor with a thud and paper went sailing in the air, landing everywhere. He went to the dresser next.

"Petey!" India cried out in alarm.

This had happened once before, about two months ago when he came home from trick-or-treating on Halloween night. He'd lost it then, too, throwing his candy everywhere and only stopping when Stella had started crying. At the time, India had considered it a one-off, but now she wasn't so sure.

He turned to her. His face was beet red and his hair was damp with exertion. There were tears in his eyes. When he saw her, the expression on his face faltered, then crumbled.

India immediately went to him and wrapped her arms around him. "It's all right. Shh."

Petey sobbed and held on to her tightly. "I miss Mom."

"I know you do, sweetie." She held him and rubbed his back until the sobbing stopped and he took in deep, big breaths of air. She pulled back and looked at him, searching his face and giving him a reassuring smile. She brushed his hair along his forehead the way her mother used to do with her when she was upset.

"Come on, sit down and talk to me," she said softly. She led him to his twin bed and they sat down on the edge of it. She put her arm around him and he leaned into her.

"I miss Mom and it bothers me that she's never coming back," he said. He started crying again and his whole body shook. "I want my mother."

And there it was. Despite his offhanded humor, his interest in all things zombie, and his love of music, at the end of the day, he was still just a little boy.

India didn't say anything at first. She let him cry it out. There was no way around grief, only through it, as painful as it was. In the past two years, she had felt the same way Petey did now, many times.

"I mean, I have no home to go to," he cried. "I have no parents."

She pulled him closer. "Of course you have a home. As long as I'm alive, you will always have a home. No matter where I live or who I'm living with. We are a package deal, buddy."

When he settled down again, she said, "It is very painful, Petey. I agree. And you're young and you don't fully understand everything. We need to find you a better way to deal with Mom's death."

"You mean other than trashing my room?" he asked, a little glimpse of the old Petey shining through, to India's relief.

"Yes, exactly. It's too—" She faltered, searching for the right word, a kind word that would get the point across.

"—destructive?" he asked, filling in the blank.

"Yes."

He didn't say anything for a moment. They sat there in the silence, both thinking of their lost mother. Everything had changed with her death. Their circumstances, their living arrangements, their lives. That first year had been awful for India and she'd been twenty-four. She couldn't imagine being Petey's age and trying to cope with the fact that both your parents were dead.

They were quiet for a few moments, then she asked, "Is there anything else?"

Petey wailed, "I'm the only kid in my class who doesn't have a parent to bring to the Christmas luncheon. How lame is that?"

He shrugged her arm away from his shoulders.

"I know, I'm sorry," she said soothingly. "I don't think Gramps will be home from the hospital just yet. He was planning on going with you." She was beginning to wonder if he'd even be home for Christmas.

"I know, and now he can't. At least having my grandfather there would have been okay."

"What about Uncle Sam?" India asked, trying not to sound desperate. Uncle Sam was Gramps's older brother.

"Uncle Sam! Are you kidding? He's deaf, he shouts, and he always smells like poop!"

India winced and she was surprised by the sound of John's chuckle. She looked up quickly to see him standing in the doorway. Jumbo stood next to him, surveying the mess that was Petey's bedroom and dying to get at it. But Mr. Laurencelli pointed at the dog to heel and the dog obeyed him. Funny, that, India thought.

"Okay, it was just a thought," she conceded.

Petey sniffled and wiped his nose with his sleeve—a young boy who had gotten a raw deal.

India swallowed hard. "I'll tell you what, I'll go with you to your Christmas luncheon at school." She'd miss Stella's Christmas play but there would be others.

Petey looked at her quizzically. "But what about Stella? She's your daughter. She should come first."

"Yes, Stella is my daughter," India said, and then she took Petey's hands in hers. He did not pull them away. "But listen very carefully, Petey."

"What?"

"Stella is my daughter,"—she paused— "And you're my brother. And you are just as important to me."

She couldn't tell if she was making any headway with this. It was imperative to her that he understood how much he meant to her.

"May I make a suggestion?" John said from the doorway.

India and Petey looked over to him.

"I would be more than happy to take Petey to his Christmas luncheon," he said.

India blinked. "Oh, Mr. Laurencelli, that's very kind of you, but we couldn't impose on you like that."

"I don't mind," he said. "But it's up to you, Petey."

"Are you kidding me?" Petey said. "Bring a billionaire to my classroom. That's class! It beats bringing a parent!"

"Oh, I don't know—" India said, but Petey's exuberance silenced her.

"If it's okay with Petey, I'm game," John said, smiling.

India looked between the two of them.

"It's definitely okay with me!" Petey said excitedly.

"Very good. What time?" John asked.

"It's at one sharp," Petey said. "And we have to bring something for lunch."

"Like what?" John asked.

"I've been assigned sandwiches."

"No problem, I'll order them. How many kids in your classroom?"

"Twenty-eight. But we only need to bring enough for twenty. There are four other kids who are bringing sandwiches, too."

"Okay, good. Now, will I pick you up in my car or will I have my driver drop us off at the front door?"

"Really? A driver?"

India sat back, listening to the two of them making arrangements. Petey couldn't contain his excitement. She'd really have to thank Mr. Laurencelli later. But at the back of her mind, she couldn't help but wonder why he was going to all this trouble for them.

"Why don't you get the room cleaned up now, Petey," India suggested. "I'll make you a cup of hot cocoa and then you can settle in my bed and watch some television for a little bit, just for tonight. How's that?"

Petey nodded.

He stood up from his bed and started by straightening out his bedspread. India picked his pillow up off the floor and laid it at the head of the bed.

"Get everything cleaned up and get ready for bed and I'll go down and make the cocoa."

India exited the room, looking curiously at Mr. Laurencelli as she passed.

He had the grace to look flustered. "I'm sorry. I came up to see if you needed any help."

She raised her eyebrows in surprise.

John surveyed Petey's bedroom. "Can I help you pick up your room, Petey?"

Now India's mouth hung open.

Petey looked at him and shrugged. "Sure, it isn't every day you get a billionaire to clean your room."

India could have sworn she heard John laugh.

TWO THINGS HAD PROPELLED John upstairs when he'd heard all the commotion: first, he'd wanted to make sure India was all right and second, he was plain curious.

Now, out of the corner of his eye, he watched as Petey picked up the loose-leaf papers that were strewn all over the floor. He liked Petey; he was a good kid.

John reattached the curtain panel to the rod, then he went over and picked up the string of Christmas lights off the floor. "Which way did you have these?"

Petey said quietly, "Over the bed."

"Why don't you climb up on the bed and attach it to the wall and I'll hold the other end," John suggested.

Nodding, the boy obediently climbed up, stood at the head-board and tacked up his end. When it came time, John fastened the remainder in place.

He gathered his courage and his voice. "When I was about your age, my mother died."

Petey stopped what he was doing and stared at John.

John continued. "She died on December twenty-first, just a few days before Christmas."

"That must have sucked," Petey observed.

John gave a hollow laugh. "It certainly did."

Petey remained standing on his bed, making him eye level with John.

"It was the most difficult thing I've ever had to go through in my life," John told him. "Nothing since has been as awful."

"Yeah, it's pretty harsh," Petey admitted.

"But you have a lot of people in this house who love you. Your grandfather, your sister, and your niece. I bet even Jumbo and Mr. Pickles love you," John found himself saying. He was surprised at the words flowing right out of him. He usually didn't do tender and sincere. He preferred gruff, difficult, and indifferent. But right now, this kid needed someone. And he was going to step up to the plate just for once in a way he wished someone had manned up for him.

Petey jumped off the bed and looked down at the floor. "But none of them are my mother."

"I know."

They sat for a moment in companionable silence.

"What I'm trying to say is . . ." John sighed. What was he trying to say? He wanted to help this kid. To give him a chance. He wanted to make sure he didn't end up like him: closed off to everyone and everything. "You have to accept that your grief will be painful. But don't let it destroy you. Let your family help you."

He didn't want to see this kid damaged like he had been. The day of his mother's death, the sun had shone brightly off the few feet of snow. The blinking lights on the Christmas tree had made the whole event seem surreal. His father had disappeared behind a closed door and that would be how John would remember him for the rest of his years growing up. They were all left to deal with their grief in their own ways. Alone. His mother's death had been awful enough, but then the lack of support and the loneliness had been his undoing. If he had to pinpoint one thing that had turned him into the man he'd become today, the ensuing years after his mother's death were the cause.

"Do you have a pen and paper?" John asked.

Petey nodded and pointed toward the desk. John bent over and tore a small piece of paper off a sheet. He scribbled something down and handed the note to Petey.

Petey looked at it, raised his eyebrows, and stared at John.

John held up his hands. "Look, I don't have all the answers, but I do know what you're going through. That's my cell number. You can call me any time," he said. He didn't know who was more surprised, himself or Petey. John rarely gave out his personal number; he was too jealous of his privacy and his desire to be alone for that.

"Thanks," Petey said.

"Now, let's finish up," John said, clapping his hands. "There isn't much more to do."

CHAPTER TWENTY

John went into work the following morning and stopped at his secretary's desk.

"Good morning, Janice," he said. He tapped his finger against the desk.

"Good morning, sir," she said. "The board members are all gathered in the conference room."

"Can I ask you to do a few things for me?" he asked.

She nodded and smiled. "You know you can."

"First, clear my schedule for Friday," he instructed.

She clicked the mouse a few times and Friday's diary appeared on her computer screen. It was also reflected in the lenses of her glasses. She frowned looking at it.

"You've got that one o'clock meeting with the owner of the beach-glass magazine," she said. She glanced around and lowered her voice. "Alone. Without Ms. Preston."

His brow furrowed. He wanted that magazine and not only did he plan to buy it but he also planned on talking the owner, Brenda, into staying on board and running it for a good salary.

"Ring Brenda, tell her a personal emergency has come up," —Janice raised her eyebrows— "and reschedule for either next week, or if she prefers, we can do it after the New Year."

Janice jotted this down on her notepad.

"Also, send her a lavish Christmas gift basket with my apologies," he added.

Janice nodded. She looked up at the screen again. "Everything else looks manageable but you do have that charity dinner with Ms. Preston."

"I told her I couldn't go to that," he said.

"That doesn't bode well for you," she said, looking at him.

"Thanks for your input," he said sarcastically.

"I'm here to serve, Mr. Laurencelli," she said.

"All right, I'll talk to Angela myself."

"Anything else?"

"Yes, let Frank know that I'm going to require the use of the car on Friday. I'll need him to pick me up from my apartment at eleven in the morning."

"Will do," she said.

He began to head toward the conference room, but he stopped and turned back to Janice.

"Do you know where I can order a couple of trays of sandwiches for about twenty kids?" he asked.

"Twenty kids?" she repeated. "How old?"

"Twelve or so," he said.

"I do know a place," she said. "Will I handle it?"

"Please, and arrange for Frank to collect them prior to picking me up on Friday," he said.

Janice nodded.

Once all that was set, he removed his coat, draped it over his arm, and walked into the conference room. Everyone was gathered around the table. He went to the chair at the head of the table. He was surrounded by men and women older than himself. Angela sat at his left. She briefly glanced at him and then looked away.

Once he sat down, he smiled and said, "Good morning, we'll keep this brief because I know everyone is anxious to get things done before Christmas."

There were a few surprised faces and raised eyebrows around the table. His board members knew that Christmas was just another day to John Laurencelli and no notice was usually taken of it. Little did they know they owed the sudden change to a single mother with a lot of people and animals depending on her, he thought wryly.

"Now before we begin, I do need to ask one small favor of you." He drew out India's sponsor card from his briefcase. "We all know how important charity is and I tell you with the straightest face that I am partaking in a charity dance Friday night. All proceeds will benefit the neonatal unit at Children's Hospital. I need sponsors."

There was mostly collective silence around the table with the exception of one nervous giggle. Angela sat there in a frozen silence.

He was amused. "What? Why are you surprised? I like to dance," he teased them, knowing that wasn't what they were so shy about.

He passed the sponsor card to his right, to Steven Monroe, a man with white hair and a mischievous smile. He'd be a good place to get the ball rolling. Steven was known to be generous and he would set the bar for the rest of them. John didn't want Angela setting the tone for their generosity.

"Now, let's get down to business . . ."

AFTER THE MEETING, Angela asked him to remain behind as everyone else filed out of the room.

She glared at him with frosty eyes. "What is this? This charity dance? This is the reason you can't accompany me to that dinner?" she asked.

"We already talked about this. You can manage by yourself. You don't need me to hold your hand," he said.

She stiffened. "I don't need anybody to hold my hand."

"Maybe that's your problem, Angela," he said, and he exited the room.

SPONSOR CARD FIRMLY in his hand, he set out from the meeting in good humor. He stopped again at Janice's desk. "One more thought, Janice."

"There seems to be a flurry of them this morning," she remarked.

"I promise this is the last one," he said, laughing. "Send out a memo to all staff, that on Friday the twenty-second, there will be a catered Christmas lunch at noon . . . Janice, is there something wrong with your eyebrows? They've been going up and down all morning!"

"It's been one surprise too many for your old secretary," she said tartly.

"I'm sure you'll recover. Your acerbic wit doesn't seem to have suffered," he remarked.

"Thank God for that," she said.

"Mmm. Yes," he said absent-mindedly. "Would it be too much to ask you to make the arrangements?"

"Would it matter?" she shot back.

"You could always delegate," he offered.

"No sir, I will handle it," she said.

"I know it's short notice but I'm sure you'll find something nice."

"Oh, I will." She looked at him guardedly. "Is that all?"

"Yes. No. In that memo, tell staff they can leave by two on Friday. They don't have to stay until six."

"Did you notice me refraining from raising my eyebrows?" she asked.

"It's appreciated."

Once in his office, he sat down behind his desk. He had a phone call to make.

"Brigid?" he asked when she picked up on the third ring.

"Wow, to what do I owe the pleasure?" she asked.

"Just a quick question to ask you what time dinner is on Christmas Eve," he said.

Her reaction, he decided, would be his Christmas present this year.

She finally sputtered out a response. "You're coming?"

He leaned back in his chair. "If I'm asking for the time, then the logical conclusion is that I'll be there."

"Six o'clock." She added, "You know the kids will be all wound up, right?"

"Are you trying to talk me out of it?" he asked.

"No. More like warn you," she said.

He thought of Petey and Stella and the rest of the residents of India's nutty household. "If three kids weren't hyper on Christmas Eve, I'd be worried about their state of mind."

Before she could say anything more, he wrapped up the call. "All right then, see you by six. Looking forward to it." Loving the fact that he had caught her off guard and promising himself to do more of it in the future, he hung up, smiling to himself and wishing he could have seen the look on his sister's face.

ON THURSDAY AFTERNOON, right before the everything-has-to-happen-on-the-same-day Friday, India received a call from Rupert as she loaded groceries for the Christmas dinner into the backseat of her car. She had come from visiting Gramps in the hospital and decided she'd get the shopping for the big day done now instead of waiting until the last minute. She also picked up Stella's birthday gift. Carrying on her mother's tradition of birthday presents, she'd gotten her new pajamas and a book.

"Swannie, are you there?" Rupert's voice was full of gravel and stones, always sounding like he'd just woken up.

"I'm here, Rupert," she said. She walked the cart back to the corral.

"Listen, are you still dancing in that thing tomorrow night?" he asked.

"The charity dance? Yes, I am," she confirmed.

"Good. Stop by, because I have something for you," Rupert said.

"What is it?" she asked.

"Just stop by. I won't keep you because I can imagine you're very busy," Rupert said.

"All right. Can I come now?" she asked, thinking she'd loop by on her way home. There was just too much going on tomorrow between Stella's Christmas pageant, Petey's luncheon, and the charity dance. If she thought about it too much, her nerves would end up frayed.

"That would be great. See you soon," Rupert said, and then he was gone.

She finished brushing off the car and climbed into it. She had had the car running for five minutes, and the heat was blasting out of the vents.

She soon turned onto Rupert's street and was able to nab a spot in front of his townhouse. He was waiting at the door when she climbed the stone steps.

"Come in, it's cold out," Rupert said.

Her boots were covered in snow and she kicked them off in the outside hall.

"Just put them on the tray there so we don't get water all over the floor," he instructed.

She followed him into his living room. It was all white woodwork and navy-blue walls. The long rolled-back sofa was lime green with navy blue pillows. There was a white Christmas tree next to the white marble fireplace, all decorated in blue lights and blue ornaments. Barbara sat in a leather recliner, reading the paper. She pressed the button on the remote control, closing the footer on the chair, and sat up.

India frowned. "Don't get up, Barbara, I'm not staying."

Barbara stood. "Would you like tea?"

India shook her head. "No, thank you. Your tree is beautiful."

Barbara glanced at it and concurred. "Thank you. Are you all ready for Christmas?"

"I'm close," India answered with satisfaction. She had managed to get most of the things on both Stella's and Petey's lists. She had planned on going up to the attic over the weekend to wrap everything. It was going to be a good Christmas. She also planned on doing some baking over the weekend. Stella had been after her to make Christmas cookies. Now if she could just get through tomorrow.

"Stella must be getting excited," Barbara said. "She's at a great age."

India smiled. "She is. Her feet are barely touching the ground."

Barbara laughed. "I bet. Children make Christmas."

"They sure do," India agreed. Stella's excitement and awe over the magic and wonder of Christmas had been pure joy for India. She knew she only had a few more years of this before Stella reached Petey's age and became worried about whether she was getting 'only' clothes for Christmas. India intended to enjoy every blessed moment with her.

Rupert reappeared, carrying a box in his hands. India regarded him with curiosity.

He handed her the box. Frowning, she took it and opened it. Her mouth fell open when she saw that it was the necklace she had modeled only weeks ago for him.

"What is this?" she finally managed to ask.

"It's something you wear around your neck," he replied smartly.

She rolled her eyes. "I know that, but why are you giving it to me?" She started to panic at the thought of possibly owning a twenty-thousand-dollar necklace.

"Don't get your panties in a bunch. I had Lenny make me an identical one with rhinestones. So this is a fake. It looked so good on your neck I thought you should wear it for the dance contest."

"It's not a contest," she corrected. She was still studying the necklace. She'd never be able to tell the difference between this one and the original.

It was Rupert's turn to roll his eyes. "Well, whatever it is. Here you go. Merry Christmas. Just a little something from me," he said.

"Oh Rupert, you're a gem!" She stepped forward and hugged him. "You are so thoughtful."

"That's what I keep telling everyone!" he said in good humor. "But do they listen? No!"

"Did your brother ever sell that necklace?" she asked.

Rupert got excited. "He did! The ad ran in the Sunday magazine and someone was at his door first thing Monday morning!"

"Lenny and Rupert managed to get into an argument over the sale of it," Barbara said.

India gave her a knowing smile. Lenny and Rupert could fight over just about anything. "How?"

"Rupert insisted that it was your neck that sold the necklace and Lenny said it was his necklace that sold itself, and before we knew it they were off," Barbara explained.

"Oh no!"

"Don't worry, love, he's still coming for Christmas dinner," Rupert interjected. "In the end, we just agreed to disagree."

"Like they always do," Barbara added.

India thanked them again and tucked the knockoff necklace into her purse. She wished them both a 'Merry Christmas,' and left.

IT WAS THE NIGHT BEFORE the charity dance. India was nervous. She felt that she could practice every day for a year and she'd never be ready. John got held up in a meeting and was late arriving at India's house. She was coming down from getting Stella ready for bed when she found John on the couch, chatting with Petey.

She hoped Petey wouldn't make too much of a fuss about having to go upstairs.

"Hello," she said.

"Hi," he said. He stood up from the sofa.

"Petey, I'm afraid you're going to have to go upstairs," she said.

Her younger brother rolled his eyes. "Aw, come on already. You've been hogging this room all week."

"I know," she said, "but this is the last night. The dance is tomorrow."

"Thank God," Petey grumbled as he stood up from the couch. He looked to John and then to India. "Maybe I should stay. I could critique your method. Give you some pointers."

"Good night, Petey. Don't forget to brush your teeth before you go to bed," she said. She was not even going to engage in that type of conversation. She was nervous enough—she didn't need her kid brother staring and making wisecracks as she and John whirled around the living room.

"It was just a suggestion," he said, heading toward the staircase.

"Duly noted, now good night," India said. She grabbed one end of the sofa and John took the other and they pushed it out of the way.

"Is she bossy when she dances?" Petey asked John.

John shook his head and winked at him. "No, I don't allow it."

"Good for you," Petey said.

"Good night, Petey," John said.

"Good night, John."

Once he was out of sight, John said, "He's a great kid."

India smiled. "He has his moments."

"How is your grandfather doing?" he asked.

"He's coming along. They're hoping he'll be able to come home over the weekend, so he should be here for Christmas."

"That's great news," he said.

"Yes, although he bears watching. He's eighty and now he has some health problems," she said.

"I'm certain he's in good hands with you," Mr. Laurencelli said.

India gave him a faint smile, wishing she shared his confidence.

"Shall we get to work?" John asked.

"Yes, let's," she said.

She turned on the stereo and met John in the middle of the living room. She should be used to it by now but she wasn't. Self-consciously, she wiped her hands on the sides of her pants. He held out his arms. She stepped right into them and thought crazily how easy it was. And how good it felt. She pushed those kinds of thoughts to the far recesses of her mind. In fact, if her mind had an edge, she wished those thoughts would just topple over it.

He placed his hand on her waist and India melted.

"Why are you trembling, Ms. Ramone?"

"I guess I'm nervous," she said.

"There's no need to be," he assured her. "We've been practicing. You know the steps and most of all, if you just follow my lead, you'll do fine."

She nodded at what he was saying. He started off and led her away. Out of habit, she looked down at their feet.

"Keep your eyes on mine at all times," he instructed.

"Oh right, I forgot," she said. She lifted her chin and her eyes met his. He was so dashing. They glided around the living room despite its confined space. She relaxed and let him lead her around and suddenly the room didn't feel so small at all. It felt as if they were in a vast ballroom.

When Patti spoke about old boyfriends—and there were plenty—and she'd complain about something they used to do, she'd often add, "Yeah, but he was a great dancer." India had never understood what she meant. Oh, she'd understood in the literal sense, but what she couldn't understand was why it had mattered. Why it was a qualitative thing. But after dancing all week with John Laurencelli, she finally understood what Patti had been saying all along. To dance with a good dancer was nice but to dance with a great dancer was an experience. John was in the latter category and he had India practically convinced that she was almost a good dancer herself. In the bleak light of day, India knew that nothing was further from the truth. That was the magic of it.

She was going to miss these dance practices. After tomorrow night, she would no longer have a valid excuse to be held in his arms.

"Ms. Ramone, you can open your eyes now," he said.

"Oh, I'm sorry, I got lost in my thoughts," she said.

"I can see that. I hope they were good ones," he said, smiling.

She looked into his eyes and said softly, "They were."

He swept her around the room and all the while her eyes remained locked on his. Soon the room fell away and she became aware of nothing else but him. The color of his eyes. The shape of his eyebrows. The texture of his skin. He was so close she could practically feel it. They came to the dip, the part where he bent her backwards in his expert hands so that she was practically horizontal. They had practiced it dozens of times. Countless times. Each time, getting better and better. This time he dipped her and held her. She could feel his strong fingers along her spine. A pleasant sensation gripped her and fanned out through her body. He held her a moment longer than they had ever practiced before. She did not break eye contact with him. She remained suspended. His face came closer to hers. Her lips parted in sweet anticipation.

"India," he said softly.

She closed her eyes in expectation . . .

"Mommy, can I have a drink?" asked Stella from the bottom step of the staircase.

John brought her back up to a standing position and coughed.

India's hands flew to her cheeks. Without looking at John, she dashed over to her daughter, took her by the hand, and walked her to the kitchen. "Of course, Stella."

She sent Stella back up to bed and returned to find John in the process of putting on his coat. "I think we've practiced enough for one night, Ms. Ramone." He bid her goodnight, promised to see her tomorrow, and left her. His demeanor had shifted so abruptly that India was left to wonder if she had imagined the whole thing.

CHAPTER TWENTY-ONE

India Ramone was unlike any other woman John had ever met. He realized he must have been traveling in the wrong circles to have missed this little gem. In a rare moment of honesty, John realized he had most likely gravitated toward a certain kind of woman to protect himself. Despite his own middle-class background, he had tended toward upper-middle-class, educated, and affected. But most of all, superficial. That was the most important thing he had looked for in all his dates or girlfriends over the past decade. Because if they were superficial, he didn't run the risk of getting attached to them. He could always keep them at arm's length emotionally and that way he didn't get too involved. He appeased them by sparing no expense on them: jewelry, clothes, luxury vacations.

He poured himself a generous portion of Macallan 25. He knew he was going to need it. He had to laugh at the irony of it. If there was a God he sure did have a sense of humor. Here he was, John Laurencelli, the most sought-after bachelor in a five-hundred-mile radius if the press were to be believed, someone who could have anyone he desired. And for the first time in his life, falling for one of the most unlikely candidates ever. India Ramone was one of the most unaffected people he had ever met. She treated him the same way she treated everyone else: with kindness. She didn't defer to his financial status. He knew the reality of her home life. She could have come to him any time for financial help. That was what John did: he helped people out financially. But she didn't. And she almost took umbrage if he should offer any help. She had a lot of pride.

She wasn't the kind of beautiful you'd see on a magazine cover, but she had a certain something that made her stand out, head and shoulders above every other girl he had known, with a sparkle in her eye, a keen wit, some eccentric ways, and a selfless desire to take care of everyone. And she did it so well. He saw how they all adored her: Stella, Petey, and Gramps. Even that goofy thing they called a dog followed her around like a mooning calf. Each one of them would be lost without India.

In a few short weeks, she had managed to turn his head. She had shown him a life different from his own that he thought was impossibly out of his reach. What it would be like to come home to someone you loved and who loved you, too.

That's when he realized that he, too, would be lost without India. He wanted to help her. Not just financially but in every way. He wanted to ease her burden any way he could. What John wanted to do was take care of India Ramone so she could continue taking care of everyone else, which is what she seemed born to do. But most of all, he just wanted to love her.

But how to convince her of this? She had never once flirted with him or given him any indication that she was the least bit interested in him. This would be his newest venture. The one he was most excited about: convincing India Ramone that he was worthy of her love.

INDIA WOKE ON THE FRIDAY before Christmas hours before the alarm went off. Today was a big day. Mr. Laurencelli was accompanying Petey to the parent luncheon. India was going to see Stella perform as a star in her kindergarten Christmas pageant. And then there was the charity dance later that night. She was nervous about it, but she knew she was going to be sorry when it was over. She had really enjoyed the dance sessions with Mr. Laurencelli. When she had been in his arms, everything else had fallen away, all her cares and worries. She felt free and relaxed and she hadn't felt that way in a long time. Had she ever? She couldn't remember. Maybe in high school before the death of her father?

It was hard not to have a crush on John Laurencelli. He would tick a lot of boxes for any girl. All these years, since Stella's birth, she had denied herself getting involved with any man. Between Stella, Petey, Gramps, and nursing school there just wasn't time. Looking back, she realized that that had just been an excuse. An excuse that served to protect her from rejection and abandonment. And then wham, out of nowhere, she'd let her guard down and fallen for a man who was completely out of her league. Out of reach. She sighed and buried her face into the pillow. Why couldn't she have fallen for someone in her own income bracket? Her own neighborhood? It would have been so much easier. If she could kick herself, she would. There was no way Mr. Laurencelli was thinking of her the way she was thinking of him. She supposed she should abandon this kind of thinking and get out of bed, as no good was going to come of it. India Ramone believed in a lot of things but she certainly knew better than to believe in fairy tales.

Knowing there was no going back to sleep at this point, she got out of bed and headed to the shower. She might as well get that done before everyone else got up.

ONCE INDIA WAS DRESSED and her hair back in her signature ponytail, she did a Christmas-pageant run-through with Stella to recite her one line and adjusted the garland that rimmed the neck of her white costume. Stella couldn't stop smiling. Gramps called while they were finishing up breakfast and reported that the doctor had been in and he could go home in the morning. India was so relieved;

he'd be home just in time for Christmas. India didn't know who was more excited: herself, Petey, or Stella.

She went to stash Stella's costume in her backpack and when she unzipped it, she found Mr. Pickles inside, sound asleep.

"Stella?"

"Yes, Mommy?" Stella answered, standing near the kitchen sink and waving her wand around absent-mindedly.

"Why is Mr. Pickles in your backpack?" she asked, gently lifting him out. He opened his eyes and stretched. He seemed a little dazed but then that was how Mr. Pickles always looked.

"He wants to go to my Christmas pageant," Stella said.

India laughed. "I think Mr. Pickles will have to stay home."

"But why, Mommy?" Stella asked earnestly. "Doesn't he like Christmas plays?"

"He does, but you know he doesn't like crowds and there'll be a lot of people there."

"Oh, I forgot about that."

"Besides, the puppy would be lonely without him." The puppy had attached himself to the low-maintenance cat and India worried they'd never find his rightful owner. India picked up the cat and handed him to Stella. "Why don't you take Mr. Pickles upstairs?"

"We should name the puppy," Stella said.

That was the last thing they needed to do, India thought. It would be harder for them to get rid of a puppy they had named.

"Barbie's a nice name," Stella said, cuddling her cat.

"We're not naming the puppy after a Barbie doll," Petey yelled from the living room.

"Go on, Stella, take Mr. Pickles upstairs."

Stella ran off with the cat and India saw that Petey was watching out the front window, waiting for John. He seemed tense.

"What if he doesn't show up?" he asked.

"He will," she said. She trusted Mr. Laurencelli; he wouldn't let Petey down.

"What if he forgot?" Petey asked.

"He won't," she said, packing the cupcakes she'd made for the party after the Christmas play.

"Yes, but what if he does?" Petey stressed.

She shook her head. "Look at the clock. You still have five more minutes."

Petey turned to look back out the window and broke into a smile. "He's here! It's a limo! I don't believe it." He ran away from the window to answer the side door and said to India as he sailed by, "See, I told you he wouldn't forget."

India rolled her eyes. Self-consciously, she smoothed back her hair. There was some apprehension after last night. She could swear he'd almost kissed her. Would he mention it or just sweep it under the rug?

Sadly, she might never know. Marta had rung her earlier that morning and said that the doctor had cleared her to go back to work. She'd told India there'd be no need for her to return after Christmas. She could have the week off to spend with Stella and Petey. India had not expected Marta to come back until after the first of the year. And though the prospect of having the week off with the kids should have delighted her, it left her feeling disappointed and hollow and a little irritated. After the charity dance, there would be no reason or really any opportunity for their lives to cross paths. As much as she didn't want to admit it, she would miss him.

India drew in a breath when Mr. Laurencelli entered the kitchen. Nervously, she leaned against the countertop.

After nodding toward India, he asked Petey, "Are you ready?"

"I am!"

"Good, I've got the trays of sandwiches for your classmates so I expect we'll be off."

He looked at Stella. "Are you all ready for your play?"

"I am!" she said. "I'm ready to be a star."

He didn't even look at India. Either India had misread what had happened last night or he was keeping his distance. Or worse, he had come to his senses. India decided to force him to say something.

"Mr. Laurencelli, Marta called me this morning," she said.

"I know, she called me, too. She'll be back the day after Christmas."

India couldn't read the expression on his face because there was none.

Neither one of them said anything.

"It will be nice for you," he said. "You'll have Christmas week off."

She didn't know how to respond.

"You've worked hard, Ms. Ramone," he said. "Enjoy your time with your family."

"Can we go?" Petey asked. "I don't want to be late."

John turned his head. "Of course. Good luck, Stella." He followed Petey out the door but turned to India. "What time shall I pick you up?"

"It starts at eight and I'd like to get there early to practice," she said.

"We don't need any more practice," he said.

"Oh, okay," she said, feeling dejected. "Then there's no need to pick me up until seven thirty."

"All right, see you then," he said, and he disappeared out the door.

India sank down in the chair at the kitchen table and burst into tears.

WITH TEN MINUTES TO spare, India was ready for the charity dance. Physically, at least. Her nerves were another story. Her dark hair in an updo, make-up applied, and the faux choker around her neck, India paced around the kitchen. As she did, her sapphire-blue ball gown swirled around her ankles. Patti had picked it out and at first, India had scrunched up her nose at it. It seemed to have volumes of material below the waist. But Patti had insisted, told her to try it on and twirl in front of the mirror so she would both feel and see the effect as she was dancing. Patti had been right. The dress was perfect for dancing. It was almost like a special effect, India thought.

Mrs. Bannon had come over to sit with Petey and Stella even though Petey had protested that he didn't need a babysitter. He'd said he was too old for that.

John walked in wearing a black tuxedo and the sight of him took India's breath away. He was stunning. He had a strange look on his face, though.

"What is it?" she asked. "Is it the dress? I told Patti I thought it was too much."

He shook his head. "No, it's not. The dress is fine. You look beautiful."

"Thanks." She blushed.

"I was admiring your necklace," he said.

"Oh, this," she said. She explained the story about how she had modeled the original and how Lenny the jeweler had made one out of rhinestones for her as a gift.

"It's stunning," he said.

Suddenly, the choker slid off her neck and India managed to catch it before it hit the floor.

"Here, let me do that for you," he offered.

She turned her back to him and held the choker in place. His fingers grazed the back of her neck lightly as he secured the clasp. She broke out in goosebumps.

"Are you cold?" he asked from behind her.

She shook her head.

"There you are," he said. He set the back of the choker against her neck and his fingers lingered for a moment, but then he abruptly pulled them away. "We better head off. We don't want to be late."

"I'm ready," she breathed out.

"Is this the coat you'll be wearing?" he asked of the long white winter coat hanging on the back of the kitchen chair. When she nodded, he picked it up and held it open for her as she got into it.

Jumbo lumbered in and gave a bark. India ran her hand over his head. "Be good now, Jumbo. Behave yourself. And no jumping on Mrs. Bannon."

She looked down at her footwear. The high heels weren't going to work in the snow.

As if reading her mind, John said, "Frank is shoveling a path to the car door for you and he'll drop us off right out in front of the venue."

"Okay. I don't like to cause anyone any more trouble," she said.

"Frankly, Ms. Ramone, you should cause people a little more trouble," he said.

She said goodnight to Stella, Petey, and Mrs. Bannon.

"Mommy, you look like a princess," Stella gushed.

Petey shook his head. "Girls."

"I won't be late, Mrs. Bannon. Thank you again," India said.

She went out the side door followed by John.

AFTER HELPING INDIA into the car, John settled into the backseat of the limo comfortably. Any attempts at small talk were answered with one-word answers. India had even refused the offer of a drink. As she stared out the window, he admired her regal bearing. When he had walked into her house earlier to pick her up, he had been both dazed and confused. She looked absolutely beautiful all dressed up, and he had to agree with Stella that she did indeed look like a princess. And apparently, she was a neck model, too. He wished Angela had left that advertisement with him; he would have liked to study it more closely. Not so much the jewelry but the neck underneath it. He looked at India, thinking how he would like to unpin her hair and run his fingers through it. He had come very close to kissing her last night and when the moment had been lost, he'd retreated home. He'd lain awake in bed, staring at the ceiling most of the night, trying to figure out how India Ramone had utterly bewitched him.

When Marta had informed him that she would return to work the day after Christmas he had tried to talk her into taking an extra week off and leaving it until after the new year. But she had insisted that she had inconvenienced him long enough. So, there it was. After tonight, he most likely would never see India again. Or Petey. Or Stella and Gramps. He'd even miss that thing they called a dog. After tonight, he'd be back to the way it used to be: alone and sitting in an empty apartment every night. It didn't bear thinking about. How his carefully laid-out life of the last ten years had been turned upside down in the past month. He shook his head at the thought of it. Taking a page from Ms. Ramone's book, he stared out the window, taking in all the windows lit up with Christmas lights and all the decorations. Christmas was definitely in the air. It was a pity that love wasn't.

THEY ARRIVED AT THE Irish Center on Abbott Road with only a few minutes to spare. Frank dropped them off at the front door and John helped India out of the backseat of the limo, insisting she take his arm as they navigated the icy sidewalk.

Patti and Marta were behind a table in the entryway, crossing names off a list as the entrants arrived. Marta was affixing badge numbers to dresses and suitcoats. Their eyes widened in surprise when they saw India with John Laurencelli. Patti dropped what she was doing to scurry out from behind the table to accost them. She wore a voluminous green-and-gold caftan with a matching turban.

While not looking directly at India but all the while staring at John, Patti asked, "What happened to Warren?"

"He broke his leg," India explained, trying to ignore the cat-that-ate-the-canary look on Patti's face.

"How unfortunate," Patti said, her face full of glee as she devoured John visually. India rolled her eyes at Patti's lack of subtlety. John, for the most part, seemed to take it in stride.

"How are you, Patti?" India asked as John helped her remove her coat.

"My night has just improved immeasurably," she purred.

"Mr. Laurencelli has agreed to be my dance partner," India informed her.

"Substitutions are always allowed, especially if it's an upgrade," Patti said, practically leering at him.

Marta came over and hugged him, apparently pleased to see him. This surprised India, as she didn't think he was the hugging type. But she had gotten him wrong since the beginning. All her preconceived ideas about him could be thrown out the window. The biggest surprise to her had been his kindness.

Patti whispered to her, "It looks like Christmas came early for you."

India immediately shook her head, wanting to disabuse Patti of any foolish notions. "No, it's not like that at all," she said hurriedly. "He's just helping me out."

Patti glanced at John then looked back at India with a gleam in her eye. "I bet he is."

India gave up, thinking Patti was nothing but a hopeless romantic and incurable to boot. There was no sense arguing with her when it was apparent she had already made up her mind about him.

Marta greeted her and told her how lovely she looked.

"Don't you think our India looks lovely, Mr. Laurencelli?" Marta asked him pointedly.

India shook her head. Marta was just as bad as her sister.

She was about to protest when John answered quietly, "I think she looks beautiful."

Suddenly her face felt hot and she felt the need to remove herself from the equation of her, John, Patti, and Marta.

"So, what do we do next?" she asked, once Marta had finished pinning their badge numbers on them.

"Just go to the back of the hall. There's an area where the dancers are waiting. You're couple number nine out of ten. You'll be called to come out."

India nodded, anxious to get away. Entering the vast hall, she saw that it was packed. There had to be hundreds of people there. A quick scan of the crowd told her she knew some of them. Didn't they have anything better to do the Friday before Christmas than watch dancing? She was not prepared for this and her resolve wavered. Now confronted with the volume of spectators, she felt panic and dread fill her. In all her worrying about the actual dancing, she'd never given much thought to the people who would be watching her.

She froze to the spot and announced, "I can't do this."

John almost barreled into the back of her with her abrupt standstill. "What can't you do?"

"This. Dancing. In front of all these people," she stammered.

"You can do this," he assured her.

She shook her head. "No, I can't."

"Give me your hand," he commanded. She did as he asked and put her hand in his.

She looked up at him, melting under his gaze, searching his face for a trace of the fear and unease that she felt. But she only saw confidence.

She swallowed hard and whispered, "I'm nervous."

He nodded. He spoke to her softly. "I know. But you don't have to be. I'll be with you every step of the way." He then chuckled and added, "Literally."

He gave her hand a gentle squeeze. "Come on, India."

She hadn't time to process that he had called her by her given name for the second time in less than twenty-four hours as he led her through the crowd to the back of the center behind the stage.

Once out back, she saw other couples in all sorts of formalwear. Some were obviously nervous by the way they paced and one man was even doing jumping jacks in his tuxedo. Another couple was practicing their moves and India thought there was some fierce competition.

She heard the screech of a microphone outside in the main room followed by the sound of Patti's voice welcoming everyone.

India felt sick to her stomach. She wanted to throw up.

As it was for charity, there would be no real winner. They would get a trophy but she didn't want to come in dead last, either. Most of all, she didn't want to make any mistakes. She could feel herself breaking into a cold sweat.

The first couple was called and as they left the back room, everyone wished them luck.

John pulled out the sponsor card from the inside of his breast pocket. "Here's your card. I managed to get some more sponsors for you."

India took the card from him and when she opened it up and saw the row of donations, none of them less than five figures, she exclaimed, "Heavens to Murgatroyd! There's got to be over a hundred thousand in sponsorship!"

John raised an eyebrow. "And that's not a good thing?"

"It's a lot of pressure," India moaned. She thought of all these people putting their money forward and her stomach twisted in knots.

"Don't worry, it's for charity," he said.

"Why would they back someone like me? Someone who can't dance?" she asked.

He gave her a mischievous smile. "Because they're businesspeople and once in a while, they like to back a dark horse."

The first couple returned with smiles on their faces. India watched as the second couple took a deep breath and went out to the dance floor as their name was called. India trembled.

"Don't be nervous, India," John said from her side.

"I'm trying not to be, but it's proving difficult," she replied.

"Why?" he asked.

She shrugged. "I'm afraid of tripping up, or worse, falling."

He was so calm; she wished it was contagious. "There's no reason you should be," he said. "You've just got to keep telling yourself that you're prepared."

"I have been telling myself that but it's not working," she said.

"Look, this is nothing compared to everything else you're doing," he said.

"What do you mean?"

"I mean everything is relative," he answered. "Look what you've accomplished in your own personal life. You're a single mother responsible for yourself, your daughter, your brother, and your grandfather. Not to mention a dog and a cat." He paused and added thoughtfully, "Though the dog is questionable."

"Yes, but even he needs a home."

"I suppose. Anyway, as I was saying, you're taking care of everyone and going to nursing school. You're handling all that and it doesn't seem to faze you."

"Because I'm used to it. Besides, I don't mind because I like taking care of people."

"After meeting Petey and Stella, I'll tell you, in case anyone hasn't, that you're doing a great job."

"Thank you."

"But the question I want to pose to you is this—while you're taking care of everyone else, who is taking care of you?"

She didn't need to think about it to know the answer. She had just decided not to dwell on it.

She was about to respond when she looked up and saw Angela Preston bearing down on them in a long winter coat and high-heeled black boots. She was all fury.

"Oh no," India whispered.

CHAPTER TWENTY-TWO

"Curiosity got the better of me and I had to check this out!" Angela said with an edge in her voice.

If John was surprised by her appearance or her demeanor he didn't give it away. He remained very calm. His expression revealed nothing. India, hating any kind of confrontation, began to tremble once again. Nervously, she watched Angela.

"That farce at the board meeting, getting all of them to sponsor her," she said. "While you're busy playing Sir Galahad."

All the couples backstage looked at them. India wanted to crawl away and hide.

"Get a hold of yourself and stop making a scene," he hissed.

Angela gave a brittle laugh. "And all this time telling me that you couldn't help me out because we've been friends for so long and you valued our friendship and the business. Your refusal to help me out had nothing to do with that; it was all about you having a thing for your maid!"

Anger washed over John's face. "Angela, this isn't the time or the place for this conversation. Not now."

This only served to infuriate Angela further and she turned on India. "You're nothing but a little gold digger! Insinuating yourself into John's life . . . Who do you think you are—Cinderella?" She paused, her eyes narrowing at the sight of the necklace on India's neck. Then her eyes widened, and she looked back to John. "How dare you?"

"What are you talking about?" John said. "It's time to leave."

She rounded on John. "Don't tell me nothing is going on between the two of you. You gave her my necklace!"

Before India realized what was happening, Angela started to reach out for the rhinestone choker around India's neck, but John intercepted her by grabbing hold of Angela's wrist.

"If you so much as lay one hand on Ms. Ramone, I will have you arrested for assault," he said firmly.

Angela's face was a mask of controlled, white-hot fury. "You wouldn't dare."

"I most certainly would," he seethed. He took her by the arm and escorted her to the back door. "Now pull yourself together and go to your charity dinner. You and I will be having a nice, long discussion after Christmas."

"But you went behind my back and gave her the necklace I wanted! I went to buy it and the jeweler told me it had been sold. It was you!"

"Have you completely lost your mind? You sound like we're back in the schoolyard."

She started to say something but he cut her off. "Drop it. That necklace is hers. It's a replica of the one you wanted," he said. "Not that it's any of your business."

He opened the back door. "Now go, Angela," John said firmly. "I don't know what's gotten into you, but if I ever hear of you confronting India Ramone again, I will have a restraining order placed against you."

Angela stepped out into the parking lot and was about to protest, but John Laurencelli closed the door in her face.

JOHN WAS APPALLED AT the scene Angela had just created. He stretched his neck, adjusted his collar and his tie in an attempt to regain his equilibrium. But he soon realized he had a much bigger problem on his hands when he saw the state India was in. She was shaking and her eyes were wet with tears. In a couple of strides, he was at her side. He could throttle Angela.

"It's all been too much," India said, staring straight ahead, not looking at him. Her voice was barely above a whisper. "School, Petey, Gramps, Warren. Trying to make ends meet, and most of all thinking I could dance in this event when I have no idea what I'm doing!"

John recognized the signs of an imminent breakdown when he saw them. He had had first-hand experience with them. People got burnt out. It happened. Life just became too much. And India Ramone was about to have a breakdown that was likely long overdue, minutes before they were set to go onstage.

She looked up at him, tears spilling from her eyes. Her voice shook. "I'm so sorry Mr. Laurencelli, but I can't do this. Not now."

He put his arm around her trembling body and took her to a secluded corner, away from prying eyes, so as to give them some privacy.

"Ms. Ramone, we are going to go out there and do our three dances just the way we practiced."

She shook her head. "I can't."

"I'm sorry, but I won't take no for an answer."

Her eyes were getting puffy from the tears and her nose was red, and he knew at that moment that he loved her. He took her hands in his and asked softly, "Do you trust me?"

She seemed surprised by the question but didn't hesitate with her answer. "Yes, I do."

"Good, because that's where we're going to start."

She regarded him quizzically.

"We are going to go out there and dance the best we ever have."

"I can't—"

"Shh. Yes, you can. Do you know why?"

She waited.

"Because out on that stage, I'm going to be there for you. You won't have to do a thing. You're going to put everything out of your mind and just come along with me for the ride," he said. "Okay?"

She didn't say anything, but he was encouraged by the fact that she didn't say no.

"I have one favor to ask," he continued, leaning into her. She looked up to him, their faces only inches apart.

"Yes?"

"The only thing I ask you to do is enjoy dancing with me," he said.

She was nodding and had stopped crying and he thought that was a good sign.

From where they stood behind the stage, they heard Patti call out couple number eight. John only had a few minutes and this was as good an opportunity as any.

"India, I . . . there's something else I'd like to say."

He searched her face, momentarily getting lost in her big brown eyes and thinking how beautiful she was.

"I asked you a question earlier," he went on. "But I never heard your answer. I asked you who takes care of you while you're taking care of everyone else."

"No one," she whispered.

"As I thought," he said.

He placed his trembling hands over hers. She raised her eyebrows and looked from his hands back up to his face.

"Are you all right?" she asked.

"I am. Actually, I've never been better." He did not take his eyes off her. "I say that because since you've come into my life, it's true."

She remained silent, waiting patiently.

"I have everything money can buy," he said. "All the comforts, all the luxuries, but what I've realized is that I'm not happy. And I didn't see that until I met you."

"Oh." It was all she could say.

"May I be blunt?" he asked.

She smiled. "I've never known you to be anything else."

"Yes, there is that," he acknowledged, mirroring her smile. "I want to take care of you, India. I want to help you. I just want to be there for you and make your life easier."

She regarded him with a mix of interest and curiosity.

He scratched his forehead, looked down, and exhaled a loud breath. "That doesn't sound right. It makes it sound as if I want to take you on as a project. Or a new business venture." He stepped closer to her.

"Just say what you feel," India prompted.

He sighed as he ran his hand over the back of his head. "The truth is, Ms. Ramone, I have fallen in love with you." She looked a bit unsure and John felt as if his heart had stopped beating.

"You realize I bring lots of baggage with me," she pointed out, thinking of her brood back home.

He laughed. "I am well aware of that. And I'm more than willing to help you carry your suitcases."

It was her turn to laugh, a deep throaty laugh as if she hadn't heard anything that funny in a long time.

"Ms. Ramone—India—do you think you could ever feel the same way about me?"

He waited with a look of both hope and expectation. She took a step closer to him, closing the gap. Tenderly, she placed her hand on the side of his face. "Yes, John, I already do."

He leaned in to kiss her, closing his eyes, and India held her breath in anticipation.

"Couple number nine." Patti's voice rang out over the sound system, summoning them to the stage.

"Interrupted again," John said.

India laughed.

"Relax and trust me," he said. Confidently, he took her by the hand and led her through the red velvet curtains and out onto the stage. "Look, India, the lights are so bright you can't even see the audience. It's almost like we're in your living room practicing all by ourselves."

He looked at her. The nervousness was gone and she had a smile full of joy on her face. And that made him very happy.

"Let's do this," he said, putting his arm around her waist and sweeping her away.

EPILOGUE

One year later . . .

John headed up the stone steps of the red-brick Italianate building. Skipping the elevator, he took the stairs to the second floor and headed down the corridor to the end office. He sat down in the empty waiting room, picked up a magazine, and leafed through it, not really interested. He waited for Petey to finish his session with the bereavement counselor. India had set it up for him after last Christmas and even he had seen the change in the boy. Petey was no longer prone to fits of anger or sullenness. He was what he should be: a normal teenage boy.

To help India out, John had offered to taxi him to and from his weekly appointments. John still couldn't believe how things had changed in a year. Last year his sister had asked him if he was happy. He knew he wasn't then, but he definitely was now. He had this amazing girlfriend and he just couldn't believe how lucky he was. But not only that, she had a great family, as well. And he was happy to be a part of it.

He wasn't waiting long when Petey came out of the room with Louise, his counselor. The few times John had met her, he had liked her and he could definitely see a genuine rapport between her and the boy. India had been right to push for grief counseling. Petey had resisted but eventually resigned himself to going.

John closed the magazine, laid it on the table, and stood up. "All set?" he asked.

Petey nodded. "Only one more session and I'm through."

John clapped him on the back. "Good for you. You should be proud of yourself."

Petey nodded. They made small talk for a moment, wished Louise a 'Merry Christmas,' and exited the office.

As John stepped out into the hall and closed the door behind him, a thought occurred to him, as it had many times these past few months. "Wait here, Petey, one minute. I forgot something."

He stepped back into the grief-counseling offices, relieved to see that the counselor had gone back into her own workspace. He had spied business cards on the reception desk and wanted to take one. As he did, Louise stepped back out.

"Mr. Laurencelli!"

He looked sheepish. He lifted up the card. "Just thought it might be handy to have."

"That's what they're there for," she said with a smile.

He turned toward the door, hesitated, then faced her again. He felt foolish and a little embarrassed. She watched him with curiosity. He decided to be brave.

"Um, I was wondering if I could make an appointment," he said.

"Of course," she answered.

"I have some unresolved issues regarding my own mother's death," he admitted, reddening. He coughed and cleared his throat to cover his embarrassment. It was the first time in more than two decades he had been able to say that.

She went behind the reception desk and pulled out a black diary. She flipped it to the new year. "After the holidays all right?"

"Perfect."

"How about January second?" she asked. "In the evening or daytime?"

"Evening, any time after six," he said.

She wrote the date and time down on a little pre-printed card, handed it to him, and smiled.

"Thank you," he said, and he tucked it into the inside breast pocket of his coat. In a safe place.

THE WEEK BEFORE CHRISTMAS, India and John walked down the street. The air was cold and crisp but the sun was warm. It was India's day off from the hospital.

"After we get married next summer, we're going to need a place to live," John said casually.

"I guess Gramps would like to have his house back to himself," India agreed. Then she added hurriedly, "Not that he ever complains about us being there."

"Of course not," John said.

"Where would you like to live?" she asked.

"As long as you're there, I'd live in a tent under a traffic light," he said. He studied her intently, never tiring of looking at her.

She giggled. "That could be a little dicey."

He smiled. "Like I said, as long as you are there, I wouldn't care one bit."

"Be serious," she said. "And your place is beautiful, but I don't think apartment living would suit Petey or Stella."

"Or Jumbo," John added. "Or Mr. Pickles. Or Barney."

India giggled again. "No, definitely not!"

"I was thinking we'd need a nice-size house," he said.

India nodded. "Yes, but not too big."

"No, of course not," John said somberly.

"Are you making fun of me?" she inquired.

His eyes twinkled. "Well, maybe just a bit. I mean, we could have a really big house. You know, with wings and everything, a movie theatre, a tennis court, an Olympic-size swimming pool . . ."

"I know," she said. "But I really wouldn't like that."

"I know you wouldn't," he said. "But if you ever change your mind . . ."

She bowed her head. "You'll be the first to know."

"And it probably wouldn't be a good idea to take Stella and Petey out of this school district," he mused.

"I'd like to avoid that if possible," she said. But there weren't a lot of big houses in the area where they lived. The thought almost seemed futile.

She paused at the corner lot where the huge abandoned two-story house still stood. It was possibly the worst-looking house she had ever seen. And she didn't know why, but it brought a smile to her face.

"Ah yes, the Van Doren mansion," John said, looping his arm through hers.

She smiled. "I can't explain it—it just brings me so much joy to look at it and imagine how it used to be and how it could be again with a little TLC," she said wistfully.

"It would take a lot more than TLC," John pointed out.

She smiled at him, content. "I realize that."

She turned to head back to the house. They had their last weekly dance lesson before the holidays later that evening so they couldn't linger too long.

He didn't follow, instead placing his hands on the rickety picket fence and considering the derelict house on the corner. "Unless you'd like to live here," he said.

India clapped her hands and jumped up and down. "Oh, could we? John, don't tease me if you really don't want to!"

"Actually, my lawyers have already located the owner and he's accepted our offer."

India squealed. "Oh, John! I can't believe this!"

"Of course, it will be awhile before we can move in," he said.

"Thank you!" she said, jumping up and wrapping her arms around his neck. She kissed him on the mouth.

"Do whatever you want. You're in charge," he told her. He paused. "Although I was thinking of yellow on the outside and replacing the white picket fence. What do you think?"

Tears sprang to her eyes. "That's what I was thinking! John, you're a keeper."

He pulled her to him and whispered, "Merry Christmas, India."

Also by Michele Brouder

The Happy Holiday Series
A Whyte Christmas
This Christmas
A Wish for Christmas
One Kiss for Christmas
A Wedding for Christmas

Escape to Ireland Series
A Match Made in Ireland
Her Fake Irish Husband
Her Irish Inheritance
A Match for the Matchmaker

Soul Saver Series
Claire Daly: Reluctant Soul Saver
Claire Daly: Marked for Collection

About the Author

Michele Brouder is originally from the Buffalo, New York area. She has lived in the southwest of Ireland since 2006, except for a two-year stint in Florida. She makes her home with her husband, two boys and a dog named Rover. Her go to place is, was and will always be the beach. Any beach. Any weather.

Made in the USA
Monee, IL
12 November 2022

17628965R00163